YA
FIC
VEGA

Vega, Danielle,
The haunted

P9-CDX-777

S WITHDRAWN 6/19

# THE HAUNTED

## DANIELLE VEGA

## RAZORBILL

An imprint of Penguin Random House LLC, New York

## alloyentertainment

Produced by Alloy Entertainment
1325 Avenue of the Americas
New York, NY 10019

First published in the United States of America by Razorbill,
an imprint of Penguin Random House LLC, 2019

Copyright © 2019 by Alloy Entertainment

Penguin Random House supports copyright. Copyright fuels creativity,
encourages diverse voices, promotes free speech, and creates a vibrant culture.
Thank you for buying an authorized edition of this book and for complying with
copyright laws by not reproducing, scanning, or distributing any part of it in any form
without permission. You are supporting writers and allowing Penguin Random House
to continue to publish books for every reader.

RAZORBILL & colophon is a registered trademark of Penguin Random House LLC.

Visit us online at penguinrandomhouse.com

Library of Congress Cataloging-in-Publication Data is available upon request.
Printed in the United States of America.
ISBN 9780451481467

1 3 5 7 9 10 8 6 4 2

Design by Kristin Boyle
Text set in Adobe Jenson Pro

This is a work of fiction. Names, characters, places, and incidents either are the product
of the author's imagination or are used fictitiously, and any resemblance to actual persons,
living or dead, businesses, companies, events, or locales is entirely coincidental.

*For my mom, who loves ghost stories*

# THE HAUNTED

# PROLOGUE

STEELE HOUSE CAST A DARK SHADOW OVER THE GRASS. Its broken windows were like deranged eyes, its sagging porch a weird, lopsided grin.

Maribeth stared at it, goose bumps crawling up her skin.

*Don't be a baby*, she told herself. *It's just a house.*

But it wasn't just a house. It was Steele House. Maribeth used to hold her breath whenever she had to walk past the vacant, overgrown yard. But she was nine now, and that was too old to be afraid of a dumb old house.

Still, she crept along the very edges of the grass, careful not to put even one toe under the shadow the house cast onto the lawn. Babyish or not, she thought if she stepped into the shadow, the house might *see* her. But this was the fastest way to get home, so she walked fast, not even looking at the house.

She was almost past the cellar, close to the place where Steele House's dead, yellow lawn turned into her house's nice, green lawn, when she heard a small, frightened *mew*.

Maribeth froze, a heavy feeling settling in her stomach. She looked at the cellar. That had sounded like a kitten.

*Mew.*

This time the sound was louder and more desperate, as if the kitten had heard her walking past and was calling to her for help.

Maribeth chewed on her lip, not sure what she should do. It sounded like the kitty was trapped.

*Just a dumb old house*, she told herself again. And then, quickly, before she got too scared, she grabbed for the cellar doors and, grunting, struggled to pull them open.

No kitten came bounding out. In fact, Maribeth couldn't see anything in the pitch-black darkness.

*Mew*, she heard once more. The sound echoed through the cellar.

Maribeth crouched down at the top of the stairs and reached her hand into the darkness. She was still wearing her church tights, and dirt smudged up the knees. Her voice shook a little as she called, "Here, kitty, kitty. I'm not going to hurt you."

She knew only part of the story of Steele House. Some people died in there a really long time ago, and now no one would live there. Her big brother Kyle and his friends sometimes rode their skateboards past the house and dared each other to throw rocks through the windows while shouting, *Who's afraid of Steele House now, suckers?* Only they didn't say *suckers*, they said a word Maribeth wasn't allowed to repeat. But they never went inside. Kyle was too chicken.

"Kitty?" Maribeth leaned as close to the doorframe as she could without going inside. She could see the top few steps into the cellar, but everything else was dark.

She braced herself. Just because Kyle was too chicken to go inside didn't mean she couldn't. She thought of how impressed he'd be when she told him what she did, and hurried down the stairs before she lost her nerve.

The air grew very still around her, as though the house was holding its breath.

Maribeth walked past a wall of shelves filled with old, green bottles, the labels long since worn away, and stopped in front of a wooden trunk with a broken lock. A doll sat on top of the trunk, slumped against the wall. Its eyes had been plucked out of its face, and there were gouges around the empty sockets.

Maribeth turned away from the doll, eyes straining against the darkness.

"Kitty?" she called. It smelled like wet jeans and the trailer park dogs and something gone rotten in the garbage, almost like something *lived* down here. Maribeth held her nose closed with two fingers. Her heart started beating faster.

Outside, the cellar door rattled in the wind.

*I should go back,* she thought. It was cold, and her skin felt itchy and shivery. She could feel something down here with her, something bad. She turned in place, but all she saw were smudged walls, and bottles, and that weird doll.

Two eyes blinked open.

"Kitty," Maribeth whispered, moving toward the eyes. They were shiny and yellow. She lowered herself to her knees and leaned forward.

The yellow eyes blinked.

"Come here," she murmured, reaching out her arm—

A boy's voice drifted down the stairs. "Hey? Is someone down there?"

Maribeth's heart sputtered. She jerked her hand away and spun around so fast she twisted her ankle. Pain shot up her leg.

The yellow eyes shifted back into the shadows.

"Who's there?" Maribeth shouted, tears tickling her eyes. Her ankle hurt a *lot*, but the fear was worse. It felt like someone had grabbed hold of her lungs and squeezed. She pressed herself all the way back against the cold cellar wall.

The stairs creaked. It sounded like someone was walking very slowly down the steps, but Maribeth didn't see anyone there. A moment later, the scent of cologne wafted through the cellar. Her nose itched. It smelled like the stuff her dad wore on special occasions, like when he took her mom out on a date.

"What's your name?" asked the voice. It was a nice voice. It reminded Maribeth of her older brothers.

"Maribeth Ruiz," she said, numb. She tried to sound more confident than she felt. Where was the voice coming from? For some reason, she looked over at the doll sitting on the trunk. The black eyeholes stared back at her, but the doll's mouth stayed still.

"Cool name," said the voice.

Fingers curled around Maribeth's wrist. They were cold and damp, like raw chicken just out of the fridge. Maribeth looked down at the fingers, but there wasn't anything there. She blinked and there was *still* nothing there.

But she could *feel* them. They pinched her wrist and squeezed the blood from her hand.

Maribeth shrieked and took a clumsy step backward. Her hurt ankle slid out from beneath her and she hit the floor—*hard*—the packed earth chilling the skin right through her tights.

The fingers still held her arm. They twisted it back at an awkward angle so that bright flares of pain pierced Maribeth's shoulder. She tried to scream, but the sound didn't make it past her throat. Her lips trembled. The fingers squeezed tighter.

The cologne scent became sweet and stronger. It clogged Maribeth's throat, making it harder for her to scream.

"You'll pay for what she did," the voice crooned into her ear.

Maribeth opened and closed her mouth, lips flopping like a dead fish. A ragged, desperate sound finally clawed up her throat, but the walls were thick, and she knew no one would hear it.

Outside, the wind blew the cellar door shut.

*Three years later . . .*

# CHAPTER 1

HENDRICKS DIDN'T KNOW WHAT PISSED HER OFF MORE: starting over or becoming a cliché.

Back at her old school, she'd waged her own private war on clichés. She'd had rules and everything: no burn books or mean-girl comments. No clamoring to be named homecoming queen. No dating the high school quarterback.

"Good thing I'm not a quarterback," her ex-boyfriend, Grayson, had said, brow furrowed. "You have anything against soccer players?"

"Only if you're the captain of the team," Hendricks had told him, teasing, and when he'd pouted she'd added, "Hey, I didn't know you were going to ask me out when I came up with the rules."

Which was true. Rule or no rule, everyone knew it was borderline impossible to reject Grayson Meyers. He had a gravity that drew people in. A smile that said *trust me*, and a deep, throaty voice that made him seem older and more mysterious than he actually was. Of course now, after everything that'd happened, Hendricks couldn't think about his smile or his voice without feeling a rush of shame.

Shame that she should've known better, should've followed her own rules. Shame that, really, all of this was her fault.

The back seat of her parents' car felt suddenly hot and airless. Hendricks closed her eyes, pretending she was in her closet back home. She imagined coats rustling against her cheeks, shoes pressing into her legs. The low drone of the car radio and her parents' murmured voices sounded far away, almost like they were muffled by the other side of a door.

*Breathe*, she told herself and her lips parted, air whooshing out. She'd spent most of the last two months hiding in that closet, and it was surprisingly comforting to imagine being there now. She'd always felt safe there. But it was over two hundred miles away. And it didn't belong to her anymore.

She opened one eye, head tilted toward the car window. Drearford's Main Street rushed past her face, blurry beyond the icy glass. People clutched their jackets closed as the wind picked up and whipped through the bare trees.

"But if we take Metro-North, we should be back around midnight," her mother was saying from the passenger seat, thumbs tapping her phone screen. "One a.m. at the latest."

"Maybe we could stay overnight, just this once. The contractors could always meet us in the morning." Her father had lowered his voice, like he thought Hendricks might not hear him.

A pause, and then, "I . . . really wouldn't feel comfortable with that, yet." Her mother spoke softly, too, but they were only sitting two feet away. Hendricks felt rather than heard the pause in their conversation, and pictured their eyes flicking to the rearview mirror, casually, like they weren't checking on her.

She kept her eyes trained on the window, watching her breath mist the glass.

Drearford, New York, was one and a half hours north of Manhattan and nearly four hours from Philadelphia. Almost—but not quite—too far to drive in a single night. Population: 12,482. Current weather: twenty-two degrees and gray. Gray like the sky was sucking the life from its surroundings, leaving trees and grass and bodies of water colorless and covered in a thin layer of frost. Philadelphia—where Hendricks had lived until a week ago—was also cold in January, but it was a bright, glittering kind of cold. This place just looked dead.

Before she could stop herself, Hendricks pictured Grayson drinking from a bottle of stolen MD 20/20, offering it to her.

"Dare you," he'd said, one eyebrow going jagged.

It had been their thing, sort of like an inside joke.

*Dare you to go to the movies with me Friday night.*

*Dare you to change your Facebook status to "in a relationship."*

*Dare you dare you dare you.*

Hendricks swallowed. The memories felt like something caught in her throat. She reached into her pocket instinctively, fingers curling around her cell phone. But she didn't pull it out.

*Clean slate.* That's how her parents sold the move to Drearford. One by one, Hendricks released her fingers, letting the phone settle back into her pocket.

"Clean slate," Hendricks whispered. Grayson had mostly stopped calling by now, anyway. Mostly.

The car pulled to a stop. Hendricks turned her head and saw a building on the other side of the street, hunching low to the ground, like a predator. A few cloudy windows broke up the dirty brick walls, and a flagpole stood directly in front of the main doors, flag flapping like crazy in the vicious wind. Hendricks's eyes flicked to the left, landing on a sign:

## DREARFORD HIGH SCHOOL, HOME OF THE TIGERS

Something heavy settled in her gut. The idea of a new high school, new friends, new *everything* hadn't felt real until this second.

She wanted to throw open the car door and run down the street. Let the wind blow her away.

*Don't think like that*, she told herself, and her eyes moved to the front seat, worried that her parents knew, somehow. She tried to keep the nerves from her voice as she asked, "We're here?"

Her mom twisted around to face her. "You know the way back home, right? Two lefts and a right on Maple?"

Their new house wasn't even a ten-minute walk from here. Hendricks nodded.

"There's money for pizza for dinner, or leftover chicken in the fridge if you feel like something healthier." Her mother chewed her lower lip. Hendricks knew what was coming. "Are you sure you want to—"

"Bye." Hendricks grabbed her backpack and climbed out of the car, door slamming behind her. They'd been over this before. Her mom wanted Hendricks to homeschool until senior year started in the fall. She tried to make it seem like this was for Hendricks's benefit, that she'd have fun helping them renovate their new house, but really, Hendricks knew her mother just wanted to be able to keep an eye on her at all times. As though that might keep her safe.

Climbing out of the car, Hendricks felt a sudden pang of guilt. It was her fault they had to start over. They'd all been happy in Philadelphia. A year ago, it never would've occurred to any of them to move.

*Clean slate*, she told herself again.

She was halfway up the steps to the school when she heard a noise, then dry leaves rustling. She froze, squinting into the shadows of a large oak tree.

A boy stood beneath the branches, cigarette pinched between two fingers. He wore the standard outsider uniform: black T-shirt over black jeans tucked into beat-up black combat boots. Curled upper lip. His skin and hair were both dark. His eyes were even darker.

He jerked his chin in Hendricks's direction, then dropped the cigarette butt into the gnarled roots of the overgrown tree and stomped it out, moving back into the shadows. The smell of smoke lingered behind him.

*More clichés,* Hendricks thought, mouth twisting. She would've hated this place six months ago.

Now, it felt strangely comforting. At least she knew her role.

A girl waited inside the school's glass double doors, arms hugged tight over her chest, shivering in her short skirt and thin tights.

*This must be Portia,* Hendricks thought. She'd gotten an email from her last night.

*Hi hi!!!* the email had read. *My name is Portia Russell and I'll be your guide to all things Drearford High tomorrow morning. Meet me inside the front doors at 10 a.m. sharp and I'll give you the lowdown on the cafeteria food to avoid and which teachers are secretly evil. (Kidding kidding!!)*

*xo—P*

Hendricks had never been the new girl at school before, so she didn't have any experience with this, but she'd been expecting a good-girl librarian type. Pretty, but in a virginal way, and more likely to spend her Friday nights studying than partying.

She'd been only half right. Portia was dressed like a good girl— cardigan, skirt, headband holding back thick, black curls—but Hendricks could see at a glance that she wasn't one. Her cardigan was a size too small, her skirt a hair too short. Her dark brown skin seemed poreless.

"Get *in* here," Portia said, holding the door open for her. "It's *freezing!* Aren't you dying?" She grabbed Hendricks by the arm and pulled her inside, giving an exaggerated shiver as she tugged the door closed. "The weather has been *so* gross lately."

"It's not so bad," Hendricks said, but only because she thought it was shitty to complain about this town when she'd only just moved here.

"If you say so. You're from Philly, right? The Walter School?"

Hendricks could hear the words *prestigious* and *exclusive* in the way Portia's tongue curled around the name. *The Walter School.* Hendricks had dressed down for her first day at Drearford High— boyfriend jeans slung low on thin hips, messy blond hair tucked in a topknot—but she could still see Portia studying her, weighing her assets, placing her somewhere on the inevitable social ladder.

Hendricks knew what she saw. Beneath the slouchy clothes and messy hair, she was still blond and thin and tan, pretty enough that Portia wouldn't be embarrassed to be seen with her, generic enough that she wouldn't be a threat.

"I've heard that place is *amazing*," Portia said, hooking Hendricks's arm with her own. "You're slumming it here. Why didn't your parents move to Manhattan?"

"They flip houses for a living," Hendricks explained. "They came up here to look at an old property and decided they liked it so much they wanted to keep it for themselves. I guess they couldn't resist the whole quaint small-town thing."

It was the truth, but only half the truth. Hendricks was quickly becoming an expert at lying by omission.

Portia paused for a fraction of a second, something flicking across her face. "Well, *this* is definitely a change," she said. "Let's get the tour out of the way so you can get in to see Principal Walker and get your schedule set up. The school's tiny, so it'll only take a second. This here is a hallway, similar to hallways you may have seen in Philadelphia. You'll find most of your classes here, or down one of two *other* hallways."

"Fascinating," Hendricks said, deadpan. Portia snickered.

"Right? It's a good thing they sent me out to meet you or you'd have never found your way around." She paused in front of an empty cafeteria. "We eat here in the winter, at that table in the back corner, but juniors are allowed to take their lunches outside so we move to the fountain as soon as it gets—"

Portia stopped talking abruptly and rose to her tiptoes, waving. The school doors whooshed open and a line of boys in tracksuits streamed into the hall. Sneakers squeaked against the floor, and deep, laughing voices reverberated off the walls.

"Hey, Connor!" Portia called, and the tallest, blondest tracksuit-clad guy broke into a shockingly wide smile and separated from the others to jog over to them. Hendricks felt her shoulders stiffen. She pretended to study a cuticle.

"Ladies," Connor said, brushing the hair back from his forehead. "How are you this morning?"

Hendricks looked up, frowning slightly. Normally, she hated it when guys called girls "ladies." They either used the word mockingly or like they were reciting a line from that playbook on how to pick up women. But Connor hadn't said it like that. His tone had been a touch formal, and there was something old-fashioned and all-American about his crew cut and cleft chin.

*Wholesome*, Hendricks thought. Then again, Grayson could seem wholesome, too. When he wanted to.

Connor dropped an arm around Portia's shoulders. "Are you going to introduce me to your new friend?" he asked.

And then he was staring at Hendricks, his face so animated that, for a moment, Hendricks wondered if she'd said something hilarious without realizing it.

"Oh, hi," she said, taken aback. "I'm—"

"He's joking." Portia smacked him lightly across the stomach. "He already knows who you are."

"Ow." Connor pretended to double over, cringing. To Hendricks, he said, "Hendricks Becker-O'Malley, right? You're sort of famous."

Hendricks felt a shot of nerves. "Famous?"

"We don't get a lot of new students." Connor tilted his head. "You know, technically, you don't exist."

This threw Hendricks off guard. She said, blinking, "What?"

"I looked you up. Hendricks Becker-O'Malley is a unique name, so I figured I'd find something, but you're not on Instagram, or Facebook, or Snap . . ."

*He'd looked her up?* Hendricks glanced at Portia, wondering what she thought about her boyfriend internet stalking some other girl. The girls at her old school would've freaked. Not that it would've stopped their boyfriends from doing whatever they wanted. But still.

But Portia's face remained impassive as she lowered her voice and said, conspiratorially, "We figured you were hiding some deep, tragic secret."

Hendricks shrugged, trying for casual. "I'm just not into social media. It . . . keeps you from living in the moment."

Which was a lie, and not even a good one, but they weren't getting her deep, tragic secret that easily. Or ever.

"Living in the moment," Connor repeated, like this was a sage piece of wisdom he'd never heard before. He jostled Portia's shoulder, adding, "See? I told you she'd be cool."

Portia rolled her eyes. "You just cost me twenty bucks, new girl. I was sure you were going to be some snooty rich kid, but Connor had a feeling about you."

Connor looked irrationally pleased with himself. "I should hit the showers before next period," he said. "We're all hanging after school. Want to join? We can introduce you around."

Hendricks opened her mouth, and then closed it. This all felt so easy, so normal. It was starting to sink in. No one knew about her here. She could start over again, be absolutely anybody she wanted to be.

Despite everything, she felt a thrill of relief.

But then she remembered—she couldn't tonight. She groaned and said, "I'm sorry, I can't. My parents have to check out a property in Manhattan, so I'm watching my baby brother."

Connor's smile flickered. Portia stared at her. "You're going to be home?" she asked. "All by yourself?"

Hendricks frowned. "Well, yeah. Why, is that bad?"

Portia touched her lower lip with the tip of her tongue. "I wouldn't want to spend the night alone at Steele House."

A nasty shiver moved down Hendricks's spine. "Steele House?"

"Didn't you know your house had a name?" Connor asked.

Hendricks hesitated. She didn't realize everyone already knew where she lived.

A bell rang then and students spilled out of the doors lining the hallway, surrounding them.

Connor ducked his head, abashed. "Okay, now I really do have to hit the showers. Catch you at lunch, O'Malley."

He said her last name with a wink, like they were sharing an inside joke. And, with another insanely wide grin, he turned into the crowd.

Hendricks didn't realize she was staring until she heard Portia's voice in her ear: "It's okay. Everyone at school is a little in love with him."

Hendricks blinked, cheeks reddening as she pulled her gaze away. "Everyone at school is a little in love with your boyfriend?"

21

Portia released a short, hard laugh. "Boy and friend, yes, but *not* my boyfriend. Connor's currently unattached, although I should warn you that we're all very protective of him. That nicest-guy-on-the-planet thing wasn't an act. He's pretty much like that all the time. Anyway," she continued, jerking her chin at a door to her left. "That's Principal Walker's office. He's expecting you. See you around."

She wiggled her fingers and turned on her heel, stepping into a classroom halfway down the hall. "Good luck," she called back to Hendricks, and pulled the door shut behind her.

Hendricks stood for a moment, frozen, after Portia had gone.

Suddenly, the school doors crashed open, hitting the wall so hard it made Hendricks jump and turn around, her heart pounding in her throat. Cool winter air gusted around her.

For a second she'd been so sure there would be someone there, coming down the hall toward her.

But it was just the wind.

# CHAPTER 2

HENDRICKS STOOD ON THE CURB OUTSIDE HER NEW HOUSE, shivering despite her puffy down coat. Portia and Connor hadn't been the only ones who'd mentioned the house to her today. Everyone seemed to know where she'd moved. Everyone seemed to know it had a name.

Steele House.

"Weird-ass town," Hendricks muttered. Nothing about the house looked special. It was two stories high, with three bay windows and a wraparound porch. Only the porch looked wrong. It was newer than the rest of the house, its white paint much brighter than the siding, the green trim shiny and glossy where the shutters had already faded with age.

Hendricks hitched her backpack farther up her shoulder and started up the steps. They were new too, but unpainted, splinters still jutting out of the raw wood. She pushed the front door open and heard the television blaring from the living room. Then there was a shuffling sound, and the television switched off.

"Mrs. Becker-O'Malley?" called a voice.

"No, it's just me." Hendricks kicked off her shoes and walked into the living room. Her baby brother's nanny, Gillian, was sitting on the floor, cross-legged, a pile of laundry heaped beside her. "My parents aren't back until late."

"Oh, right." Gillian folded the sweatshirt she'd been holding. She was in her twenties, a junior at St. Joseph's University, but she was pint-sized and looked a lot younger. She wore an old band T-shirt tucked into thrift-store Levi's. Her short hair was dyed lavender and pulled back from her face in a vicious ponytail, spiky strands escaping around her neck.

"Also, nobody's going to care if you watch TV," Hendricks added, plopping onto the floor to help fold.

Gillian looked embarrassed. "I wasn't really watching anything, I just wanted the noise. Brady went down for his nap about twenty minutes ago, and it gets so quiet in here. Well, mostly."

She pulled a doll out from behind a pillow on the couch, sheepish. "This was in Brady's room, but it started, um, *talking* earlier? It was really creeping me out, so I—"

"Hid it," Hendricks finished, taking the doll from Gillian. "Good call."

It had been her grandmother's, one of the first talking dolls on the market, and she knew it was special, but she'd only ever found it disturbing. There were deep cracks all along its porcelain face, cutting across its mouth and nose. And the doll wasn't smiling. Its lips were pressed together, tight, like it was hiding something.

But the worst thing about the doll was that its voice box was broken, which meant it started talking on its own sometimes.

Truly, Hendricks thought, these were the things nightmares were made of. It was like her parents *wanted* their son to develop a phobia.

Gillian looked around, shivering. "It's kind of a strange old house, isn't it?"

"Yeah." Hendricks put the doll aside and absently balled a pair of socks. "A bunch of kids at school said it had a name. Steele House?"

"Really?" Gillian raised an eyebrow without looking up. "Do all the houses around here have names?"

"I was sort of hoping you could tell me."

"Sorry. I've only been here since fall semester, so I'm not up on the local history yet. When do you think it'll be finished?"

Hendricks shrugged. The house was mid-renovation. There were heavy plastic sheets hanging over the doorways and covering the windows, and some of the drywall hadn't gone up yet, leaving the boards beneath gaping and bare. Her parents had been so desperate to get out of Philadelphia that they'd decided to move in before their new house was even finished.

*Because of me*, Hendricks thought. She suddenly, desperately wanted to be alone.

"I can take it from here if you want to head out," she said, pulling a fresh stack of laundry onto her lap. It smelled so strongly of the lemon-scented soap her family always bought that, for a second, she wanted to bury her face in the fabric and breathe. It was the first thing that'd felt familiar all day.

It took her a second to realize Gillian was talking again. " . . . have this pop quiz in astronomy, which I only took because I thought we'd be, like, looking at stars and shit, but apparently it's mostly math. So I have to study."

"Good luck," Hendricks said. Gillian made a face as she stepped outside, and then Hendricks heard the porch creak as she jogged down the steps. She slipped a hand into her pocket, her cell phone warm beneath her fingers.

If anything about this move had been normal, now was when she'd be texting all the people she'd left behind.

Oh my God this place suuuuucks!

Followed by the inevitable sympathetic responses.

**Come back! We miss you! Wish you were here!**

Half of her wanted to take the phone out, to check her messages. There would be a few, she knew. Her old friends had tried to keep in touch after what happened, but she'd ended up pulling away. Everything felt tainted by Grayson.

She pulled her hand out of her pocket, chest twisting.

*Clean slate.*

She held those words in her head as she pushed herself to her feet, looking around for something to like about her new home. A plastic sheet hanging over the front window rustled, and then went still. Hendricks frowned, the skin on the back of her neck tingling. But it was just the wind.

She walked into the kitchen, eyes moving over the brand-new steel appliances. It was all very modern, everything sleek and clean, the lines sharp. But the old parts of the house were still there, not quite hidden beneath the slate tile and the sculptural light fixtures. The floorboards creaked and the walls groaned and cold air leaked in from the windows, no matter how tightly you closed them. It made Hendricks think of an aging actress who'd gotten too much Botox, desperate to maintain her youth.

Water dripped, steadily.

Hendricks listened, something crawling very slowly up her spine. The sound was hollow and heavy and it seemed to be coming from directly behind her. But the only thing behind her was wall.

Her dad said the acoustics in this place were weird. Old-house noises, mixed with half-finished construction. And then he'd shrugged and thrown his hands up, a smile quirking his lips, like this was all charming, somehow.

*It's not charming*, Hendricks thought. *It's creepy.*

She went to the sink and jerked the faucet handle down. The dripping sound stopped, but now there was a smell coming up from the drain. A dank, rotten smell, like food going bad in the garbage disposal. But the sink didn't have a garbage disposal.

"Gross," Hendricks muttered, stepping away from the sink. Her nose itched as she walked down the hallway.

She suddenly understood why Gillian had been so weird about the television. It wasn't a normal sort of quiet in this house. It was the kind of quiet that was made up of a dozen small noises. Wood creaking and faucets dripping and windows groaning from the wind.

She needed something—music or reality television or even the news—to drone it all out. She went back into the living room and started digging around in the couch cushion for the remote.

There was a sound above her.

Hendricks looked up at the ceiling, frowning. The sound had been a clear, even creak. Like a footstep.

As she stared upward, she heard another creak. And then another. They moved from one corner of the ceiling to the other, like someone was walking down the second-story hall. And then, abruptly, they stopped.

Hendricks stood, her sudden fear blotting out everything else. She told herself Gillian must've forgotten to mention that a construction worker had come by. Workers had been in and out of the house since they'd moved in, setting up the internet and checking the wiring and fussing with the boiler.

Her eyes ticked off everything near the front door. No muddy worker boots on the welcome mat, no dirty parka hanging from the hooks on the wall. She looked out the window and saw that there wasn't a truck in the drive, either.

Her skin began to creep. Hendricks crossed the living room and walked into the kitchen. There was supposed to be a door separating the staircase from the kitchen, but it hadn't been put up yet. Instead, a sheet of plastic blocked the way. Hendricks yanked it aside.

"Who's there?" she shouted up the stairs.

The house was silent in response.

Hendricks was very aware of the sound of her heartbeat, the way her breath seemed to catch in her throat. Slowly, she made her way to the second floor, and leaned her head against Brady's bedroom door. She could hear the soft whir of his white noise machine, but that was all.

Then, behind her, a long creak. She jerked around.

No one there.

She stared into the shadows for a long moment, her heartbeat slowing, her breath growing calmer. And then—

*BANG! BANG! BANG!*

This time, the sound seemed to come from downstairs. Hendricks took the stairs two at a time and whipped open the plastic partition. She was trying to think of what she could use as a weapon—her dad's golf club in the hall closet, the butcher knife in the kitchen—when her eyes landed on the window, and she saw Portia standing on the porch. *Laughing.*

Hendricks threw the front door open, her pulse still fluttering. "You scared the *shit*—"

Connor stood directly in front of her door, wearing jeans and a faded T-shirt instead of his track uniform. He held a basket of clearly homemade muffins, and his cheeks were slightly flushed, but that might have been from the cold.

"Hey," he said, smiling sheepishly. "My mom wanted me to bring these over. Sort of a welcome-to-the-neighborhood thing."

He gestured to the muffins. As though Hendricks could have possibly missed them.

Portia stumbled over to his side, smile wide. "I'm sorry, I couldn't help myself. You said you were going to be all alone in there, and . . ." She shook her head and rose to her tiptoes, craning her neck to see past Hendricks. "Aren't you going to invite us in?"

Hendricks stepped aside, dumbfounded, holding the door open.

"Nice," Portia said, but in a way that seemed to mean something else. Connor shot her a look.

"It *does* look nice," he said, handing Hendricks the muffins. "Your parents must've put a lot of work into this place."

Hendricks closed the door and followed them into the living room. "What do you mean?"

"It used to be different," Connor explained. "Nobody lived here in a long time, and it was pretty dangerous to come inside."

Portia snorted. "Yeah, we all thought the walls might fall down on you or something. But it sort of looks like a real house now."

Her eyes narrowed on the hall closet and she pulled it open— quick—like she expected there to be someone waiting for her on the other side.

"Looking for something?" Hendricks asked.

Portia shrugged, seeming disappointed as she closed the door. She pulled out her phone. "I thought that led to the basement."

"There isn't really a basement, but the storm cellar door is outside."

"Right," Portia said, distracted. "I knew that."

And, again, that feeling like she was missing something. Hendricks frowned. "*How* did you know that?"

"I told you, this place was empty for years and then, out of nowhere, your parents buy it and fix it up." Portia hesitated, her eyes moving around the room. "Or, you know, tried to fix it up or whatever—"

The phone in her hand vibrated, cutting her off. She zeroed in on the screen again, chewing on her lip. "You said your parents were out, right?"

Hendricks heard an ominous chime.

"Yeah," Hendricks said. "Why?"

Portia's thumbs flew across the phone screen, and a whoosh sound told Hendricks she'd sent a message. "Some of our friends wanted to check out your place."

Hendricks felt a sudden sinking in her gut. "So?"

"We thought since you couldn't come out to meet everyone, we could invite them over here," Connor said.

His face had transformed into another megawatt smile, and, once again, Hendricks felt like the funniest, most charming person in the room.

*Dangerous*, she thought. The ones who made you feel like the only person in the room were the ones you really had to watch out for.

# CHAPTER 3

HENDRICKS TOOK A SIP OF BEER, HOPING IT MIGHT CALM her nerves, but the beer just sloshed around her stomach, making her feel worse. She bit the inside of her cheek so she wouldn't make a face.

She couldn't even remember who'd brought the beer. It'd just appeared in her kitchen, along with three other Drearford High students whose names she'd immediately forgotten.

"And *this* is Casey Claire," the girl beside her was saying, pointing to a blurry photo on her phone. Hendricks nodded, trying to keep her expression politely interested. The girl she was talking to was Asian and beautiful, with thick, waist-length brown hair with bleachy blond highlights and eyeglasses shaped like octagons.

Hendricks struggled to remember the girl's name. It was some sort of bird. Robin, maybe. Or Sparrow.

The girl kept talking. "Casey laughs like a drunk hyena, but her mother is sleeping with the volleyball coach, so you have to be nice to her if you want to make the team."

*Wren?* Hendricks thought, pursing her lips. *Goose?*

"Hey, Raven! Toss me another beer!"

*Right.* Raven.

Raven removed a Natty Light from the cardboard box on the

marble island and tossed it across the kitchen to a dark-skinned boy with thick black hair and the kind of perfectly straight teeth people paid six hundred dollars a cap for.

Hendricks didn't have to strain to remember his name. *Blake.* He looked like a Blake. Pretty and dumb. The captain of some sports team. Baseball? Lacrosse? Raven had mentioned that, too, but it'd already slipped right out of Hendricks's mind.

He stood beside another boy, this one good-looking in the exact same way that Connor was good-looking. Hendricks thought they must be brothers, and her suspicion was confirmed when the boy curled an arm around Connor's neck, putting him into what seemed like a friendly headlock. If headlocks could be friendly.

Hendricks frowned, watching the two boys wrestle around her kitchen. Brothers did that, right? Or should she be concerned?

She anxiously twisted the tab on top of her beer can, eyeing the staircase that led to the second floor. She'd already checked on Brady—twice—and she knew he was fine. But all the noise still made her feel guilty.

Finally, Connor said, "Come on, Finn, knock it off!" and awkwardly untwisted himself from the headlock. His hair was mussed, his cheeks pink from the exertion. "The new girl's going to think we were raised in a barn."

Finn stumbled back a few feet, colliding with a kitchen counter. He straightened, looking embarrassed. "Sorry," he said to Hendricks.

"It's okay," she said, but her stomach gave a lurch. She looked down at her hands, which were clutching her beer can like it was a lifeline.

Everyone was being totally nice, so why did she feel like everything she'd eaten that day was moving around inside of her, floating on a sea of warm beer?

Maybe it was just that it felt like things were happening very fast. It was only her first day, and already she was surrounded by people who claimed they wanted to be her friends. It seemed too easy. There had to be a catch.

A lump thickened inside her throat. Could they know about what happened to her? Her old friends had done this, too, acting too nice, like she was something that had to be handled delicately. It was one of the reasons she'd been cool with moving away. No one wanted friends who treated you like something that could be broken.

Her brain raced, wondering how anyone in Drearford might've found out. There wasn't anything online, she'd made sure of that, but Philadelphia wasn't far away. Maybe someone here knew someone from her old school, someone who'd been at the party . . .

"Are you cool?" Raven glanced up from her phone, frowning. "You look a little overwhelmed."

*Overwhelmed.* That was a good word for how she felt.

"Maybe a little," Hendricks admitted, and she tried to hide her nerves with another swallow of beer.

"I hear that." Raven slid her phone into her pocket and leaned against the counter. "I was new last year. It's the worst."

Hendricks raised her eyebrows. "You've only been here a year?"

Raven seemed so settled. Hendricks assumed she'd grown up here like everyone else.

But Raven was nodding. "My family moved up from Brooklyn at the beginning of sophomore year. The small-town thing isn't really my scene, so I figured I'd totally hate it, but then Portia convinced me to try out for cheerleading. She said it would do amazing things for my brand." Raven lifted her eyebrows. "I'm not even kidding. My *brand*. She actually said that."

Hendricks snorted. Raven was currently wearing a pair of ripped-up jeans over black tights, topped with a little-boy's summer camp T-shirt that looked like it came from the Goodwill, and a chunky, beaded necklace. Her octagon-shaped glasses made her dark eyes look big and round.

Everything about her screamed *artist*. She was about the last person you'd expect to be a cheerleader.

"Well?" Hendricks asked. "Did you?"

"*Yeah*." Raven dragged the word out, turning it into two syllables. "I did. And you want to know the most batshit part? She was completely right. Cheerleading might be basic or whatever, but it's also *dance*. It's creative. I . . . sort of love it." A shy smile flicked over Raven's face.

"You're right. That is batshit," Hendricks said, and Raven laughed out loud. She laughed like a little kid—mouth open, head thrown back, no self-consciousness at all—and it made Hendricks grin in return, relaxing a little.

"Are you talking about the cheerleading thing again?" asked Portia, appearing beside them. "All I did was make one *tiny* little suggestion. And if I hadn't, you'd probably be like that Lauren Groggin chick." To Hendricks, "She performs spoken-word poetry at the coffee shop every Friday night and wears a cape unironically."

Raven snickered and said, "Hey, some of her poems are sort of good."

"That doesn't mean I want to hear them while drinking my cold brew." Portia's eyes twinkled. "So how are we going to help the new girl?"

It took Hendricks a second to realize they were talking about her again. "What makes you think I need help?"

Portia flicked a hand, dismissive. "Everyone needs help," she said, which Hendricks had to admit was sort of randomly deep.

"We could use another cheerleader on the team," Raven offered, turning the tab of her Natty Light. "Cassidy fell last week, and she says she only twisted her ankle, but *I* think—"

But Portia was already shaking her head. "Hendricks isn't a cheerleader."

"Why not?" Hendricks asked. She couldn't be sure, but that had sounded like an insult.

Portia rolled her eyes. "Ugh, no, I didn't mean that to be bitchy. It's just . . . you're sort of weird."

Raven snorted.

"I meant *good* weird," Portia insisted. "Like an alien from a planet where teenagers wear a lot of oversized sweaters and forget to brush their hair but have unfairly clear skin."

"And at least fifty percent of that was a real compliment," Raven pointed out. "I think that's a personal best."

Hendricks was momentarily at a loss for words. She'd never really liked that expression before, *loss for words*, as though the words could just fall out of your head and be gone forever, but it was an accurate description of how she felt. She knew there was a normal thing to say in this scenario, and there might have been a time when she could've figured out what it was, but for now all she could do was open and close her mouth, like a fish.

"Maybe I don't even mean weird. You're more different. Like, I can't figure out your deal at all, and normally I'm really good at that," Portia said.

"My deal?" Hendricks asked.

"Who were you at your last high school? I need a cliché."

Hendricks's eyebrows drew together. "I don't think I was a cliché."

"Everyone is some cliché. Like, Raven's the arty chick, and I'm sort of the queen bee mean girl. Except I don't think I'm mean—"

"You're more blunt," Raven said, thoughtful. "Tactless, sometimes."

Portia flapped her hand, like tact was a silly, quaint idea she didn't care for. "So what cliché are you? A jock? Or, maybe, one of those overachieving honor student kids?" When Hendricks didn't answer, Portia's eyebrows went up. "Come on, give me something to work with. Shy and deep? Moody bad girl?"

Hendricks tugged at a cuticle. She'd never been part of a clique, never thought of herself as a cliché. She'd started dating Grayson freshman year, and then his friends became her friends, and the girl she'd been in middle school—the girl who wasn't afraid to talk to anyone, to try anything—sort of . . . faded.

It had never seemed weird to her before. But now she thought of it and felt a strange churning in her chest. *Who was she?* Just someone's girlfriend. And now she wasn't even that anymore.

"Of course, Connor likes you, which will help," Portia continued, lowering her voice. She glanced across the kitchen, where he and the other two boys were engaged in a conversation about some sort of team sport, and said, "Connor liking you is, like, a stamp of approval at Drearford."

She nudged Hendricks with her elbow, eyebrows wagging.

Hendricks swallowed, her eyes darting to the boys, and then back to Portia. This was the beginning of a longer conversation, and the kitchen didn't seem like a private enough place to get into it.

Portia took her silence as a cue to continue. "In the interest of full disclosure, Connor and I dated for a few months back in tenth, before I came out. Now we're just friends, so you totally have my blessing." Turning to Raven, she asked, "Don't you think they'd be cute together?"

"Blessing?" Hendricks repeated.

Raven pursed her lips, like she was thinking this over. "Yeah, I see it. Portia's whole thing with Connor was that he was too laid back and easygoing, while she's this crazy, mega-achieving super student, you know?"

"And also, he's a guy," Portia added.

Raven cocked her head, considering Hendricks. "But Hendricks looks like she could use a little fun."

Hendricks chewed on her lower lip, amazed that Raven—and *Portia*, apparently—had picked that up in just a few minutes of knowing her.

"My last school was pretty intense," she admitted. Understatement of the year. "But I don't know if I'm up for dating anyone right away. I kind of just want to . . . date myself."

*Date myself?*

Did she really just say that?

"See what I mean? Good weird," Portia said.

"Oh yeah," Raven added. "She's the best weird."

Hendricks took another sip of beer, trying to relax.

Across the room, Connor caught her eye and dazzled a smile at her. Hendricks smiled back, but her heart gave a complicated tug inside her chest. For a second, she imagined answering Portia's question honestly.

*Who am I? I'm the popular jock's girlfriend. I define my entire personality around him.* It was so pathetic that it made her blush, even though she hadn't said any of it out loud. Some clean slate. She pictured a rock rolling down a hill, moving too quickly, gathering mud and moss and debris—

And then slamming into a tree and breaking into a million pieces.

# CHAPTER 4

IT WASN'T UNTIL HER NEW FRIENDS HAD GONE THAT Hendricks realized how long this night was going to be. It was January dark outside, not even seven o'clock, though it looked much later. The stars hadn't come out yet, but streetlights winked through the trees.

She drummed her fingers against the counter. Her parents weren't going to be home until midnight, at the earliest.

What was she supposed to do here for five hours?

Her eyes fluttered closed. She sucked down a lungful of air and held it. She was all too aware of the sounds of the house. The groaning walls, the creaking windows . . .

And were those footsteps again? Or just her heart pounding in her ears?

Hendricks's eyes popped back open. For a moment she forgot how to breathe.

She grabbed a beer and Brady's baby monitor and headed out the back door.

Outside, everything was black and bright with cold. Hendricks's breath hovered in a cloud before her lips after she exhaled, and her skin grew rigid and coarse with goose bumps, but at least the noises were normal. The wind wasn't nearly as spooky when it wasn't tapping at her window.

Out of nowhere, a voice said, "Hey."

Hendricks started, her heart jackhammering. "Who's there?"

"Calm down," the voice said. "I didn't mean to freak you out."

Hendricks squinted and stepped into the dark . . .

A guy sat at the edge of what was supposed to be a pool, legs dangling over the sides. The tarp that'd been covering the empty hole lay crumpled in the grass. His clothes were black and slim-fitting. Hipster cool, but Hendricks doubted that was the look around here. He wore his hair short on the sides and longer on top. It was a city trend, a sort of throwback to the fifties. Like Elvis, or James Dean.

Hendricks frowned, recognizing him from this morning. He was the guy who'd been smoking outside the school when she'd walked in to meet Portia. "What are you doing out here?"

He held up his hand, and she saw a cigarette pinched between his thumb and forefinger. Silver smoke curled into the sky.

"Oh." Her shoulders relaxed. "Are you looking for Portia and those guys? Because they already left."

His expression went stony. "No," he said, his voice landing hard on the word. "I'm not."

He brought the cigarette to his lips. It was too dark to see him clearly, but the smoldering red embers illuminated a full mouth and hooded eyes.

"Then why are you here?" The question came out sounding more accusatory than she'd meant it to.

If the boy was offended, he didn't show it. "I live just through there." He jerked his head toward the trees that separated their backyards. "This place used to be the perfect smoking spot, before you moved in."

He said this easily, but there was something going on in his eyes that made Hendricks think there was more to the story. She found herself wondering where he existed on the social totem pole of Drearford High. She doubted it was very high.

"Anyway," he continued, his tone light enough to make Hendricks think she'd imagined the moment of weirdness. "I'll stop coming over now that you guys have moved in."

He put his cigarette out on the heel of his boot and pushed himself to his feet. He looked at her for a long moment. It felt like a look of pity mixed with something else that Hendricks couldn't place. She had the sudden urge to say something to get him to stay, but all she came up with was "Yeah."

"What's up with your yard, anyway?" he asked.

Hendricks looked around. The yard was going to be beautiful, someday. Her dad had spent months planning the landscaping: a patio surrounded with trees, stone pathways twisting around bushes and flowers. The cement had been poured, the stones set, but they couldn't start planting until spring. The pathways curled around empty plots of fresh dirt. Lights surrounded the perimeter of the pool, but there were no bulbs, and, anyway, Hendricks didn't think the electricity out here was set up yet.

"We're renovating," she said.

The boy pushed the hair off his forehead. "Weird. I'd figured whoever bought this place would knock it down. Build something new."

"Why?"

"Don't you know anything about this house?"

"No," she said. "Why? What's the deal?"

"A little girl was murdered here about three years ago." For a second it looked like he might say something else. But then he shrugged with one shoulder, seeming to decide against it.

Hendricks bit the inside of her cheek, working to keep her face impassive. "That's fucked up."

But it struck her harder than she thought it would. *Little girl*. She pictured Brady, all safe and snuggly in his crib upstairs. No wonder this house felt wrong.

The boy removed his cigarette and exhaled a cloud of smoke. "The guy who did it is dead now. So there's that."

"That doesn't make it okay," Hendricks said.

"No, it doesn't." The boy said this like it was a fact, with no apology in his voice. It made Hendricks uncomfortable for reasons she couldn't name.

*Complicated*, she thought. She shivered.

"Yeah. Well, see you around, I guess." Hendricks started to turn, then hesitated, eyes resting on the boy's shadowy face.

She tilted her head. "Got a name?"

"Don't bother. If you plan on hanging with Portia and that crowd, you'll just have to forget it again."

He tucked his half-finished cigarette behind one ear and disappeared through a gap in the fence before Hendricks had a chance to respond.

Hendricks heard Brady crying as soon as she got back inside, and mentally pinched herself. She must've had the monitor's volume turned down.

He'd been sound asleep the last time she'd checked on him. But how long ago was that? An hour? More?

How much did she suck?

"I'm coming, Bear." She pushed the plastic away from the stairs and hurried past the drywall-dusted brick and exposed beams. Brady's sobs had the raw sound they got when he'd been crying for a while already.

When Hendricks reached his nursery she saw that he was

standing up in his crib, his chubby face bright red and tear-stained. His creepy talking baby doll was jabbering away on the windowsill.

"A . . . B . . . C . . . D . . . will you sing with me?" The doll had an unnaturally deep voice that grated like rocks on sandpaper.

"Sorry, Bear," Hendricks muttered. She made her way across the room to turn the doll off. The voice petered out gradually, becoming high-pitched and strained before dying away. The sound always reminded Hendricks of someone being strangled.

"Ha-ha," Brady said, sticking out his arms for her.

Ha-ha was Brady's name for Hendricks. In this case it was also a sentence, which, roughly translated, meant "Hendricks, take me out of baby prison and play with me."

Hendricks shook her head, sadly. "No, Baby Bear, no Ha-ha. You need to go back to sleep."

Brady pointed at the floor. Hendricks followed his stubby finger and saw a ratty, hand-knit blanket at the foot of his crib. Their mother had made it, and Brady couldn't sleep without it.

Hendricks plucked the blanket off the floor. "Now lie down," she said. Brady plopped to his bottom and curled onto his side. He reached a chubby hand through the slats in his crib. She let him take the blanket. "And close your eyes."

He hugged the blanket to his chest and clenched his eyes shut tight.

"Big faker," Hendricks said, standing.

She rubbed her hands up and down her arms. Goose bumps covered her skin. It was *freezing* in here. She squinted around Brady's room. Her eyes landed on the open window behind the world's creepiest baby doll, propped against the wall. Gillian must've forgotten to latch it.

She pushed the window closed, snapping the latch shut with a click. Much better. From the sound of the wind outside, it was going to storm tonight.

"Go to sleep now, Baby Bear," Hendricks said, stepping back into the hallway and gently closing the door behind her.

She headed to her room to watch TV on her laptop. She must've dozed off after a while, because the next thing she knew she was blinking into her pillow, her body heavy and tired.

She couldn't say what had roused her, but when she rolled onto her side she saw that her cell phone was lit up. Groggily, she picked it up and stared at the screen. A text from her mother:

We're on the train! Be back in an hour. XO.

The timestamp read 11:12.

*11:12?* Hendricks frowned. She couldn't remember the last time she'd fallen asleep before midnight. It must've been the beer; it had left her feeling groggy. She'd mostly stayed away from parties over the last two months.

She kicked her legs over the side of the bed and stood, stretching. She needed a glass of water, and she should probably double-check the kitchen to make sure all the beer cans had been properly disposed of. She padded out of her room and into the hall, rubbing her eyes. She blinked. And then froze.

Brady's door was open, and his baby doll was lying on the floor in the middle of his room.

"Sing with me," the doll crooned in its gravelly voice. "A . . . B . . . C . . . D . . ."

# CHAPTER 5

ABOUT SEVEN MONTHS AGO, AFTER A LATE-NIGHT STUDY session at Starbucks, Hendricks had found a single white peony inside her mom's old Jeep. It had been propped on the dashboard just behind the steering wheel, its petals all glowy in the moonlight. Grayson was always buying her peonies. She'd texted her friends Fallon and Kimiko on the drive home, and they'd both been in awe.

*How sweet!* Fallon had written back, and Kimiko had sent six heart-eyed smiley-face emojis.

It *was* sweet, Hendricks had told herself. But she'd felt something dark gathering at the edges of her mind, and it wasn't until she was home that she could pinpoint exactly what was bothering her.

Grayson didn't have a key to her car. And the car had still been locked when she'd gotten there.

So how had he gotten inside?

Now, Hendricks's skin crawled, and a bad taste trailed down the back of her throat. The taste was like pennies, or blood. She brought her fingers to her neck, swallowing hard.

"It fell," she said out loud. The certainty in her own voice made her feel a little better. Of course it fell. Not even Grayson would drive four hours to move a doll around.

She scooped the doll off the floor and turned it off, her movements jerky. She was about to put the toy back in his room but then, thinking better of it, she opened the door to the hall closet and stowed the doll in there instead. She hurried back to her bedroom, completely forgetting about her glass of water.

But she didn't sleep. She stared up at the ceiling, her heart racing. Shadows danced across the bedroom walls, casting shapes that shifted on the surfaces surrounding her.

*It's just moonlight and clouds*, Hendricks told herself. But she had the disturbing thought that there was something else there, something that skittered back into the darkness a moment before she turned to look. Her breath grew very still.

And now she could hear the wooden walls groaning around her. Wind pressing into the windowpanes, making the glass creak.

*Old-house sounds.*

But it didn't sound like normal house sounds. It sounded deeper, sounded ragged.

Like someone breathing.

The next morning, Hendricks hovered outside the Drearford High front doors like a phantom. She felt gauzy and immaterial, as though the bitter January wind might blow her away.

A teacher Hendricks only vaguely recognized walked past. "Good morning, Hendricks!" she chirped, pushing through the front doors.

Hendricks started, and it took her a beat too long to say "Morning" back. It was surreal. She'd been a student at her old school for almost three years and most of the teachers there still called her Henrietta.

*Must be the small-town vibe*, she thought, heading inside.

It wasn't just the teacher. Half the kids in the hall looked up as she made her way toward her homeroom. They jerked their chins at her, their hands lifting in a wave.

"Hey, Hendricks."

"Morning, Hendricks!"

"See you in class."

Everyone knew who she was. It felt like standing under a spotlight.

*Oh God.* Had they been *talking* about her?

Hendricks felt a wave of heat sweep over her cheeks.

"Hey, girl." Portia suddenly appeared, an arm snaking around Hendricks's elbow. She had a tray of iced coffees balanced in her other hand. "Come sit with us. I picked up Dead Guy on my way in."

"Dead Guy?"

"It's what we have instead of a Starbucks. The local coffee shop is called Dead Guy Joe." Portia made a face. "So gross, right? They should seriously make the owner change it. Anyway, at least they have cold brew. I didn't know what you drink, so I loaded yours with sugar and milk."

*Thoughtful.* Hendricks smiled. "Good guess." She slid the coffee out of the tray, grateful. "Thanks."

"Don't mention it." Portia's eyes flicked over Hendricks's outfit, taking in her ratty sneakers and oversized fisherman's sweater, courtesy of her favorite thrift store back in Philly. Portia's eyebrow gave a subtle twitch. "By the way, I'm absolutely loving this whole 'I don't care that I look homeless' vibe you've got going on. *Very* street-style chic."

Hendricks honestly didn't know whether she was meant to take this as a compliment or an insult.

Portia wore a pair of dark wash jeans and a formfitting sweater. The silver polka dots on her sweater perfectly matched her heeled silver booties. She looked like she had an entire wardrobe department helping her get dressed in the morning.

Before Hendricks could formulate a response, Portia was maneuvering her through the cafeteria to the table in the back corner where Raven and Connor were already sitting.

"Refreshments," Portia announced, plopping the remaining coffees in the middle of the table. "And look who I found wandering the halls, frightened and alone."

It took Hendricks a second to realize she meant her. "Oh," she sputtered. "Hi!" Followed by an awkward wave that she immediately regretted.

Raven mumbled something that didn't sound like words, managing to lift her head only long enough to grab a coffee. Connor flashed a wide grin.

"Hey," he said. "Good party last night."

"Yeah, thanks," said Hendricks. She started to pull out a chair, but Portia slid into it first, pushing Hendricks aside with a hip bump.

Hendricks frowned and tried to catch her eye. Portia was picking a piece of lint off her sweater and seemed not to notice.

*Okay.* Hendricks slid into the empty seat beside Connor instead. *That was weird.*

Raven blinked, slowly, as she aimed the coffee straw at her mouth. "Mmm. Better."

"Raven's a zombie in the morning," Portia explained.

"Need brains," Raven murmured. Her eyelids lowered as she slurped coffee. "I mean caffeine."

"Connor's the morning person among us," Portia said. "Don't you get up at, like, six for crew?"

"Five," Connor corrected, leaning back and stretching his arms behind his head. The gesture pulled Hendricks's eyes to his biceps, where they remained until Portia cleared her throat.

"Crew," Hendricks repeated, cheeks flaring. "That's, like, boats and stuff, right?"

"Boats and stuff." The skin at the corners of Connor's eyes crinkled when he laughed. "You guys don't do crew back in Philly?"

"Nah, we're more into hockey."

Connor was nodding. "Right, you've got the Flyers down there. I have a buddy who's into them."

Hendricks didn't follow any sports, but she nodded like this was something they had in common, silently praying he didn't ask her any follow-up questions.

Connor slid his elbows onto the table, leaning toward her. "You know, I've wanted to see the inside of your house since I was a little kid."

Hendricks felt her posture stiffen. "Because of the murder?"

The skin between Connor's eyebrows creased, and a look of horror crossed his face. "That little girl? No, that's seriously morbid." After a beat, his grin returned. "It's just, my older brothers and I built this tree house out in Ridgefield woods when we were kids. It's about a mile away, maybe? Anyway, you can see directly into the upstairs bedroom of Steele House from that tree house, and I used to stare at it when I was real little, thinking someday I might buy that house and, like, live there." Connor shrugged and looked down at his hands. "But you got there first."

He said it like he was saying "Good for you," not like he was jealous. Hendricks found herself returning his smile.

She used to be good at flirting. She hadn't had a lot of practice in the last few years, but she could feel it coming back to her, like a language she'd forgotten she could speak. "Let me get this straight. You can see *into* my house from some tree a mile away?"

She'd injected just the right amount of teasing into her words, and Connor's smile froze.

"Oh. Shit. Yeah, but, like, I'd never go there *now*. Damn." He sat up, brushing the hair from his forehead with a flick of his hand. "You might want to get some curtains, though. I didn't even think of that."

"Yeah, heavy ones." Hendricks felt her nose start to wrinkle and immediately heard Grayson's voice in her head: *I didn't realize you were so forward.* A wave of shame rolled through her, and she shrugged.

Connor, nodding, didn't seem to notice her sudden discomfort.

"Um, and maybe an alarm system," she continued, which wasn't a bad idea, actually.

"And maybe a sign that says, '*I know you're looking into my room, creeper,*'" Connor added.

"Or, 'I know you're looking into my room, *Connor.*'"

Connor raised his hands, all innocence. "I told you I wouldn't go up there anymore!"

Hendricks laughed, softly, trying to push Grayson's voice out of her head. He wasn't her boyfriend anymore, she reminded herself. She didn't have to care about what he thought.

Connor glanced over his shoulder then, at the sound of voices rising up on the other side of the cafeteria. When he looked back at her, his expression had changed. His mouth was drawn into a tight line, and a crease had formed between his brows. He looked nervous.

Hendricks felt her muscles knot.

"So." Connor wrapped a hand around the back of his neck. "It might be too early for this."

Hendricks frowned. *Please don't,* she thought.

Out loud, she said, "Um, too early for what?"

"I'd like to ask you out on a date tomorrow night."

Her skin felt suddenly hot. She pictured the inside of a toaster, how the filaments would glow red as it began to heat up. She imagined her cheeks looked like that.

"You'd like to ask me on a date for tomorrow night?" she asked. "Or tomorrow night, you'd like to ask me out on a date?"

"Which one are you more likely to say yes to?" Connor asked, wary.

Hendricks didn't answer right away. Grayson's voice drifted through her head again: *I dare you to go to a movie with me Friday night,* and with it came the same confusing rush of emotions that always accompanied memories of those early days in their relationship.

Shame. Disgust.

And, worst of all, *sadness.* Despite everything, she actually missed that Grayson, the one he'd been in the beginning, before everything went so badly wrong.

How messed up was that?

"I . . . I don't know," she said after a moment. "Can I think about it?"

Connor smiled and said, "Of course." He didn't sound offended at all. He picked up the abandoned straw wrapper from her coffee and twisted it around his finger. "Take all the time you need."

*How's forever?* Hendricks thought. *Does that work for you?*

From the corner of her eye, she caught Portia aiming an extremely jagged eyebrow in her direction.

*Told you so,* the eyebrow said.

# CHAPTER 6

BRADY SMUSHED A CHUBBY HAND INTO THE PILE OF FOOD ON his high chair tray, somehow managing to wedge a single pea between his fingers. Laughing, he launched it at Hendricks.

*Thwack.* Right in her hair.

"Ha-ha!" he said, lifting his hands.

This time, the word translated to "Food is boring. Time to play!"

"No, not until you finish your dinner," Hendricks's dad said, fixing Brady's bib. Hendricks didn't know why he bothered. Brady's T-shirt, face, and hair were already covered in mushed-up potatoes and peas. Ironically, the bib was the only part of his outfit that was still sort of clean.

"Yeah, you're supposed to *eat* the peas, Bear," Hendricks said, finger combing her hair until a fat little pea plopped onto her plate. "See?" she said to her parents. "This is why you should just feed him with a spoon."

"It helps with his fine motor development if he does it himself," her mother said, distracted. She was staring into the kitchen, her head tilted. "Are we sure about the subway tile, Frank?"

"I thought you said it was classic," Hendricks's dad said.

"Now I'm thinking it's a little boring." She gestured with her fork. "What about something with a little color?"

"We have another four bedrooms and two bathrooms to get to,

Diane. I think we're going to have to live with it." Turning to Hendricks, he added, "So. How's the first week of school going?"

"Good," she said, cheeks flushing as she looked back down at her plate. A pea escaped from the prongs of her fork and she stabbed it, viciously. "Surprisingly good, actually."

"Really?" Now, her mother was studying her, a wrinkle creasing the skin between her eyebrows. Her voice sounded casual, but Hendricks wasn't fooled. "Why surprisingly good?"

She probably thought Hendricks didn't notice the look that passed between her and her dad. They hadn't talked to her about it, but she figured they thought it was too early for her to start dating again.

*You don't have to worry about that*, she thought.

"Did you meet anyone interesting?" her dad asked, taking a sip of wine.

Hendricks might've groaned, but she was in too good a mood. Instead, she flicked her fork so that the pea shot across her plate and landed in a pile of mashed potatoes.

*Score*, she thought.

"Define *interesting*," she said.

Her mother started to reply, then merely pressed her lips back together, and Hendricks knew she couldn't bring herself to ask, *Did you meet a boy?*

She bit her lip. Was it that obvious? She kept replaying the moment in the cafeteria this morning, how Connor's face had gotten all scrunched up and nervous before he'd asked her out, how he'd been so cool when she told him she needed some time to think about it before giving him an answer.

She wasn't going to say yes. Yes was a bad idea on so many levels. But that didn't mean she couldn't enjoy this part, the part before anything had even happened, when there weren't any expectations. She knew that as soon as she told Connor she couldn't date him it would all be over. She had to savor this while she still could.

"You know, I actually have a ton of homework to do," Hendricks said, grabbing her dinner plate and pushing back from her chair. "I should take the rest of this upstairs."

"Would you like me to bring you some tea?" her mother called as Hendricks left the room.

Hendricks had a feeling that her mother was going to bring her tea regardless of what she said, probably picturing the two of them lying across her bed and having a "serious conversation" about dating and boys. An unexpected lump rose in her throat.

"I'm good, but thanks." And then she went to her room and closed the door behind her.

Setting her dinner plate on her dresser, Hendricks picked up her book bag and flopped onto her bed. She considered actually doing her homework, but she didn't have much yet. Most of her teachers had told her that she should just listen to the lectures and try to follow along.

Instead, she went to her closet and dug around inside, locating a familiar orange soccer jersey.

It was Grayson's. Or, at least, it used to be. He'd given it to her last year, after one of his friends had accidentally spilled his beer all over her at a party, ruining her shirt. Even now, after everything that had happened between them, it hurt Hendricks's heart to imagine giving it up.

She didn't want Grayson back. But that didn't mean she didn't miss him sometimes. Maybe not *him*, exactly, but how it'd felt to be with him. For a little while, she'd had one person who loved her more than anyone else. She'd had a person to go out with on Friday nights, and hang out with her at parties, and call before she went to sleep at night. It'd been nice. She missed it. She brought the jersey to her nose and breathed it in. It still smelled woodsy and clean, like Grayson.

For a second—just a second—she considered what it would be like if she told Connor yes.

Where would he take her on their date? Was this the kind of place where guys took girls to old-fashioned soda shops to split a milkshake? Or did that sort of thing only happen in movies?

She shook her head, suddenly disgusted with herself. What was wrong with her? She'd *just* gotten rid of Grayson for good. Was she really sitting here with his old jersey, feeling all sad and mopey about how things used to be? Did she really want to jump into another thing so soon?

*No*, she thought firmly, she really, really didn't.

She needed a distraction to keep her from obsessing. She tossed the jersey back into her closet and emptied her new schoolbooks, notebooks, and pens onto the faded duvet.

*French*, she thought, sliding her textbook toward her. She'd study French.

Her eyes glazed over as she flipped through the pages, trying to find the chapter they'd been talking about in class.

She wasn't facing the window, but she could see the gauzy curtain from the corner of her eye. The moment she looked down at her book, she was sure she saw the curtain flick, as if it had been reaching for her while her eyes had been turned away. But when she jerked around to look at it directly, it was still.

Her skin crept.

*There's nothing there*, she thought, feeling stupid.

But she stared at it for a while longer. Just to be sure.

It was a white curtain, made of a thin material intended to let in the sunlight. But there was no sunlight now, only flat darkness. It made Hendricks think of shrouds used to cover dead bodies. Without meaning to, she pictured bloodstains and a gaping mouth. She felt her body temperature drop by several degrees.

Somewhere in the back of her mind, she considered the idea that the curtain *had* been reaching for her, but that it'd gone still again the second she turned to look at it. It was a silly, childish thought, and she was embarrassed the second it went through her head. But she couldn't unthink it.

Something shifted in the hall outside her door. Hendricks jerked around, and her hand slipped. The corner of the page cut deep into the pad of her finger.

"Shit," she said, watching a line of red appear on her thumb. She stuck her thumb into her mouth to stop the bleeding. She didn't think they'd even unpacked the Band-Aids yet . . .

A laugh sounded on the other side of her door. Hendricks's head shot up, the hairs on the back of her neck twitching.

That laugh . . . it had sounded just like Grayson.

But Grayson was in Philly. So that wasn't possible.

She crept across the room, easing her door open. The hall was empty. Moonlight snuck in through the opposite window, painting the fresh floorboards and giving the plastic sheeting still hanging from the unfinished walls a strange, silvery sheen. Otherwise, everything was dark.

"Mom?" Hendricks called, thinking her mother had brought up tea after all. But she could hear her mother's voice downstairs, calling for her dad to help with the dishes. Besides, the laugh had sounded like a boy's.

The cut on Hendricks's thumb smarted. The taste of blood was coppery on her tongue. She stepped into the hall, shivering a little. This old house was so drafty. Even though she could tell that the hall window was closed, there was still a breeze rustling the plastic against the walls, snaking around her ankles.

"Hello?" she murmured, lips moving around her thumb. Something uneasy prickled below her skin. She almost expected an answer, but the hall stayed quiet.

Slowly, the muscles in Hendricks's shoulders began to relax. Maybe she'd drifted off while reading her French book and ... dreamed the laugh. Shaking her head, she stepped back into her bedroom, one hand already pushing the door closed.

A voice, low and deep, said, "What are you doing here, loser?"

Hendricks jerked around, her heart hammering.

"Who's there?" She tried to keep her voice even, but she could hear the tremor that had crept into her words. Her brain flashed to Portia banging on the window the day before. Maybe she'd convinced one of the guys at their lunch table to swing by and mess with her.

She stepped fully into the hallway now. The new floors out here were still splintery, and Hendricks could feel tiny shards of wood separating from the floorboards, pricking her toes. She heard the low hum of her parents' voices drift up from the living room, but there was another sound beneath that. Hendricks paused, head cocked, listening.

More laughing.

Goose bumps crept up her arms. Now that Hendricks was listening for it, she couldn't deny what she heard. Someone was in her house. Someone was in her house *laughing*.

A shudder went down her back. Her eyes were drawn to the

shadows behind the plastic covering her walls. She clenched and unclenched her fists and realized that sweat had broken out on her palms.

The laughter seemed to be coming from the bathroom. Hendricks crept down the hallway, every moment expecting the floorboards to creak and groan beneath her feet. But they were new, and her movements were silent. She stopped outside the bathroom and pressed her ear to the door.

She heard voices now. It sounded like two guys talking.

Hendricks swore, quietly, her whole body relaxing as she realized what must've happened. She'd been listening to a podcast about sheet masks while she got ready for school that morning, and she must've forgotten to turn her Bluetooth speaker off. It was probably picking up her dad's phone downstairs. It did that sometimes.

Relieved, she pushed the door open and flicked the light on, eyes already scanning the sink for her bright-blue speaker . . .

She caught sight of her reflection in the mirror above the sink, and felt her stomach drop.

Her long, blond hair had been chopped short. Spiky locks stuck straight up in some places. In others, it'd been hacked so close to her scalp that she could see spots of raw, bleeding skin.

Hendricks's chest tightened. She lifted a shaking hand to her head, cringing as her fingers brushed against a deep gash where her hair had been cut too close to her skin. Blood bubbled up beneath her fingers and trickled over her face in dark rivulets.

And that wasn't all. Someone had drawn on her face with blue Sharpie, circling her forehead, her nose, a spot on her chin.

*Acne*, they'd written. *Nose too big. Mole.*

The familiar hot burn of shame rose in her cheeks. She might've thought she was imagining this, somehow, except that she could feel the blood trailing down her skin, and the steady throb of pain from the deep gash in her scalp.

Hendricks staggered backward, crashing into the bathroom door. *He's here,* her mind screamed. It was the only explanation. He'd crawled through her window; he'd done this to her while she was sleeping. He'd always said she'd be ruined if they ever broke up, that no one would want her if she left him.

Now he'd made sure of it.

Hendricks drew in a long, sobbing breath and grasped for the doorknob behind her back. She threw it open and raced back to her room, slamming her door so hard the wall shuddered.

That's when she saw the dinner knife she'd brought up from downstairs. It was protruding from the back of her door. Like a warning.

The scream seemed to rip out of her. It clawed up her throat and exploded from her lips, so loud that her ears were still ringing seconds later.

Footsteps pounded down the hall. Hendricks lurched away from her door, but it was her dad who tore into her bedroom, not Grayson.

"What happened?" He was already looking around for the intruder, his mind clearly following the same path that Hendricks's had. "Is that little prick here?"

Hendricks shook her head and motioned to her face, her hair.

Her father only blinked at her, frowning. "Hendricks?" he said. "What's going on?"

"Don't—don't you see what he did?"

The perplexed look didn't leave her father's face. Confused now, Hendricks spun to face the mirror hanging above her dresser.

What she saw caused the blood to chill in her veins.

Her reflection was normal again. Her hair hadn't been hacked off. It was still in a bun, a bit messier now that she'd been digging her

59

fingers into it, but it was all there. There was no Sharpie on her face, no blood dripping down her cheeks. Everything looked exactly like it was supposed to.

"No," Hendricks breathed, leaning closer to the mirror. She ran her hands over her face, her lips. She pulled her hair out of its bun, fingers shaking. "You don't understand, a second ago it was different."

Her dad was staring at her, frowning slightly. "What was different?"

Hendricks's throat felt tight. She didn't want to admit what she'd seen. What she'd *thought* she'd seen. It was too crazy to say out loud.

"I don't know," she mumbled, twisting her hair back into a bun.

Her father didn't look convinced. Awkwardly, he said, "That counselor we talked to said stuff like this might happen, remember? Something like forty percent of people with PTSD experience auditory or visual hallucinations."

"Jesus, Dad, I don't have *PTSD*," Hendricks said, her voice thick. "It was a trick of the light or something."

"I'm just saying, I know you told us you didn't want to talk to anyone about what happened, but maybe—"

"I'm *fine*."

There was a long pause. Hendricks's dad appeared to be having some sort of internal battle with himself.

The word *therapy* had been thrown around a lot over the last few months. Hendricks had told her parents that she didn't want to sit on some old man's couch and talk about her feelings, that she wouldn't even know where to start, and they'd agreed to let her try to handle things on her own for a while. But Hendricks knew they weren't so sure that was the right choice. Sometimes she wasn't so sure herself.

"Okay," her dad said, finally. "Just try to get some rest?"

Hendricks heard what he wasn't saying. *I'll let this go once. But if it happens again, we're getting your mother and doctors and prescription medication involved.*

She nodded, stiffly, staring at him until he backed into the hallway.

When she closed the door, she saw that the steak knife was still embedded in the wood.

# CHAPTER 7

THE NEXT MORNING, HENDRICKS HURRIED DOWNSTAIRS while her parents were getting ready for work. She heard their voices drift beneath their closed door.

"Someone needs to talk to her about her anxiety, Diane," her dad was saying.

"I just don't know whether that should be us," her mom responded. "I still think a therapist would—"

Hendricks hurried down the stairs, tuning the rest of their argument out. She didn't need a therapist, and the only way she could think to avoid that argument was to avoid her parents completely. She grabbed an apple from the fruit bowl on the kitchen island and scrawled a quick note.

*Told Portia I'd meet her before school. See you later!*

It was a lie, but whatever. Her parents would just be relieved she had a Portia. She shoved the apple into her mouth and, clenching it between her teeth, she slipped into her coat and shot out the door.

The day was gray and blustery, but warmer than it had been when she first got here. Warm enough that Hendricks left her coat unzipped, enjoying the feel of the breeze against her hot cheeks.

Someone was walking just ahead of her, head hunched so she

couldn't see his face. She followed him for a block and a half before she recognized the black clothes, the retro haircut. It was that guy from after her party, the one who'd been smoking by her pool and wouldn't tell her his name.

"Hey!" she shouted, jogging to catch up with him. "Wait up!"

His posture stiffened. He hesitated, but didn't turn around.

"Are you following me or something?" Hendricks joked, bumping her shoulder into his.

He touched his arm, like her little shoulder bump had actually hurt him. His face was guarded as he jerked his chin at a run-down house on the corner. "I told you, we're neighbors. Sort of."

*Right*, Hendricks thought, nodding. She remembered him saying something about living in the house just behind hers.

"Maybe we should build one of those soup-can telephones," she joked. "You know, like in old television shows? You connect the soup cans with strings and it's supposed to . . . do something."

She trailed off, frowning. He'd started walking again, his face tilted away from hers. "Yeah, whatever," he said.

"It was a joke," Hendricks said, catching up with him again. "Because everyone has cell phones now. Why would you need to build a soup-can—"

"Not *everyone* has a cell phone." He hit the word *everyone* hard and cast a look her way, clearly indicating that she was being insensitive, somehow. She felt her cheeks color.

"Sorry," she muttered. She wasn't sure why he was being so cold or why she was apologizing. He'd been nicer the other night.

She cleared her throat, trying again. "So I haven't seen you around school."

He frowned, slightly. "Yeah, I can think of about ten thousand places I'd rather be than that hellhole."

"Wow, a kid who dresses all in black and hates school. Original."

"Wasn't aware that I was going to be quizzed on my originality on this fine Thursday morning." He stopped walking and turned to face Hendricks fully, his dark eyes fixed on her, searching. "Did you need something?"

Hendricks felt something thrum below the surface of her skin. She was suddenly tongue-tied. "I—I just wanted to say hi."

He didn't smile. "Hi."

Hendricks chewed her lip. Why did it feel like he was sizing her up? Trying to decide whether she was worth his time?

Was it what she was wearing? She glanced down at herself. She had to admit, she hadn't put a lot of thought into her outfit this morning. The boyfriend jeans weren't the current style, but they were Citizens.

Grayson used to tell her he liked the way they hung off her hips. Of course, he'd also said that she should wear something formfitting on top or else it looked "sloppy."

Hendricks had paired the boyfriend jeans with her old track sweatshirt and a pair of beat-up Vans. She hadn't even bothered with her hair, which was still wet from her shower and bunched in a knot on the top of her head.

They were almost eye level. He was only an inch or two taller than Hendricks was. This close, she could see a faint spray of freckles on his nose. There was something vulnerable about them. They didn't match with the black T-shirt and beat-up leather jacket.

She shifted her eyes away. "Anyway. I'll see you around. Or not, seeing as you hate school and won't tell me your name."

She turned away from him, trying to walk fast enough to leave him behind without being totally obvious about what she was doing. She thought she felt the faint pressure of his stare on the back of her head. It gave her a strange thrill, but she didn't want to give him the satisfaction of looking back. Let him watch her walk away.

She'd managed to put half a block between them when he called after her, "Hey! Hold up."

Hendricks hesitated. Then she turned back around.

He made his way toward her slowly, not bothering to rush, which just made her feel like a spaz for speeding away from him.

He waited until they were side by side again before asking, voice low, "Was someone . . . screaming at your place last night?"

The blood drained from Hendricks's face.

"I—I saw a spider," she blurted.

"A spider," he repeated. He didn't sound convinced.

Hendricks searched his eyes, her heart stuttering. His expression didn't give anything away, but she felt his interest sharpen. He cared about what had happened last night. He cared more than he wanted her to know.

"What's your name?" she asked again.

He held her gaze for a beat, long enough that she thought he might answer. Then he pulled a crumpled carton out of his jacket pocket and shook a cigarette loose.

"You know what?" he said, sticking the cigarette between his teeth. "Fuck school."

And he brushed past Hendricks, heading back down the sidewalk the way he came.

# CHAPTER 8

RAVEN LOOKED SCANDALIZED. "HENDRICKS, PLEASE TELL ME this guy you're talking about isn't *Eddie Ruiz?*"

School had just ended, and they were crowded around Portia's locker, waiting for Portia to reapply her lipstick. Some kid Hendricks didn't recognize raced down the hallway past her, and she had to dart to the side to avoid getting hit in the face with his backpack.

"Watch it, Gavin!" Portia yelled after him, her eyes never leaving the foggy mirror attached to the inside of her locker door. The boy turned in place, running backward, and cast an apologetic expression in their direction before bursting out of the school doors. Portia made an annoyed sound in the back of her throat and muttered, "Rude."

"Eddie Ruiz," Hendricks murmured, distractedly watching Portia dab at her lips, making sure she'd gotten her cupid's bow just right. She'd never seen anyone outside of a YouTube tutorial spend so much time on her lipstick. It was hypnotic.

She shook her head and turned back to Raven. "Is that his name? He wouldn't tell me."

"Well, *obviously* he wouldn't tell you. He was probably relieved to find someone in this town who didn't already know who he was." Portia sniffed, and stuck the cap back on her lipstick. "God, he's probably wanking it to you, right now."

"That's nasty, Portia," Raven said, and Portia grinned, clearly pleased with herself.

"Wait, who is he?" Hendricks asked. "Why wouldn't he want me to know his name?"

"Eddie's from the wrong side of the tracks," Portia explained, "but not in a sexy, eighties-movie way. In a gross way."

"He said he lived around the corner from me," Hendricks said.

"It's a metaphorical wrong side of the tracks. You should steer clear of him." Raven fished around in her backpack and, a moment later, she pulled out a root-beer-flavored Dum Dum. "Believe me, you don't want his drama."

She carefully unwrapped the sucker and stuck it into her mouth. Portia made a face and said, "Ew, where did you even get that?"

"I had a doctor's appointment this morning."

"What kind of a doctor hands out *candy?*"

Hendricks let them bicker. She shifted her gaze to the school doors beyond Portia's hair, searching the yard for Eddie's familiar black-on-black ensemble. But, of course, she wouldn't see him. He'd skipped today.

*I can think of about ten thousand places I'd rather be than that hellhole,* he'd told her. Well, at least now she understood why. No wonder she never saw him in school.

"That whole family is so messed up," Portia was saying when Hendricks tuned back in. "A lot of people think Eddie is, like, some sort of psychopath. Like maybe he kills kittens and—"

"*Anyway,*" Raven cut in, giving Portia a pointed look. "Maybe we can save the Eddie rumors for another day? We don't want to completely freak her out."

Portia shrugged. "Whatever. She's going to figure all this out eventually." Smirking, she added. "Our town has some serious baggage."

Raven rolled her eyes and said, lips moving around her sucker, "Our town is perfectly normal and boring, thank you very much. Hey, are we still headed to your place?"

"What? Oh yeah, definitely," Hendricks said.

Her parents were taking Brady in for his eighteen-month checkup, so the house was going to be empty when she got home. She winced, remembering how her blood had gone cold when she'd gotten the text that afternoon. She didn't want to be alone in the house, even if was only for an hour. The events of last night were still fresh in her mind.

And so she'd invited Portia and Raven over. Problem solved.

She added, "My parents won't be home till after six, so you can camp out until they get back."

*Please*, she added silently.

"Lead the way." Portia slammed her locker door, and the three headed for the school's main entrance. They were the last ones in the halls. Portia had spent a full twenty minutes perfecting her lips. "And by the way, the Ruiz family isn't our only bizarre story. What about those boys who disappeared in the nineties?"

Raven blinked at her. "Huh?"

"Those boys! Come on, you know who I'm talking about. They disappeared when our parents were in high school. Didn't you ever hear the story?"

Raven pulled the sucker out of her mouth and pointed it at Portia. "Girl, you know my parents didn't go to high school here."

"Oh, right. Well, my mom told me that her freshman year, three of the coolest boys in school just vanished, and no one ever heard from them again." Portia snapped her fingers. "They were *gone*, just like that."

Raven snorted. "Bullshit. My dad tells the same story about some guy at his high school, and he grew up in Hong Kong. I call urban legend."

"It's *totally* true. My mom showed me her yearbook and everything. There's, like, a whole memorial page dedicated to them."

"Then they ran away to become contract killers or something."

Portia rolled her eyes. "Yeah, Rave, *all three of them* ran away to become contract killers and never came back."

Portia and Raven kept up a steady stream of casual bickering for the rest of the walk to Hendricks's place. Hendricks felt a pang of jealousy listening to them. She used to have that, back at her old school. She sighed, thinking of it. It kept hitting her at strange times: that was all gone now.

And so she was more than a little relieved when the three of them finally climbed the steps to Steele House. At least being home meant she could play hostess. She might not have much to add to the conversation, but at least she'd have something to do with her hands.

"You guys want something to eat?" she asked, heading for the fridge.

Raven finished crunching through her sucker. "Maybe something healthy? I have to cheer tomorrow."

Portia snorted. "Yeah, like that sucker was healthy?"

"It was from my *doctor*."

Portia rolled her eyes and turned back to Hendricks. "So," she said, all casual. "Did you bump into Connor at all today?"

Hendricks had just opened the fridge to grab them some cans of LaCroix, but she froze, one hand wrapped around the door handle, icy air cooling the heat rising in her face.

"Um, just once, in the hall after bio." She set the cans of

sparkling water on the kitchen island and loaded her arms up with baby carrots and red pepper hummus. She knocked the fridge door shut with her hip and saw that Raven and Portia were both staring at her.

Not sure what they expected, she blurted, "He said he had to do a makeup test over lunch and wanted to say hi." A shrug. "That's all."

That wasn't all, not entirely, but Hendricks wasn't sure how to tell them about what had actually happened. The whole thing had lasted maybe three minutes, but it had been the first three minutes she and Connor had spent alone, and Hendricks had used it to officially turn down his date offer. It had been . . . awkward.

She blushed now, thinking of it.

After a beat, Raven rolled her eyes. "Jesus, Hendricks, put us out of our misery. Are you going out with him or aren't you?"

Hendricks dumped the food on the island and ripped the bag of baby carrots open. She made a face. "He told you about that?"

"Connor and I have known each other since preschool." Portia popped her LaCroix open, and fizzy, grapefruit-flavored water gathered on top. She slurped it up, smudging the rim of the can with pink lipstick. "He was the first person I told about being gay, and I was the first person he called when Finn got into that car crash last year and stopped breathing for like two minutes. We tell each other everything."

Raven snorted. "Yeah, Connor and I have known each other for thirteen months and he tells me everything, too." Portia shot her a disgusted look, and Raven added, "Come on, he tells *everyone* everything. The boy does not know what a secret is. Be prepared for the whole school to know everything about your entire relationship."

Hendricks swallowed too quickly and sparkling water went down her windpipe, making her choke. She threw a hand over her mouth, tears springing to her eyes. That wasn't good news. If everyone was going to talk about her dating Connor, what would they say once they'd heard she turned him down?

She shifted her eyes to her fingers, clenching the sides of her can, and tried to ignore the squirming in her stomach. "Look," she started. "I like Connor, I do, I just don't think I'm ready to date anyone yet."

Portia rolled her eyes. "I seriously don't get that. What, were you and your last boyfriend engaged or something? Did you exchange cheesy promise rings and swear that you'd wait for each other?"

Hendricks felt her cheeks flush. "No."

"Then what's the holdup? I can tell you like him, too. I've seen you staring at his arms. And you guys would be so cute together." And then, eyes wide, "Your couple name would be *Condricks*."

Hendricks opened her mouth, and then closed it again. She had no idea how to respond to that.

Maybe Portia was right. Maybe dating someone new wasn't the worst idea in the world. It could be, like, a rebound, something to keep her from obsessing about Grayson.

But it also sort of felt as if she was trading one boyfriend for another.

It was hard to know what the right choice was. Sometimes she felt a little unhinged, like she was making everything that had happened so much bigger than it needed to be. Other times, she felt like she should be double-checking that every door and window was locked, never walking alone at night, hurrying past empty streets. She didn't want either of those to be true.

Now, Portia was frowning at her. "Seriously, though. You never talk about your old school."

Hendricks shrugged, staring down at her LaCroix.

"Your old friends, hobbies, ex-boyfriends. You know, *life.*"

Hendricks felt a little sick.

Raven's eyes darted to Portia, wary. "Come on, Portia, give her a break."

"I'm just trying to get an idea of who she is," Portia continued, unapologetic. To Hendricks, "You show up here, all mysteriously in the middle of the year, and you're not on social media and you don't say anything about your old school, like, *ever*. You have to admit it's a little spooky. Are you a vampire? Have you been a sixteen-year-old girl for the last two hundred years? Do you reinvent yourself whenever you move to a new town so no one discovers your secret?"

"No," Hendricks said.

"Then what's the deal?" Portia asked.

"There's no deal. In middle school, I had a bunch of girlfriends. I was into *everything*—sports, school plays, the newspaper." Hendricks felt her cheeks grow warmer. "I was a bit of an overachiever, I guess. When I met Grayson . . . I forgot who I was for a while. He became *everything*. But no one knows who I used to be here, so I sort of thought I could start over."

*And figure out who I am without Grayson*, she added silently.

It was the first entirely true thing she'd said since she moved here, and it made her feel vulnerable and raw.

Luckily, Raven cut in before Portia could add anything else and said, voice flattened, "Was that enough for you, Portia? If you don't leave her alone, I'm going to make you talk about Vi."

"Fine," Portia said with a sigh. But two bright-red spots had blossomed on her cheeks.

Hendricks raised her eyebrows. Grateful to have the conversation steered away from her, she asked, singsong, "Who's Vi?"

"No one," Portia said at the same time that Raven said, "Portia's first girl crush who she makes googly eyes at when she thinks no one's looking."

Portia rolled her eyes. "*Betty* was my first girl crush."

"Okay, she's your first girl crush who isn't a character on a CW show," Raven corrected.

Portia glared daggers at her, but Raven just shrugged. "What? You told me about her easily enough."

"Yeah, after playing beer pong at Blake's all night." Portia shifted her eyes to her hands. To Hendricks's surprise, the blush had spread to her entire face. "You can't expect me to talk about her *sober*."

Hendricks had an idea. "You know, my parents decided to turn that weird basement into a wine cellar. My dad's sort of a collector, and they have cases and cases of the stuff just sitting down there. I don't think they'd notice if a bottle went missing."

*And I would feel way more comfortable talking about Connor if I was a little buzzed*, she thought.

Portia's eyes widened. "Seriously?"

"They don't count the bottles?" Raven wrinkled her nose. "My parents count the bottles of this gross Bud Light Lime low-calorie crap they buy. As if I'd ever be desperate enough to drink that."

"My parents don't count the bottles." Hendricks held up her La-Croix. "We could make spritzers. I used to do it back in Philly all the time. You wouldn't think grapefruit and red wine go together, but it tastes *amazing*."

73

Portia and Raven shared a look. "Yes, please," Portia said.

Hendricks ducked out the front door, arms hugged over her chest to protect against the chill. The wind sighed through the trees and rattled the fallen leaves strewn across the street. It struck Hendricks as a strangely mournful sound, like the breath you took just before you started to cry. She found herself checking over her shoulder as she wandered around to the side of the house, half expecting to see someone on the curb behind her, watching. But there was no one.

The entrance to the wine cellar looked like a trapdoor angling up from the ground, the latches held shut with a chain that was supposed to be attached to a padlock but was currently attached to nothing. The old padlock had broken and Hendricks's dad hadn't gotten around to buying a new one yet.

Hendricks had one hand reaching for the chain when the chain *moved*, slithering between the latches, muscles thick and undulating in the dim, gray light. She heard the low *hiss* of a tongue, followed by a dry papery rattle.

She recoiled, jerking backward so quickly she nearly lost her balance. Her pulse spiked in her throat.

"Shit," she said through her teeth, wrapping her arms around her chest. "Shit, *shit*."

She kept her eyes trained on the snake, trying to steady her breath.

But . . . she frowned, tilting her head. It wasn't a snake at all, but just a chain wrapped loosely around the trapdoor latches.

She took a cautious step closer, leaning forward. Then, still unsure, she grabbed a stick from the ground and poked it.

The chain didn't move.

"Jesus," she muttered, embarrassed. Hands still twitching, she uncoiled the chain from the latches and pulled the door open just enough to slip inside. It thumped shut above her head, ominous.

Darkness fell over her. Alone now, Hendricks felt her chest release, air whooshing out from between her lips. She stayed at the top of the stairs for a moment, just breathing.

This was going well, she told herself, trying to calm her nerves. Or, at least, she thought it was going well. Raven and Portia seemed to like her.

Except . . . God, how could you tell for sure whether someone liked you? She didn't actually know what Raven and Portia thought about her. They were asking her questions. But maybe that's just because they knew Connor liked her. Maybe they were upstairs right now, talking about what a freak she was.

"Wine," she said out loud. That was her only job for the moment. Choose a bottle of wine that her father wouldn't notice missing and do her best to prove that she wasn't a freak.

The cellar was dark, with a low ceiling and packed-dirt floors. Hendricks flipped the switch at the top of the stairs, and the single light bulb blinked on, filling the small room with a tinny, electric buzz.

Hendricks hesitated, second-guessing her decision to come down here alone. Even in the middle of the afternoon, with the light on and her two friends just a few yards away, this place was a little freaky. It hadn't been renovated like the rest of the house had. The walls were old brick, covered in a thin layer of dirt and something reddish that was probably rust but looked like blood. The stairs were the kind without any backs, so she could easily imagine someone reaching through the slats to grab her ankles. The dirt floor gave her the sense of things buried just below her feet.

And that little girl had died down here. They should've just filled the whole room up with cement.

She inhaled and started down the steps. The cellar smell seemed to intensify as she descended. It was decaying leaves, and wet dirt, and something else. Something sweet.

*Cologne*, she thought, her nose twitching. It reminded her of the cologne Grayson used to wear. Hendricks hugged her arms to her chest, pushing that thought away. It was just PTSD or whatever, like her dad said. It was all in her head.

She made her way over to the wall of wine to examine the labels. She needed something sort of cheap, but she didn't know anything about wine, so she decided to hunt for the crappiest-looking label she could. Crappy label meant cheap, right? Well, she hoped so. She picked up something called *Quintessa*. Shrugged. Worth a try.

She was halfway up the stairs when she heard a sound below her, coming from the crawl space behind the stairs.

*Mew.*

She froze, the hair on the back of her neck slowly rising. She automatically shifted away from the back of the steps, suddenly certain that something was going to slither out of the darkness, grasping for her feet.

The sound came again, clearer now: *Mew.*

Hendricks relaxed. It sounded like a cat. She crept back down the stairs, her shoes kicking up little plumes of dirt when she hit the floor. The light bulb swayed a little from its chain on the ceiling, making the shadows around her seem to move.

She squinted into the dark space beneath the stairs, eyes straining.

She'd had a cat back in Philly. It was an old, fat cat named Blanche that her parents had adopted before she was born. Blanche had died when Hendricks was nine, and it had devastated her. She remembered crying so hard she felt like she couldn't breathe.

"Kitty?" she called. She crouched beside the stairs. "Here, kitty, kitty."

Two eyes blinked open.

Hendricks flinched, her heart jumping. She couldn't see the eyes, exactly, but she could see the light reflected off them.

She held out her hand. "Here, buddy," she murmured.

The cat crept closer, and now she could see that half of his fur was matted against his skinny body, the rest long gone. His skin was patchy and red below, stretched tight over his ribs. She felt a sudden, sharp stab of pity. The poor guy looked like he'd gotten into a fight.

"You hungry?" she asked, scooting closer. "Want me to get you some water?"

The cat hissed, and Hendricks yanked back her hand, fear prickling up her skin. Even in the darkness, she could see the sharp points of his teeth.

"Okay," she said, voice a little softer. He was just scared. "How about some tuna—"

The cat shot forward, and Hendricks stumbled backward, falling off her feet and hitting the ground hard on her tailbone. The cat leapt at her, and she braced herself, muscles tensing as she waited to feel its claws dig into her skin—

But the cat never landed on her.

He went straight *through* her.

Hendricks's heart stopped. She jerked around just in time

to watch the cat bound across the floor and disappear through the shelves of wine.

She pushed back up to her knees, trembling all over. *That didn't happen*, she told herself. It was a trick of the light. Or maybe the cat knew about some hole or crevice in the wall, and it only *looked* like he'd disappeared because—

"You bitch! I'll make you pay."

It sounded like a boy's voice, and it boomed off the cellar walls. Hendricks spun in place, her heart beating hard and fast in her chest. But there was no one there.

*There was no one there.*

Her breath was ragged, and her chest felt suddenly tight. It wasn't possible. That voice was still ringing in her ears. It had been *real*. She curled her fingers tighter around the wine bottle she was still holding.

"Who's there?" she demanded, her own voice small and trembling. Without realizing what she was doing, she raised the bottle over her head, like it was a weapon.

She waited, listening for the voice to speak again.

Suddenly, the basement seemed filled with a thousand noises. Creaking and dripping and wind whipping at the trapdoor.

And, below all that, *hissing*.

Hendricks turned, slowly, toward the staircase, her eyes narrowing. There was something down there. As her eyes adjusted, she could just make out the shape of something moving through the darkness.

Her palms grew sweaty, and the wine bottle slipped from her grasp, shattering as it hit the dirt floor. She leapt backward, swearing. She jerked her head up again, expecting the thing below the stairs to leap out at her, to strike—

Without warning, every single wine bottle in the basement exploded. The sound was like firecrackers or gunshots, so loud that it kept popping in Hendricks's ears. Glass shards flew at her, slicing into her cheeks and arms.

She threw both hands over her head, cowering, as wine rained down on her.

# CHAPTER 9

HENDRICKS TOOK THE STAIRS TWO AT A TIME, WINE AND blood dripping from her hair and sweatshirt. She threw the cellar door open and crawled outside. She didn't shiver as the January air whipped over her bare arms; she didn't even feel it. She didn't feel the wine seeping through her bra, or the cuts that covered her arms. All she felt was numb.

*What the hell had just happened?*

Her father's words from the night before floated through her head—*something like forty percent of people with PTSD experience auditory or visual hallucinations*—and she hesitated at the front door, hand poised halfway to the latch.

Was that it? Was she crazy now?

She swallowed. The thought of seeing Raven and Portia and trying to explain all of this made her feel vaguely ill. But it's not like she had another choice.

Steeling herself, she pushed the door open.

Raven and Portia were leaning over the kitchen island, chatting happily. When they saw Hendricks, they stopped mid-sentence.

"Whoa," Raven said, and Portia's jaw dropped. Actually *dropped*, like she was a cartoon. Hendricks might've found it comical if everything wasn't so messed up.

"Oh my God," Portia said. "What the shit? What *happened* to you?"

*Lie.*

The voice seemed to whisper directly into Hendricks's head.

*Yeah, no shit,* Hendricks wanted to shout back.

"I . . . am in so much trouble," she said. "I—I was trying to get this bottle of wine out and it accidentally dislodged the whole shelf. It's a mess."

Raven made a cringing face. "That sounds really bad. Are your parents going to be pissed?"

"Probably," Hendricks said. But when she looked back at Portia, she saw that her head was cocked to the side and she was studying Hendricks's face like she didn't believe her story.

Out loud, all she said was "Right."

"We'll hang some other night this week, I promise," Hendricks said.

"You're coming tomorrow, right?" Raven asked.

Hendricks frowned. "Tomorrow?"

"Party at the quarry. We were talking about it at lunch, remember? I'll text you the details."

"Yeah, sure," Hendricks said, but she was already ushering the two girls toward the door.

"And good luck with the wine," Raven said, waving as she headed outside.

"Yeah, good luck," Portia added. But she pressed her lips together, like she was holding something back.

Hendricks pushed the door closed behind them. Wine still dripped from her hair, seeping through the shoulders of her sweatshirt.

She walked to the pantry in a trance and reached around inside until she found a thick roll of paper towels. But instead of pulling them out, she just stood there, staring.

How was one measly roll of paper towels going to help anything?

The entire basement was covered in glass and wine. Even if she managed to clean everything up, her dad was going to notice that *every single bottle of his wine was missing.*

Hendricks lifted a shaking hand to her mouth, breathing hard. Her mind was going a million miles a minute.

*How did the wine explode? What the hell just happened?*

The front door slammed open and closed.

"Hendricks!" her mother called. "Are you home?"

"Shit!" Hendricks muttered. She started to turn, but she was shaking badly, and fumbled the paper towels. They fell to the floor, rolling to a stop at her feet. Hendricks looked down, and that's when she noticed that a puddle of wine and blood had formed around her, the red liquid staining the soles of her shoes.

Floorboards creaked, and the muffled sounds of voices drifted toward her. Hendricks grabbed the paper towel roll and hurriedly swiped it over the floor, wine dripping through her fingers and staining the creases of her knuckles.

There was a screech of hinges as the kitchen door swung open. Her dad said, "Hendricks? Honey, you left a trail of something that looks like grape juice all over the—"

Hendricks heard a quick intake of breath just behind her and froze. Her cheeks flared with heat. She was too embarrassed to turn around, so she kept trying to sop up the wine.

"I—I'm sorry," she stuttered, blinking back tears. "It was an accident, I swear, I'm *sorry.*"

The door swung open again and now her mother called, "Hendricks? Honey, you have to be more—Oh, honey. What on earth happened?"

Hendricks was already shaking her head. "I don't know. I—"

Her voice cracked and, in an instant, it was like something inside

82

of her snapped. All of the stress and horror and anxiety of the past few days was suddenly too much.

What kind of person sees cats disappear into walls? Or imagines that someone chopped off her hair? What kind of person hallucinates voices?

A crazy person, that's who.

*No*, she told herself. She *saw* the wine bottles explode. And the wine was still here, pooling beneath her knees, so that meant she couldn't have imagined it, right?

Hendricks's hands were trembling again. She dropped the paper towels and brought them to her face, covering her eyes.

She found herself blurting, "I had some friends over, okay? I went to get us a bottle of wine, but then I got down there, and . . ."

She hesitated for a moment. *Clean slate.* This move was for her. She didn't want to cause any more trouble for her parents.

And so she said, slowly, "I was trying to get a bottle from the top of the rack and I knocked the whole thing over." She felt something inside of her lurch, and she found herself adding, "I know I shouldn't have even gone down there, and I definitely shouldn't have tried to take your wine, I just . . . I guess I just wanted them to think I was cool."

She felt like an idiot saying it out loud. But at least it wasn't a lie.

"Oh, honey." Her mom reached out and squeezed her shoulder. "We know. We want you to make friends here, too."

Hendricks looked up, tentatively, and saw her parents exchange a look. There was an edge of concern to her father's expression. Her mother gave a very small shake of her head.

Hendricks squeezed her hands into fists, her fingernails digging into her palms. They were trying to decide whether they believed her, she knew.

*Please believe me.*

"You knocked the *whole* thing over?" her dad asked, grimacing. Her mom shot him a look and he quickly morphed the expression into a pained smile. "It's fine. I'll . . . figure something out."

"Let me run you a bath," her mother said. And with that, Hendricks knew her story had been accepted. "You're completely drenched. And is some of this blood?"

"Maybe," Hendricks admitted. "There was a lot of glass."

"Take a seat first and I'll check your scratches for glass," her dad said. "Then we can clean up the cellar together. How's that?"

*Terrible*, Hendricks thought. She didn't want to go back down there. Ever.

Some small part of her worried it would be like what happened last night, in the bathroom. What would she tell her dad if they opened the cellar door and everything was normal? No spilled wine, no broken bottles?

She pressed a hand to her chest, horror rising inside of her like nausea. It couldn't have been her imagination. She could still hear the sound of the wine bottles shattering against the wall. She could still remember that thing moving below the stairs, and how that cat had darted straight through her.

Hendricks's father checked her for scratches. When he was done, she followed him out of the kitchen, through the back door, and around the yard to where the cellar doors were still propped open, revealing the deep black darkness of the room below. All the while, she felt Steele House towering above her. It blocked out the darkening winter sky, casting deep shadows onto the grass, mocking her.

# CHAPTER 10

THE QUARRY PARTY STARTED AFTER DARK, BUT IT WAS
January, so that came early. At seven o'clock, Hendricks called, "See
you later!" to her parents and headed outside. She'd thrown on her
heavy winter coat, but the weather had warmed up a bit. It felt like
it was maybe fifty degrees out, warm enough that she left her parka
unzipped and unwound the thick scarf from her neck.

The quarry was technically outside of Drearford, but it wasn't
exactly far away. Hendricks followed the sidewalk to the end of her
block and turned left, into the woods. According to the little map
Raven had drawn her at lunch, Hendricks had to walk through the
woods to what looked like an old, gnarled tree.

Hendricks stopped and pulled out her phone, flipping on the
flashlight app so that she could take a closer look at the map.

Raven had actually written, "Walk until you hear running water."

"Seriously?" Hendricks shook her head. She slipped the phone
back into her pocket. Back in Philly, they hadn't had to rely on hand-
drawn maps and goofy instructions. You could use Google to get anywhere. But this place was different. The woods weren't plotted online,
they were just a big gray nothing on Google Maps. It was pretty spooky.

Hendricks listened to the woods around her. She heard animals
rustling in the tree branches, and her shoes kept crunching on dead
leaves. The hair on the back of her neck lifted.

But it turned out that she didn't have to listen for running water, or watch out for old trees. She heard voices as she descended deeper into the woods, and then she saw the red flames of bonfires flickering through the shadows. A minute later, she broke into a clearing, hemmed in on three sides by woods, while the fourth dropped off into a crevasse that led to a still, black body of water. It seemed like every single kid from school was here, drinking beer from red Solo cups and dancing to the music blaring from a wireless speaker balanced on an old wooden picnic table. Portia and Raven were standing near the keg.

"You came!" Portia squealed, throwing her arms around Hendricks's neck. Hendricks stumbled back a little.

"You're *drunk*," she said, unwinding Portia's arms from around her neck. Portia smelled like a distillery.

"Tipsy!" Portia corrected, holding the Solo cup above her head. "Ladies get *tipsy*. Not *drunk*."

And then she dissolved into giggles.

"She pre-gamed while we set up the fires," Raven explained, grabbing Portia's elbow to steady her. "She found out that Vi's not coming and took it pretty hard."

"Looks like I need to catch up," Hendricks said. She filled a Solo cup with foamy beer from the keg and took a sip. It was a little flat, but still good.

Raven grabbed Hendricks by the elbow and steered her toward the nearest bonfire. Hendricks expected Portia to follow them, but Portia just slumped against the picnic table, her eyes glassy.

"She refuses to leave the keg," Raven whispered, as soon as they were out of earshot. "She's taking this thing with Vi pretty hard."

"What's their deal?" Hendricks asked.

Raven shrugged. "They've made out at a couple of parties, but

**86**

Vi's not really interested in anything official. And Portia's not good at casual, so the whole thing is sort of a disaster."

"Poor Portia," Hendricks said, following Raven's gaze. Portia was staring into her Solo cup now, her shoulders sagging. Hendricks felt a stab of pity.

They stopped outside a circle of people crowded around the bonfire. Hendricks stood on her tiptoes, trying to see what they were all looking at. Finn stood beside the fire, one leg propped up on a charred log, smoke billowing behind him.

"Maribeth Ruiz was only nine years old when she was discovered in the cellar beneath Steele House"—Finn paused, firelight dancing in his dark eyes—"*dead.*"

The beer on Hendricks's tongue suddenly tasted sour.

*Please no*, she thought.

No matter where she went, she couldn't escape Steele House.

"Eddie found their older brother Kyle kneeling over her body, covered in blood, muttering the same thing over and over."

Hendricks didn't want to hear this. She still had to walk past that cellar every day, and after what happened last night, she didn't need another reason to be freaked out by it.

She started backing away, but a few more kids had crowded in behind her, and there was nowhere for her to go.

"'I'm so sorry.'" Finn made his voice high-pitched. "'So, so sorry.'"

A guy Hendricks vaguely recognized from their lunch table snorted and shouted, "Yeah, so sorry he hung himself in the living room before the police could arrest him!"

Hendricks's stomach dropped.

*What?*

A few people laughed as Finn glared at him. "Dude, I was getting to that part."

Hendricks found that she couldn't breathe. She didn't realize the girl's murderer had killed himself in her house, too. She didn't realize he'd been the girl's own *brother*.

A sour taste filled her mouth. She had a sudden, terrible vision of what had happened: Kyle Ruiz kneeling in the cellar, covered in blood, his eyes menacing. A little girl lying, motionless, on the floor in front of him. And then Kyle climbed the stairs to her living room. Found a rope—

Something tugged at her brain: *Ruiz*, she thought. *Where . . .*

The memory came to her suddenly. Raven looking at her, scandalized: *please tell me this guy you're talking about isn't Eddie Ruiz?*

The cup of beer suddenly slipped from Hendricks's fingers and hit the dirt, spilling everywhere. Raven jerked back. "Shit!"

People turned, their eyes going wide when they saw who was standing outside the circle. Finn muttered something that sounded like "Sorry, didn't mean to freak you out."

Hendricks barely heard him. Nerves crept up her arms.

Was Eddie hiding his name because he didn't want her to know that the girl who'd been murdered in her basement was his little sister? That his *brother* had killed her, and then killed himself?

"Excuse me," she muttered, pushing through the crowd of people. The staring and the whispering . . . it was too much. She needed a moment to catch her breath.

The woods were just ahead, looking enticingly dark and isolated. Hendricks made a beeline for the trees. Dead leaves crunched beneath her feet. An owl hooted overhead. Hendricks didn't stop until she was sure she was out of sight of the rest of the party. Then, she propped an arm on a tree trunk and doubled over, breathing hard. She could feel the tears pricking at the corners of her eyes, not for any particular reason but for all of them.

She didn't want to live in a house where such gruesome things had happened. She didn't want to know that Eddie's little sister had died in her basement, and that his older brother committed suicide just a few feet from where she watched television and ate dinner. It was awful enough knowing any of this had happened at all. It was so much worse knowing it had happened to someone she knew.

*Stupid tears*, she thought, angrily brushing them away.

Behind her, a twig snapped.

Hendricks straightened and whirled around, heart pounding. Connor was standing in the trees, holding two cans of beer.

*Shit.* Had he seen her crying? She tried to nonchalantly wipe her face with the sleeve of her coat. "Oh, hey."

"Figured you could use this," Connor said, handing her a can of Natty Light.

"Thanks."

"Don't mention it." He nodded into the trees. "Want to take a walk?"

Hendricks shifted from foot to foot. It felt like a pity walk, which made her want to refuse on the spot. But getting away from the rest of the kids at the party sounded okay. She cracked her beer and shrugged. "Sure."

"That wasn't about you, you know? That story, or the way they were all staring," Connor said as they wandered through the trees. "Nothing too interesting happens in this town. I mean, other than the murder, and now you moving here. They're all just curious, that's all. I'm curious." Then, blushing, he added, "About *you*, I mean. Not the murder."

Hendricks glanced at him. She couldn't help feeling the tiniest bit charmed by the color rising in his cheeks.

She'd been worried that he'd be insulted after she turned him down. She studied his face now, looking for signs of frustration in his jawline, the possibility of dark thoughts moving through his brain.

But he only twisted the tab of his beer, shuffled his feet through the dead leaves. Maybe he wasn't the kind of guy who let rejection turn him ugly.

"Okay, shoot," she offered. "What do you want to know?"

Connor smiled. "You're going to let me quiz you? Really?"

"How about this, I'll match you question for question. Deal?"

"All right, deal."

"Then go for it."

Connor pursed his lips and propped a finger at his chin, like he was pretending to think. "Okay. Siblings?"

It was such an innocent question that Hendricks found herself smiling and looking down at her shoes. "Just the one," she said. "You remember I was watching my little brother Brady when you guys came over? He's eighteen months old."

"Oh, yeah." Connor's eyebrows went up. "Big age difference."

Hendricks shrugged. "Yeah, well, my parents had me when they were really young. They'd never say it out loud, but I'm pretty sure I was a surprise baby. They were still in college, and they got married really quickly after. I think they wanted to wait until they were ready for number two. Do things right."

"Scandal," Connor said, but his voice was lighthearted. "Okay, my turn now, right? I have three older brothers and a little sister."

"*Four* siblings?"

"Right? It's crazy, but my parents were like yours, they started early. *Unlike* yours, they kept going."

Hendricks laughed out loud.

"Amy's the youngest," Connor continued. "She's only five, and she's practically an angel." He laughed, then ran his hand through his hair.

"A bratty angel who always has scabs on her knees, but still. And then, let's see, Patrick is three years older than me. He's at St. Joseph's now—that's only like forty-five minutes away, so he still comes home for dinner most nights. Donovan skipped college, and he's helping my pop out at the auto shop. My family owns O'Flannery's Cars? It's this garage up by the highway?"

"That's cool," Hendricks said.

"Yeah, so Donnie's helping my dad over there. And Finn's a senior this year. He wanted me to tell you that he's sorry for bringing up the murder back at the bonfire. He wasn't thinking, and that house has just been empty for so long."

Hendricks nodded. "I didn't think he saw me standing there." Then, wanting to keep the subject off her, she asked, "So what's his plan? College like Patrick? Or auto shop like Donnie?"

Connor grinned. "Auto shop for sure. He's good with his hands, but he's never liked books or sitting still. And he and my pop and Donnie get along real well."

"What about you?"

Connor looked at his feet, blushing again. "Ah, well, I don't know. College seems cool, but this place is my whole world, you know?" He knocked shoulders with Hendricks playfully. "Or maybe you don't know, you being a big-city girl and everything. I just don't think I could leave my brothers. It would feel totally weird being all on my own. Like losing a limb or something. Even living forty-five minutes away, to go to St. Joseph's, seems too far."

Hendricks was quiet for a long moment, thinking. She might not have a big family of brothers to look up to, but she could still remember a time when she'd thought like that, when the idea of going to a new school in a new city was completely unfathomable.

She released a deep, sad sigh. Now everything was so different,

91

but that didn't mean she didn't miss her old life. Connor got it right. It felt like losing a limb. The ache of it kept her up sometimes.

"Philly was home for a long time for me," she admitted, finally looking back at Connor. "Maybe it wasn't a small town, but I know exactly what you mean. I'm not sure I'll ever fit in here."

They'd circled through the woods and made their way back to the quarry's edge. Hendricks peered into the black water below, wondering how far the drop was.

Twenty feet? Thirty?

Connor cleared his throat. "You know, there *is* one thing you can do to become a real Dreary resident."

He nodded at the water.

Hendricks laughed, certain he was kidding. "It's like fifty degrees out!"

"Everyone who lives here has jumped in the quarry. We've all been swimming here since we were in diapers. It's a rite of passage."

Hendricks chewed on her thumbnail. She snuck a glance at Connor. She was still pretty sure he was joking—

But what the hell?

She shrugged off her coat and handed it to him. "Hold this?"

He took it but looked a little confused. "Hendricks, come on, it's way too cold."

Hendricks gave him a conspiratorial wink. "Everyone who lives here has done it, right? You don't know me that well, but I used to be a bit of a daredevil."

She felt a spark of joy as soon as she'd said the words out loud. It was true. She hadn't thought about this in years, but back before she'd started dating Grayson, Hendricks had a reputation as the girl who'd try anything. She used to be fearless. It made her a little sad to think about it now.

*Where did that girl go?* she wondered. She missed her.

And so she crept up to the edge of the cliff, the toes of her sneakers sending tiny pebbles crumbling down and down and down. Black water glimmered below her. She swallowed. It was a dizzyingly far drop.

"Hendricks." Connor touched the back of her arm with his fingertips. "You don't—"

But Hendricks would never know what he'd been about to say because, by then, she was already flying through the air.

# CHAPTER 11

HENDRICKS SANK INTO THE BLACK WATER, PRESSURE mounting in her ears, her clothes quickly growing heavy. She closed her eyes, enjoying the silence.

Then she began to kick, pumping her arms to make it back to the surface.

A second later, she heard another splash.

She broke through the water gasping for breath, and a moment later, Connor appeared beside her.

"You jumped too!" she exclaimed, treading water.

"You thought I'd let you go alone?" His chin dipped below the water for a moment before he pushed himself back up. "Let's get out of here! It's freezing."

"Race you to the shore?" Hendricks offered, eyebrow going up.

"You're—" But Connor started swimming before he finished.

"Cheater!" Hendricks called, paddling after him.

Soaking wet and laughing, Connor and Hendricks ran back for the coats they'd left at the edge of the woods, and then hurried to his car, an old beat-up Honda Civic with a cracked windshield that was parked at the edge of the woods. Connor unlocked the door with trembling fingers, while Hendricks waited at the passenger door, jumping up and down and shivering.

"Come on come on come on," she said, until she heard the click of the door unlocking.

They both threw themselves into the car, and Connor jammed the keys into the ignition, twisting the heat up to high. Hendricks shrugged off her hoodie and kicked off her shoes, leaving them in a sopping pile at her feet. Her shirt was thin but would dry much faster.

Hendricks closed her eyes and rested her head back against the seat, exhaling. Heat hissed through the vents on the dashboard, slowly coaxing feeling back into her arms and legs.

"This car used to be my older brother's," Connor told her, teeth chattering. "Well, it was my mom's first, and then she gave it to him."

"Which brother?"

"It was Pat's, but then he and Donnie fixed up this 1970 Plymouth Roadrunner, so he drives that now. And then Donnie drove it for a while, but he got my dad's old Ford truck last year. So now it's mine." Connor's smile widened. "We call it the mom car. We all have to drive it at some point."

"Finn doesn't get a car?" Hendricks asked, silently congratulating herself for remembering all of Connor's brother's names.

Connor snorted. "Finn has a Vespa. It was his act of rebellion when he turned sixteen."

"Getting a scooter is an act of rebellion?"

"You'd get it if you knew my dad. Cars are life."

Hendricks grinned, picturing what it must be like at Connor's house: the older brothers and the close-knit family with parents who really cared whether you chose to ride a scooter or drive a car. Her parents cared about her, of course. Hendricks knew that. But their house sometimes felt so empty, with just the three of them and Brady. It must be nice to have a really big family.

She turned her head to the side. Connor had one ear pressed to the headrest, and he was looking right at her. The car's heater had fogged the windows.

Their faces were really close.

Hendricks was suddenly aware of how alone they were. She swallowed and said, "So, um, what kind of car would you get if you could get any car in the world?"

Connor's face broke into a wide smile. "You really want to know?"

Hendricks nodded.

"A Mustang," he admitted, sheepish. "My dad had one back in high school. There are all these old pictures of him posing with it, but he sold it when he and my mom got married, so they could put a down payment on their house. He says he never regretted it, but he still has a framed photo of himself with that car on our mantel back home." Connor shrugged. "I think he'd be weirdly proud if I drove one too, you know?"

"That's really sweet," Hendricks murmured.

"You think so?" he asked. But he was staring at her mouth, clearly distracted.

Hendricks tried to remember what they were talking about, but her mind had gone completely and perfectly blank. Her gaze lingered on the curve of Connor's lips, and her heart stuttered as he leaned closer, bringing a hand to the side of her face. His palm was warm and a little damp.

Their first kiss tasted like lake water and bonfire smoke. Hendricks felt it tingle through every part of her body. She brought her hands to his chest.

"Sorry," he whispered, pulling away.

Hendricks frowned. "Why?"

He released a deep sigh. "Because you said you weren't interested, and I promised myself I'd respect that."

Hendricks felt her shoulders grow tight, but he didn't say this like he was trying to make her feel guilty, or like he was pointing out how inconsistent and crazy she was being. He seemed too confident to play games like that. She felt a sudden rush in her chest and realized, for the first time, that she really liked him. Maybe it was the lingering adrenaline from her jump in the lake or the beer making her head go fuzzy, but she couldn't remember why she'd been so reluctant to agree to a date.

*Clean slate*, she thought.

"I never said I wasn't interested," she said.

"You changed your mind about that date?" Connor said.

Hendricks raised an eyebrow. "*This* wasn't the date?"

Connor gave her a withering look. "How could this be the date? I didn't even buy you dinner."

"Not every date includes dinner."

"Mine do." The green glow of his dashboard lit up his hands on the steering wheel, and the rumpled lines of his damp sweatshirt. "So I'm going to drive you home now instead of trying to get to second base."

"How very old-fashioned of you," Hendricks teased. But she was grateful he was cool with going slow. She didn't think she could handle second base right now.

They pulled onto a narrow dirt road, lined with trees. The wind caused the branches to sway eerily. Watching them, Hendricks couldn't quite convince herself that someone wasn't hidden just behind the tree trunks. Waiting. She shivered.

"Are we anywhere near the famous tree house?" she asked.

"The one that looks directly into your bedroom?" Connor grinned. "I'm trying to forget its exact location. Don't want to get any ideas."

"Ha, ha."

Connor slowed his car, approaching a stop sign, and put on his turn signal. "It's through there," he said, pointing.

Hendricks squinted, but it was impossible to see anything past the first line of trees in the dark.

Connor turned the car onto another narrow road, and the woods whipped past her window, a shadowy blur of leaves and branches and—

*Eddie.*

"Connor, watch out!" Hendricks said, grabbing his arm. Eddie was walking along the side of the road, his shoulders hunched up around his ears, his hood pulled low over his head. It was almost impossible to separate his all-black uniform from the shadows.

Connor swore under his breath and swerved to the side, his car's tires rolling off the edge of the road with a sudden jolt.

Eddie looked up as they drove past. The car's headlights had hit him square in the face, illuminating his dark eyes and the unlit cigarette dangling from his mouth. Hendricks wasn't sure if he'd spotted her sitting in the passenger seat of Connor's car, but she could've sworn she saw a smirk twisting his lips.

And then he was behind them.

Hendricks leaned back against her seat, her heart beating hard. She didn't think they would've hit him, but it had been shocking when he'd just appeared out of nowhere like that. And, Jesus, what kind of person wandered around narrow dirt roads in the woods in the middle of the night? Wearing all black? It was like he had a death wish.

She waited for Connor to make some awful comment about Eddie or his brother, or what happened to Maribeth, but Connor just shook his head, whistling through his teeth.

"Man, I've always felt so bad for that guy," he said, eyes flicking up to the rearview mirror. "If something happened to my little sister, I'd never get over it."

There was a sudden rushing sound in her ears. Once again, she found herself picturing Kyle Ruiz kneeling in her cellar, blood dripping from his hands. Maribeth Ruiz lying, motionless, on the floor in front of him. Only now they both resembled Eddie.

How did Eddie live with that? It was too terrible to even think about.

She glanced at the side mirror, watching Eddie grow smaller and smaller behind them.

# CHAPTER
## 12

HENDRICKS'S PARENTS WERE STILL UP WHEN SHE PUSHED THE front door open and trudged past the living room, holding her dripping shoes in one hand. They were curled on the couch, sipping wine and watching something Hendricks couldn't see from her angle in the hall. David Attenborough's slow, accented voice drifted out of the speakers.

Hendricks cringed. It looked like they were on a date.

As gross as it was, it was also sort of adorable.

Her dad pointedly glanced at his wristwatch. "You're home an hour before curfew," he said.

"I don't think that ever happened in Philly," her mother added, her eyebrows going up.

"Don't get used to it," Hendricks said, heading for the stairs, "I'll let you guys do . . . whatever it is you're currently doing."

"Did you have fun tonight, honey?" her mom asked.

"Yeah!" she called back down from the staircase. "I did."

She rounded the corner into her bedroom, and just before she pushed the door closed, she heard her dad say, "Did she look *wet* to you?"

Hendricks quickly changed into her pj's and hurried through her bedtime routine, pulling her hair into a sloppy topknot and applying a sheet mask that looked like a tiger. She quietly hummed the song that had been playing on Connor's car radio and danced in place as she brushed her teeth.

She couldn't help it. For the first time since moving to dreary little Drearford she was starting to feel like maybe this place could be home. She'd jumped into the damn quarry, after all! Connor said that made her legit.

She grinned as she spit toothpaste into the sink.

She crawled into bed, flicking all the lights out and snuggling down in her pillows. Darkness gathered around her, and the beer she'd had at the party made her feel pleasantly sleepy and warm.

*Mew.*

Her eyes blinked back open. It was the kind of sound that you were sure you'd heard one moment, and the next you couldn't quite figure out whether it had been real, or part of a dream.

Hendricks stared into the darkness for a long time, eyes strained, muscles tense.

*You didn't hear anything,* she told herself. *It was just your imagination. Just a dream.*

Her eyelids started to get heavy again. She felt herself sink deeper into the pillows, her breathing gone shallow . . .

And then the mattress shifted, as if someone had lowered themselves to the foot of her bed. Hendricks felt something brush her foot, leaving her skin prickling.

A sickening wave of fear rolled through her. She jerked her head around, suddenly wide awake. She couldn't see anything, though she blinked and squinted into the darkness.

She knew there was something there, though. She could still feel it, how the mattress dipped, just slightly, beside her foot, curving toward the weight still sitting there.

Her chest grew tight, and a sound like static filled her ears. She clenched her eyes shut.

*This isn't real,* she told herself, balling the edge of her blanket in her fists. *It's just anxiety, PTSD, it's not—*

Then, all at once, the weight was gone.

Hendricks could breathe again. Still shaking, she tried to close her eyes, but her entire body had gone cold. She couldn't imagine falling asleep now.

Then—

"Who's a good kitty?"

Hendricks sat straight up, her heart pounding. She'd definitely heard *that.*

It sounded like it came from the hall.

She crawled out of bed and crept to her bedroom door. Minuscule hairs rose on the back of her neck. She pressed her ear to the wood. Listening.

She heard the distant murmur of the television downstairs, the steady *whirr* of Brady's white noise machine, wind rattling the windowpanes. But that was all.

She exhaled, slowly, her breath ragged. She hadn't heard anything. But she had to see what was out there, to know for sure.

Jaw clenched, she lowered her hand to the doorknob and turned, careful not to let the latch click. She eased the door open, and the movement rustled the plastic sheets hanging over the walls. She froze, skin creeping.

She stared at the thick shadows just beyond the plastic. There was nothing there, just insulation and raw wooden beams and wiring and stuff.

But she imagined someone hiding in the narrow space between the insulation and the plastic.

Her stomach warped. She dug her fingernails into her palms and tried hard not to blink.

*It's not Grayson,* she told herself. *Grayson's in Philly.*

Quickly, before she could talk herself out of it, she crossed the hall and ripped the plastic back.

No one there.

Her heartbeat began to slow.

Then, out of nowhere, a raspy girl's voice said, "Don't hurt him. Please."

"What are you going to do about it?" said a boy's voice, deep and cruel, and seeming to come from just behind her. Hendricks clenched her jaw as her spine crept. She whirled around, but the hallway was still empty.

She turned in place, eyes moving over the shadows blanketing the floors. Was it a trick of the acoustics, like her dad had said? Was she hearing the television from downstairs, and the house was only making it seem like the voices were coming from behind her?

She wanted to believe that. But she couldn't make herself go back to her bedroom. The hallway was narrow and short. A linen closet cut into the wall about halfway down, but the doors hadn't been put up yet, so Hendricks could see clearly that there was nothing—or *no one*—hiding in there.

She clenched her hands into fists, holding her breath as she listened for any other sound or movement.

"Fine, I'll let him go," said the boy's voice.

She heard the sound of something thudding into the wall—a wall that wasn't actually *there*—and she flinched so violently that she lost her footing and tripped over her feet.

She landed hard on her back, head smacking into the floor. For a moment, she saw stars.

The plastic hanging from the wall above her rustled, slightly.

"Hendricks?" called her dad from downstairs. "Is something wrong?"

Hendricks's breathing had gone jagged. She wanted to call back down to him, to tell him that something seriously messed up was going on, but she felt frozen.

Hot breath misted her cheek. She could smell something sweet in the air around her—*cologne*—and for a moment the scent was so heavy it clogged her throat. She began to choke.

And then her mind skipped—

She wasn't in Drearford anymore. She was at Katie Mulligan's after-prom party back in Philly, and she was heading for the front door, reaching for the latch.

And then Grayson was behind her, one hand braced against the door so she couldn't open it. With his other hand, he moved the hair away from the back of her neck, and whispered in her ear:

*Don't you dare embarrass me here.*

Hendricks could still smell the stink of his cologne, the lingering, sour scent of beer on his breath. She could feel his hands, cold and strong, around her wrist—

Her eyes opened, and she was back in Drearford, lying on the floor of her new house. She felt powerless, frozen. In the air above her, a heavy weight was pinning her down. She felt like she was drowning.

*No,* she thought. *Not again. Not here.*

And then it—whatever *it* was—was gone. She was grasping at nothing.

"Hendricks?" Her dad now stood at the foot of the stairs. "Did you drop something?"

"I'm okay," Hendricks called back. She pushed herself up to her elbows and looked around the empty hallway, her heart beating in her ears. Whatever she'd heard, whatever she'd felt, it wasn't there anymore.

She made her way back to her room and crawled into bed, pulling the covers all the way up to her chin. And that's when she noticed that the screen of her cell phone was lit up. She had a missed call.

Fingers trembling, she picked up the phone. She knew, before she ever saw his name on the screen, who the call was from.

Grayson.

# CHAPTER
## 13

HENDRICKS LAY IN BED FOR A LONG TIME, UNABLE TO FALL asleep. Whenever her eyes started to droop, she'd jerk back awake, certain she felt that same pressure on her chest, that she heard Grayson's voice in her ear:

*Don't you dare embarrass me here.*

She touched a hand to her neck, swallowing back a sob. She hated how even the memory of his voice had the ability to humiliate her, to turn her quiet and small. She used to think that it was because she cared about him so much, that his opinion of her meant more than anyone else's did. She didn't think that anymore.

*But all of that was a long time ago,* she reminded herself. She had left Grayson behind. She was moving on.

Only . . . she was sure someone had been here. A shiver went through her again. Not Grayson, maybe, but someone else.

Or some*thing.*

"Hey, girl! You took off Friday night," Raven said, jabbing her milk carton with a straw. "I thought we were going to party."

Her straw bent in half and Raven moaned, tossing it aside. "Dumb straw," she grumbled.

Hendricks blinked blearily, paying more attention to the straw than to what Raven was saying. She hadn't slept well over the weekend, and it was catching up with her. Half the day was already gone and she'd spent it in a haze. Grayson hadn't called her again, but she still flinched every time her phone buzzed, certain she was going to see his name flash across her screen.

It was like he knew about the kiss. Like he knew she was moving on.

She picked up Raven's abandoned straw and began weaving it between her fingers. After a moment of silence, she looked up and realized Raven and Portia were waiting for her to respond. "What?"

Portia and Raven exchanged a look. "Friday night? Your disappearing act?" Raven prompted.

"Keeping secrets already, new girl?" Portia asked, eyebrows lifting.

*Right.* Friday. Without really meaning to, Hendricks glanced at Connor at the other end of the table. He was in the middle of a conversation with Blake and Finn, but he caught her eye. She noticed the blush creeping up his neck, and the corner of her lips twitched. That, at least, was a happy memory.

"Yeah," she said, pressing the straw into the pad of her thumb.

"You guys could not be more obvious," Portia said.

Raven leaned forward, lowering her voice. "Did anything happen?"

"Sort of . . ." Hendricks kept her eyes aimed at the table, her cheeks flushing with heat. "We kissed."

Raven and Portia responded perfectly, both of them squeezing her hands, their mouths shaped like Os, eyes wide and excited. Portia even squealed a little bit—but she did it quietly, so Connor wouldn't look over and guess what they were talking about.

Hendricks opened her mouth, and then closed it, her heart crashing in her ears. She wanted to be excited along with them, but the memory of Grayson's call and everything else that had happened Friday night was still fresh in her mind, dragging her down like a weight.

She felt like a fraud. She was trapped between two realities. In one, she got to be a normal teenage girl who gossiped with her friends over lunch and kissed boys in cars after parties in the woods. But in the other reality, she was barely holding it together. She couldn't stop obsessing about her manipulative ex-boyfriend. Even worse, she saw things that weren't there.

Hendricks's jaw clenched at that thought. *No.* Whatever she saw Friday night had been there. She might still be messed up about Grayson, but she wasn't crazy. Something was going on with her house. Something not normal.

She was grateful when Portia looked around the table and said, "Did anyone else notice that Viviane I'm-too-cool-to-show-up-at-a-party-or-even-text Thompson decided not to come to school today?"

"I think she's just going by Vi now," Raven said.

"Whatever," Portia muttered, and Raven laughed, snorting milk out through her nose. Portia looked scandalized, which just made Raven laugh harder.

While they were distracted, Hendricks slipped her phone out of her pocket and settled it in her lap. No new calls, thank God. After a pause, she typed "haunted Drearford" into her search engine.

She steeled herself as the results loaded, eyes flicking around the table to make sure no one could see what she was doing. She couldn't believe she was searching this, but she'd been thinking about it all morning. She couldn't wait another minute to see if there was any information out there.

Ghosts made sense. Portia said that no one had lived at Steele House for a while, and there was Maribeth's murder, and . . .

Well, the place was just *strange.*

"I'm going to hire a clown," Portia was saying. "One with a big, frizzy wig."

"Oh God, please don't," Connor moaned.

"What do you think, Hendricks?" asked Raven.

Hendricks blinked, but she hadn't been following the conversation closely enough to know exactly what they were talking about. She shrugged, murmuring, "Sounds like a good idea."

Her eyes shifted back down to her phone as she scrolled through her search results with her thumb. *Useless*, she thought, frowning. All that came up were cutesy rumors of ghosts wandering through old hotel rooms or appearing on certain streets at midnight on Halloween. Dumb tourist stuff. Nothing like what she'd seen Friday night.

"Okay, I got it." Connor's voice cut through her thoughts. He shifted in his seat, his foot brushing up against Hendricks's. "How about drag racing? Out behind Cooper's farm."

"God no," Portia said.

"Yeah, no one actually likes drag racing except for you," Raven pointed out.

"*I* like drag racing," Finn cut in.

"Yeah, and it's my birthday!" Connor tapped Hendricks with his arm. "What do you think, Hendricks?"

She looked up from her phone, suddenly aware that everyone was staring at her. She blinked. "I'm sorry, what do I think about what?"

"Drag racing." Connor grinned. "Yay or nay?"

"Uh, nay," Hendricks said, sliding a hand over her phone screen to hide her search results. "I'm not really a NASCAR fan."

Raven snickered, and Portia flashed him an I-told-you-so smile, saying, "Three against one."

"Uh, two," Finn said, nudging Blake with his elbow. "Dude, get in on this."

Blake just shook his head. "As long as there's beer, I don't care what we do."

Hendricks chewed on her thumbnail, eyes back on her phone. There was nothing there. Frustrated now, she squeezed the phone in her hand, and her gaze drifted across the cafeteria.

Eddie Ruiz appeared on the far side of the room. He tossed a crumpled paper bag into the trash and then beelined for the door, shoulders hunched up around his ears, as if he might be able to turn himself invisible if he huddled far enough into that leather jacket.

A group of kids Hendricks didn't recognize said something as Eddie walked past. The kids laughed. Hendricks's muscles tensed, but Eddie didn't react. He just kept walking.

Hendricks watched him, frowning slightly. Eddie had seemed curious about her scream the other night. Almost as though he'd been expecting something weird to happen at Steele House. Was it just lingering hatred of the place, because of what happened to his brother and sister there?

Or . . . could he know something?

The thought gave her chills.

"Well?" Portia snapped, and Hendricks jerked her gaze away from Eddie. "Do you want to come or don't you?"

"Um, where?" Hendricks asked. She noticed that Connor, Finn, and Blake were no longer sitting at the table with them.

*Crap.* She hadn't even seen them leave.

"Connor's birthday." Portia spoke with exaggerated patience, like Hendricks was a toddler. "It's only the thing we've all been talking about through lunch."

"Oh yeah." Hendricks could feel her cheeks coloring.

"Anyway, Raven and I are leaving right after school so we can check out a venue." Portia popped her gum. "Want to come?"

"We're getting shakes after," Raven added, lazily winding a long lock of bleached hair around her finger. "You haven't been to the

Fremont Diner yet, have you? They have the *best* chocolate shakes."

"If you like drinking two thousand calories in less than twenty minutes," Portia added.

Raven rolled her eyes at her. "As a matter of fact, I *do*."

Hendricks chewed on her lip. She *did* want to go. She couldn't think of anything she'd rather do right now than inject herself with more chocolate and sugar than the human body should physically be able to handle. She could picture squeezing into a booth with Raven and Portia, telling them all the details about what went down with her and Connor last Friday.

It sounded so normal. For a split second Hendricks considered going with them, pretending that the night had ended when Connor dropped her off at her front door.

But then she thought of that weight on her bed, that deep, raspy voice. Her skin crawled.

"I—I'll have to take a rain check," she said, gathering her things. "You guys have fun, though."

Portia flashed her an exaggerated pout. "You're ditching us?"

Hendricks felt a pang in her chest. *There will be time for normal later*, she told herself.

*After* she figured out what or who was haunting her.

# CHAPTER 14

HENDRICKS HEADED STRAIGHT HOME AFTER THE FINAL
bell, but instead of turning up her front walkway, she continued on
and cut through the thick row of trees that separated her back yard
from Eddie's.

Eddie's house didn't look like hers. The paint had long ago faded,
showing weathered gray siding and rusted gutters. Old plastic toys
littered the yard, and a car without wheels sat on cinder blocks beside
the back shed. A few of the upstairs windows had cardboard taped
over the glass.

Hendricks hesitated. She wasn't sure what she'd been expecting.
Her house and all the other houses on her street were so nice. She'd
sort of figured that all the homes in Drearford were like that.

She felt a little embarrassed as she picked her way through the yard.
The porch had collapsed on one side, so she had to be careful about where
she put her feet as she climbed the stairs and knocked on the front door.

The door swung open almost as soon as she moved her hand
away, and Eddie appeared behind the screen. Hendricks jerked backward, her heartbeat jump-starting. She had a feeling he'd been watching her walk across his backyard.

"Can I help you?" Eddie crossed his arms over his chest, leaning
against the doorframe. He didn't bother opening the screen door that
separated them.

Hendricks's chest felt suddenly tight. She didn't know how to start. How do you bring up *ghosts* with someone you barely know?

She wetted her lips. "Hey, Eddie."

Eddie studied Hendricks's face, suddenly wary. "Nice going, Veronica Mars. You figured out my name."

He seemed annoyed. Great.

No longer worried about how it might sound, Hendricks blurted, "I wanted to ask you about my house, not your name, *Eddie.*"

Eddie waited an uncomfortably long time to reply. Then, exhaling through his teeth, he said, "Any specific reason you want to know, *Hendricks?*"

Something about the way he said her name caused her to frown slightly. But of course he knew her name—everyone at Drearford seemed to know her name. Eddie had just never said it out loud before.

She shrugged, trying for casual. "I'm just curious."

"Why?"

"I don't know. It's my *house.*" She shoved her hands deep into her coat pockets and forced herself to say the thing she'd come here the say. "The other day, when we were talking before school, it sounded like you might . . . I don't know. Know something about it."

She felt her cheeks grow warm. This had all sounded perfectly rational in her head, but now she realized she was coming across as vague, bizarre even.

Eddie cocked his head. For a moment it looked like he might say something deep and profound. But then the moment passed and the two of them just stood there, not speaking.

Hendricks had forgotten why she'd thought it would be a good idea to come here.

"This was a mistake." She turned and started to pick her way back down the porch steps.

The screen door screeched open and closed, and then Eddie was beside her. It was the first time Hendricks had seen him without his leather jacket. His black T-shirt was thin and worn, the neckband gaping wide enough to show the sharp edge of his collarbone just beneath. It looked like it had been washed and worn hundreds of times.

The expression on his face was still guarded, but there was something else going on below, something he was trying to hide. He started to reach for her arm, apparently decided against it, shoved his hands into his jeans pockets instead. "Did you . . . see something?"

"No," Hendricks blurted. But why did she come here if she was just going to lie? Swearing quietly, she shook her head and added, "I mean, I don't know. Maybe."

Eddie's eyes bore into hers. "*What* did you see?"

"What did *you* see?" Hendricks shot back. She wasn't going to say it first.

Eddie swallowed and shifted his eyes to his feet. He was barefoot, Hendricks realized, his toes curling into the porch like he was cold.

It was the shivering toes that softened her. Hadn't Raven said that the rest of the town thought of Eddie as a Boo Radley type? That meant he was an outcast, and so it made sense that he didn't want to trust her, that he was wary of telling her anything that could get him laughed at.

If she wanted his help, she was going to have to give something up first. "Things have been sort of . . . weird at that house."

"Weird how?"

Hendricks cringed. "Please don't make me say it out loud."

Eddie searched her face. She couldn't tell what he was thinking. Did he think she was making fun of him? Did he trust her?

"Okay," he said finally, and the timbre of his voice was lower than it had been a moment ago. "So I visited my brother Kyle, once, before he got out on bail." He paused, like he expected Hendricks to ask him what Kyle had been arrested for. When she didn't, he shook his head angrily and muttered, "This fucking town."

"I'm sorry," Hendricks said.

She didn't know what she was apologizing for, but Eddie seemed to appreciate it. He scrubbed a hand back through his dark hair, leaving it mussed.

"Yeah, well, Kyle insisted that he didn't see anyone else around that house. It was sort of a sticking point with the prosecutor. He kept saying that Kyle couldn't expect people to believe he was innocent if he couldn't give them another explanation. Kyle always said he didn't have one, but the day I went to the jail, he told me something different."

Hendricks felt the skin on her arms creep. "Different how?"

"He told me he felt something in the basement with him."

Cold flooded through her. Hendricks said, "Something?"

"Something like . . ." Eddie leaned closer and Hendricks noticed that he smelled like clove cigarettes and sandalwood. Nothing like Grayson's overpowering cologne. He swallowed, his Adam's apple bobbing up and down in his throat. "Something like a ghost."

*Ghost.*

She'd been thinking it, but it felt different to actually hear it spoken out loud. She felt Eddie watching her, trying to gauge her reaction, and she wanted to tell him she was right there with him, that she'd been thinking the same thing.

Instead, she took a step backward. It was too hard to think when they were standing so close.

"What?" Her voice cracked.

Eddie's face fell. "Hendricks—"

She lifted her hands, stopping him. She didn't understand why she was reacting like this. She *shouldn't* be reacting like this. Ghosts meant that she wasn't crazy. They meant that Grayson wasn't hiding in her linen closet.

But as soon as the word had left Eddie's mouth, she'd felt something deep inside her bones start to tremble. She didn't believe in ghosts. She'd never believed in supernatural stuff like that. The possibility of them being real made her want to laugh and scream at the same time.

She stumbled down the rickety porch steps. She heard a buzzing in her ears. When her feet hit the sidewalk, she started to run. Eddie called her name, but she didn't turn back.

She dashed around the side of his house, through his backyard, and past the trees that separated his world from hers.

# CHAPTER 15

HENDRICKS REPLAYED HER CONVERSATION WITH EDDIE ALL
through school the next day.

*He felt something in the basement with him. Something like a ghost.*

She tried to push the words out of her head as she doodled in
the corner of her notebook, half-listening to the lecture on Alex-
ander Hamilton in AP history. But she couldn't help it. She felt
like something in her chest was slowly winding tighter and tighter,
making it hard for her to breathe. Could she really trust Eddie?
Something deep down told her he was telling her the truth.
Which meant—

Whatever she'd heard or felt had actually been there. It'd been
real.

*Ghosts* were real.

At lunch, Hendricks squeezed between Raven and Portia and
dropped her plastic lunch tray onto the table. "Anyone have any idea
what this gray stuff is?" she asked, nodding at her plate.

"California loaf," Raven said.

"Yeah, that's what the sign said." Hendricks pulled her chair out
and plopped down. "But it didn't explain exactly what California loaf
was. Any guesses?"

"It's like meat loaf, but they don't include actual meat," Connor
explained.

Hendricks frowned at her non-meat meat loaf. "That's horrifying. And what's up with the sides? Aren't they, like, required by law to include something that grows from the earth in our lunches?"

Portia blinked. "What?"

"Like a vegetable," Hendricks clarified.

Raven poked at the swirl of red sauce on top of her California loaf. "Ketchup. Tomatoes. There's your vegetable."

"I think I'm fasting today," Hendricks muttered, pushing her tray away.

"That's too bad." Connor rubbed the back of his neck. "I was going to say that you should join the rest of us at Tony's after school."

"Tony's?"

"The pizza place on Main Street," Raven informed her, pulling her hair into a complicated-looking bun on top of her head. "We all hang out there most days."

"Most days?" Hendricks arched a brow. "This is the first I'm hearing about it."

Portia looked pleased with herself. "Well, we had to make sure you were cool first, obviously."

Hendricks scoffed. "And the verdict?"

Connor shook his head at her. "You passed," he said. "Obviously."

Hendricks frowned down at her gray non-meat product. Her stomach growled. She supposed she could wait another couple of hours if it meant she could eat some real food instead of whatever "California loaf" consisted of.

"Count me in," she said.

Tony's was a traditional, old-school Italian spot: plastic red-and-white-checked tablecloths, candles wedged into Chianti bottles, and massive framed posters of different shapes of pasta hanging on the brick walls.

But there were also old arcade games lining the back wall and a sign announcing karaoke in the basement.

"This place is cool," Hendricks said, looking around appreciatively. The air was heavy with the smells of garlic and baking bread, and nineties hip-hop blared from the speakers—Hendricks only knew what it was because her dad was always blasting Notorious B.I.G. in the car.

She recognized a few people from her classes as she followed Raven, Portia, and Connor to a table near the back of the restaurant, a few feet away from where Blake and Finn were playing video games. Just like in the cafeteria, they seemed to have their own booth reserved solely for them. Heads swiveled to watch the four of them walk past, and Hendricks felt a little thrill of appreciation. It sort of felt like being a celebrity. She couldn't help enjoying it.

Portia and Raven started fighting over a plastic menu the second they slid into the booth, voices overlapping as they argued about pizza toppings. Hendricks was about to scoot in across from them when Connor touched her arm.

"Don't bother," he said, nodding at the girls. "They don't exactly take requests."

Hendricks blinked. "They're not going to let me order my own toppings?"

Connor shook his head. "We can't be trusted to choose correctly. It'd be best if you just leave it to the professionals." He jerked his head over to the arcade games. "Come on. I bet I can kick your ass at some vintage arcade games."

"You wish. What do I get if I win?"

Connor pursed his lips. "Shiny quarter?"

"You're on."

They walked over to a big, boxy game called *Teenage Mutant Ninja Turtles*.

"This one's my favorite," Connor said, digging into his pocket for change. "It's so cheesy. They couldn't do 3-D yet, so whenever anything on the screen is on fire, you have to walk your turtles through the fire, but they don't get burned or anything. It's great."

Hendricks frowned at the name of the game. "Wasn't this a movie?"

"Yeah, well, Michael Bay tried to do a movie but it was a total flop. The really old ones from the nineties are okay. But the cartoons are the best. My dad has a bunch saved on his computer, and he got us all into them when we were little."

The game blared to life, and Connor scooted aside. "Come on, I'll show you how to play," he said.

Hendricks stood in front of the game, Connor at her shoulder. She grabbed the controller, and he wrapped an arm around her back, one hand hovering near her hand on the controller.

"Do you, um, want me to show you how?" His voice was a little throatier than it had been a second ago.

"Yes, please," Hendricks said, and Connor curled his hand around hers.

He showed her how to navigate the funny turtle characters all over the screen with the joystick, and Hendricks snorted as he told her the whole mythology of the turtles, from the green ooze to the Shredder and intrepid reporter April O'Neil.

"That show sounds bananas," Hendricks said when he'd finished. A ninja dude had just killed her turtle, and the screen showed a black game over. "How did it ever get on the air?"

"I have no idea. But you're wrong, it was amazing." Connor

shook his head, grinning. "They don't make cartoons like that anymore."

Hendricks noticed that his arm was still around her, even though she was no longer playing the game. It felt sort of nice.

She twisted around, so that she was looking at him. Their faces were only inches apart.

"You mean they don't make cartoons about turtles with superpowers?" she asked, faux-shocked. "What are they thinking?"

Connor swallowed. He was looking at her lips. "Exactly."

*Kiss me*, Hendricks thought.

And then Connor was leaning closer, bringing a hand to the side of her face. His eyes started to close—

A fraction of a second before their lips touched, Hendricks pictured Grayson's thick lips and long eyelashes. His breath always tasted of cinnamon because of the Big Red gum he chewed. She could practically feel his hand wrapped around the back of her neck, his voice in her ear . . .

*Don't you dare embarrass me here.*

Without thinking, Hendricks jerked backward.

"I—I'm sorry," she mumbled. "I like you. It's just that my last thing was . . . well, it was—"

"Complicated?" Connor offered.

Hendricks exhaled. "Yeah. I sort of want to take it slow for now. Is that . . . could that be okay?"

Connor took her hand and squeezed. "It's cool. And hey, look, pizza's here."

Hendricks pressed her lips together, holding back a smile. "Yeah. We should go, um, eat that."

Her face felt like it was on fire.

"Bacon, mushroom, and ricotta," Raven announced when

Hendricks and Connor returned to the booth. "Believe me, you'll die."

"No pepperoni?" Hendricks asked, trying to keep the disappointment from her voice.

"Do we look basic?" Portia asked, sliding a cheesy slice out of the pan. "Trust me, this is better."

Hendricks opened her mouth, fully ready to argue that nothing was better than a traditional pepperoni pizza, when the restaurant's front door swung open and Eddie walked in.

The argument died on her lips. She grabbed a slice of pizza to give herself something to do with her hands.

Portia smirked at him. "Think he wants some of the pizza grease to use in his hair?"

Hendricks stopped chewing. The pizza was a tasteless lump on her tongue. Eddie's hair wasn't even greasy. She had a sudden flash of how he'd looked the day before, when they'd been standing on the porch outside his house. His hair had been soft. It'd smelled like baby shampoo.

She started chewing again, saying nothing.

"Leave him alone," Connor said, picking at a mushroom on his pizza slice. "He's not bothering you, he's just grabbing some food."

"He's probably looking for a job," Raven said. "I bet his brother's legal bills were expensive."

Portia snorted. "Can you imagine paying someone to defend that freak?"

"They don't have to worry about it anymore," Raven added.

Hendricks swallowed her pizza, and it settled in her gut like a rock. She pretended to study the Tony's logo on her napkin so she wouldn't have to look at him. But as soon as she decided not to look at Eddie, it was the only thing she wanted to do.

Her eyes flicked up, largely against her will, at the exact moment that Eddie glanced over at her table. A jolt went through her as their eyes met.

And then, to her horror, he started making his way across the restaurant.

Hendricks could feel her friends watching him approach, mouths agape. Her skin flushed with heat.

*Go away*, she thought. *Please just go away.*

"Hey," Eddie said, stopping in front of their booth. He cupped the back of his head with one hand, looking between Raven and Portia. "I, uh, just wanted to make sure you were okay. You left in kind of a hurry."

"Excuse you," Portia snapped.

Raven looked at Hendricks, frowning. "Why wouldn't you be okay?"

"I—" Hendricks started, not sure what to say.

Portia swiveled around to face her. "Oh my God, did he *do* something to you?"

Raven's eyes went wide, and now Connor was frowning and half-rising from his seat. "Is he bothering you, Hendricks?"

He'd squared his shoulders, and there was something forceful about his voice. Hendricks's muscles tensed.

"No," she said, touching his arm to get him to sit back down. "*No*, it's not like that. We're just neighbors."

"Don't talk about me like I'm not standing here," Eddie said, his voice flat. He met her gaze, and then looked away.

It hit Hendricks that it must've been incredibly difficult for him to approach her here, while she was sitting with these people. She felt a deep twist of guilt.

She didn't know Eddie, though, Hendricks reminded herself. It wasn't her responsibility to defend him to her friends.

Eddie didn't look Hendricks's way again as he stalked to the front of the restaurant. He just pushed the door open with his shoulder and was gone.

But for a long time she watched the spot where he'd stood.

# CHAPTER 16

"HELLO?" GILLIAN SHOUTED, AND HENDRICKS HEARD A FLAT, slapping noise, like hands pounding against wood. "Hello?"

"Gillian?" Hendricks let the front door slam shut behind her. Gillian wasn't sprawled across the couch, like she usually was. "Where are you? Are you okay?"

"Hendricks?" The pounding grew more frantic as Hendricks hurried across the living room, following the sound to the little closet beneath the stairs. She pulled the door open and Gillian stumbled out, gasping.

"Oh my God." Gillian snaked both hands up around her head, her lavender hair sticking through her fingers. Her eyes were wide and red. "I thought I was never going to get out of there."

"Did you lock yourself in?" Hendricks asked, confused, but Gillian didn't seem to hear her. She hurried across the room, snatching Brady's video monitor from the coffee table with shaking hands.

Hendricks felt a cold wave of fear hit her.

*Oh my God, Brady—*

But Gillian's shoulders slumped, and a relieved breath escaped her lips.

"Thank God," she said, staring down at the grainy video of Brady on the monitor screen. "He's still napping. This is going to sound crazy, but it was like I was . . ."

She trailed off, swallowing hard.

Hendricks felt sick. She put a hand on Gillian's shoulder. "Like you were what?"

Gillian blinked like she was coming out of a trance. "It was like I was trapped," she said after a moment. "It was like I was intentionally trapped . . . by the house, or something. I—I heard something beneath the stairs and I thought it might be something from outside, like a raccoon? So I went to check it out and—and the closet door just slammed shut behind me. And then I couldn't get out again."

Gillian looked at Hendricks and forced a smile. "Sorry, I didn't mean to scare you. The closet must lock from the outside or something, it just really freaked me out."

"Yeah," Hendricks said, distantly. The back of her arms began to creep.

Gillian shoved her schoolbooks into her backpack, a camo-print Herschel bag that was already so full the seams were beginning to unravel. "I think I just need to get out of here now that you're home. This place is so freaky." She headed out the front door, still shaking her head.

Hendricks's muscles grew a fraction tighter with each pound of Gillian's combat boots down the front porch steps.

Wind sent tree branches tapping against the windows. The kitchen faucet dripped. Somewhere in the distance, a car backfired.

They were all normal, everyday sounds. But beneath them, Hendricks thought she heard something else. The house seemed to constrict, like it was inhaling.

*It was like I was intentionally trapped . . . by the house.*

Hendricks glanced at the closet door. She was pretty sure it didn't lock from the outside.

The hair on Hendricks's arms rose straight up.

"No, guys, you don't need to come over tonight, I'm perfectly fine," she muttered under her breath, replaying her last few moments with Portia, Raven, and Connor back at Tony's pizza place. They'd offered to hang out until Hendricks's parents came home, but Hendricks had still felt weird about how they'd been making fun of Eddie, and she told them she was cool on her own. Now, she wished she'd taken them up on their offer.

She headed for the kitchen, flicking switches as she went until every light on the main floor was blazing. She thought all that light would make her feel better, but it just made the flat, black darkness outside the windows seem flatter and blacker. She thought she saw movement in the window above the sink, but when she jerked around to see what was there, she saw only her own reflection staring back at her.

An uneasy prickling grew under her skin. Anyone could be outside, looking in.

"Stop," she told herself, dragging her eyes away from the windows.

She slid her elbows onto the kitchen island, anxiously tapping her fingers against the butcher-block counter. The clock on the microwave read 4:43, which meant that her parents would be home in about an hour. It seemed like an impossibly long time from now, so she distracted herself by rooting around in the fridge. She hadn't eaten lunch that day, and she'd barely been able to finish her slice of pizza after talking to Eddie. She should be starving, but she found herself zoning out, staring at a bottle of almond milk for a full minute without really seeing it. The icy refrigerator air sent shivers down her spine.

*Mew.*

*No no no no,* Hendricks thought. Her grip on the refrigerator door tightened. Her knuckles turned white.

"Who's a good kitty?" said a deep voice. It was muffled. Coming from upstairs. Then a small, high-pitched giggle reverberated around the house.

Hendricks's throat constricted. Heart hammering, she walked over to the staircase, stopping just before the thin plastic sheet. She held her breath, listening.

For a long moment, all she could hear was the blood pumping in her ears, the slow rasp of her breath in her throat. Then—

*Bang!* Something heavy crashed to the floor in the room directly over her head.

Brady's room.

A wave of fear and panic crashed over her. Hendricks ripped back the plastic and took the steps two at a time, the grating laughter still echoing in her ears.

She was at Brady's door a second later, fumbling for the door-knob. It wouldn't open.

"Brady!" she shouted, slapping frantically at the wood. "Brady!"

Frustrated tears sprung to her eyes. She threw her shoulder against the door, but she was too small to force it open. The wood shuddered in its frame but held. Her heartbeat thrashed in her chest like a wild animal.

"Let me in!" She banged on the door wildly, screaming his name.

She grabbed for the doorknob again, and this time, the door swung wide open, sending her stumbling into the nursery.

A boy stood in the middle of Brady's room. He was Hendricks's age, or close to it, and he didn't look like a ghost, except that his baggy jeans and loose-fitting polo shirt seemed a little dated. His hair was parted in the middle and hung down around his ears, reminding Hendricks of pictures she'd seen of her dad in high school.

The boy stared at Hendricks with intense, black eyes, head cocked at an unnatural angle.

Brady's crib lay on its side in the middle of the floor, surrounded by his toys and stuffed animals. But the boy with the black eyes was holding Brady in his arms. He absently stroked the top of his head, his fingers flattening Brady's baby-fine hair.

"Who's a good kitty," the boy said.

Brady squirmed against his chest, his face reddening. "Ha-ha," he said, spotting Hendricks at the door. He held his arms out to her and repeated, insistently, "Ha-ha. *Ha-ha.*"

Hendricks's fear became cold and hollow inside of her. She noticed Brady's blankie lying on the floor at the boy's feet and felt her breath catch. He needed that blankie. He must be so scared without it.

She crouched, reaching for it, when another, higher voice spoke. "Don't hurt him. Please."

Hendricks whipped her head around, searching the room. She didn't see another ghost.

"Poor Saggy Maggie. What are you going to do about it?" The boy's mouth took on a cruel slant. "You going to cry?"

Hendricks knew the ghost wasn't talking to her, but she felt the sobs well up inside her throat anyway. For a moment, she couldn't breathe.

She could smell something now. It was a familiar, damp smell that grew heavier the longer she focused on it.

It was earthy, at first, reminding her of the yard after it rained. And then it seemed to grow sweeter, stronger.

Now it was flowers rotting in a vase. Fresh manure. An animal carcass in the garden.

And, underneath that, the cloying smell of Grayson's cologne.

Hendricks gagged, and lifted a hand to cover her nose and mouth. Tears were rolling down her cheeks. "Please," she choked out. "Please, let my brother go."

129

The boy looked directly at her, as though seeing her for the first time. His smile stretched tight over his teeth.

As Hendricks stared back, the boy's face changed.

His skin went first, bloating and warping before Hendricks's eyes. Pockmarks opened up on his formerly clear face. Then, with a sound like raw meat dropping to the floor, a ragged strip of skin fell from his skull, revealing bone and muscle and tissue beneath.

Hendricks felt bile rising in her throat. She balled a hand at her mouth, choking it down.

The boy's lips curled back, revealing rotten teeth and bleeding gums. A maggot squirmed through the mess of soft pink muscle and tissue.

And his eyes . . . the pupils weren't the only things that were black anymore. The darkness had expanded, seeping into the whites, so that two oily pits stared out from his skull. There was nothing remotely human about them.

"Fine," the boy said, looking down at Brady. His hair moved through the air like he was underwater, snaking and drifting behind him. "I'll let him go."

And he lifted Brady's wriggling body over his head. Brady was shrieking now, his face scrunched in fear. Hendricks could just make out the sound of her name through his screams.

"Ha-ha! Ha-ha!"

And then the boy threw him against the wall.

# CHAPTER 17

HENDRICKS WAS SLUMPED IN A PLASTIC WAITING ROOM chair, her knee bouncing anxiously. She looked up when the doors to the intensive care wing whooshed open and her parents stumbled out.

"He's okay." Her mom pulled Hendricks to her feet and folded her into a bone-crushing hug. "The doctor said he broke his leg badly when he fell, and that he'll need to be in a spica cast for six weeks."

Her dad closed his eyes for a beat, breathing hard. "Because he's so young, the doctors want to keep him at the hospital for a couple of days to make sure his leg sets properly. But he's okay."

*He's okay.* For a moment, Hendricks leaned into her mother's shoulder, breathing in the familiar floral and fruit scent of her perfume. But then she remembered how terrified Brady had looked when he was lying on the floor back home. The way tears had filled his eyes as he'd reached for her. *Ha-ha.*

Brady might be okay, but all of this was still her fault. If she'd only gone to his room when she first heard the laughter, none of this would have happened.

Hendricks sucked in a deep breath. "I'm so sorry," she said carefully. "I should have been with him, I should have been watching him—"

"Honey, it's not your fault," her mother said. "This kind of thing happens with toddlers."

Hendricks's throat felt thick. "You don't understand," she said quickly. "Brady didn't climb out of his crib. There was something in the room with him, something like a . . ."

She stopped talking, her mouth suddenly dry. How was she supposed to tell her parents that a *ghost* hurt Brady?

Her mom frowned. "Something like what?"

"*Something*," Hendricks said, more insistently this time. Her cheeks were burning. She didn't want to say it out loud, but she needed them to understand. There was something wrong with that house. They couldn't go back there. "It was something not . . . not normal."

Her mother was studying her now, a strange expression on her face. "Honey, you aren't making sense."

"Did an animal get into his room?" her dad added, scratching his chin. "That damn window. Didn't I say I was having a problem getting it to stay latched?"

"It wasn't an animal. It was a thing. I think . . . I think it was a ghost."

Her parents exchanged a loaded look. Hendricks could see immediately that they didn't believe her.

"Haven't you heard about that little girl that died?" she rushed to add. "There's something really *wrong* with that house. Something bad."

Her mother pinched her nose between two fingers, like she felt a migraine coming on. "It's just an old house. I know it's creaky and drafty, but—"

"You guys aren't listening to me." Hendricks was vaguely aware that her voice was getting louder. A few of the nurses on the other side of the room looked up and were frowning slightly in her direction. Fast, before she could lose her nerve, she said, "I'm telling you I *saw* something in Brady's room. This wasn't the first time! This has been happening since we got here. The house is dangerous."

132

An uncomfortable silence followed her outburst. Hendricks could feel people staring over at her, wondering. Her skin itched.

"Why don't you head on home and get some rest." Her dad leaned close to her, voice lowered. "It's been a long night."

*Rest?* "But I—I want to see Brady!"

"He's sleeping now," her mom said. "Go home, and we'll call you when we know anything new."

Her dad patted her once on the shoulder, and then he and her mom walked over to the nurses' station.

Hendricks trudged through the front doors of the hospital in a haze, flinching when the automatic doors whooshed open and allowed a flurry of cold air to sweep in and wrap itself around her. For a long moment she just stood beneath the neon hospital sign, staring dazed into the darkness of Drearford, unsure what she was supposed to do next. The idea of going home to rest was ludicrous. But where else was she supposed to go?

Drearford was a small town, and the hospital wasn't far from where she lived. She hadn't really needed to call an ambulance; she could've carried Brady here. Even now, she could see the gray shingles of Steele House peeking out over the tops of the trees, just a few blocks away. Hendricks wrapped her arms around her chest, shivering. The last thing she wanted to do was go back there.

Without really thinking, she started walking. She didn't bother making her way over to the sidewalk but stepped right onto the neatly maintained lawn, dead grass crunching beneath her sneakers. When her shoes hit the concrete of the parking lot, she started to run.

Something was happening. Her parents might not believe her, and she might not know what the hell was going on, but she couldn't just ignore it anymore.

Wind cut straight through her thin shirt, making her shiver. The moon hung high in the sky, and it painted the sidewalks silver and black. Hendricks could hear animals rustling around in the bushes as she ran. Owls hooted. Dogs barked.

It didn't take her long to reach Steele House. She cut through her backyard and darted around the side of Eddie's house. She took the stairs two at a time, not caring about how loud her footsteps were against the wooden stairs, how it seemed like Eddie's entire house was shaking beneath her.

"Eddie!" she shouted, banging on his front door. "Open up! Please!"

Just as before, the door flew open, as though Eddie had been expecting her. "What do you want?"

Hendricks flinched at the anger in his voice. "I—I didn't know where else to go."

"Well, you shouldn't have come here." Eddie started to close the door but Hendricks reached out, stopping him.

"Wait, please. I need to talk to you."

His face remained impassive. "I tried to talk to you earlier."

"I'm sorry about that," Hendricks said, staring down at her hands. She felt Eddie's eyes move over to her, and she forced herself to keep talking before she could chicken out. "Those guys were being assholes, and I should've stuck up for you—"

"Whatever," Eddie said, cutting her off.

Now she did look at him. "No, it's not okay."

He met her eyes. "You're right. It's not."

Hendricks shivered. She'd run all the way over in nothing but a T-shirt, even though the wind made the hair on her arms stand straight up. She twisted her finger in the hem of her shirt, trying to ignore the cold. "You were right," she said. "About Steele House. It's haunted."

Something in Eddie's expression softened. He pushed the screen door open and joined her on the porch. "You saw something?"

"Yeah." Hendricks closed her eyes, fighting tears. "And whatever it was, it tried to kill my little brother."

Eddie looked like he was about to respond but instead he pressed his lips together, jaw tight.

"Let's get out of here," he said suddenly.

Hendricks knotted her hands together as they drifted into Eddie's backyard, squeezing until the blood drained from her fingers. Something inside of her had been tightening and tightening all night. She had thought that seeing Eddie and telling him what happened might cause it to release, but it didn't. She felt tense as ever.

"I hate this place," Eddie muttered out of nowhere. He wasn't wearing a coat, and Hendricks could see goose bumps pop up along his arms.

She lifted an eyebrow. "You hate Drearford? Or just this street?"

"All of it." Eddie hugged his chest, shoulders hunching up around his ears. "You feel it, don't you?"

He glanced at her sideways, and Hendricks shrugged. There was something wrong with her house for sure. But Eddie made it sound like the whole town was haunted. Drearford felt *cold*, but otherwise it was like any other town. Maybe a little grayer and darker, but that was just because it was January and they were so far north.

"I guess," she said quietly.

Eddie shook his head. "You don't get it. There's something *rotten* here."

*Rotten.* The word sent an unpleasant feeling squirming up Hendricks's back.

"Are you sure you're not just saying that because of what happened to Maribeth?"

Eddie shook his head. "No. It got worse after Maribeth, but the town has always been . . . *wrong*." He blew air out through his teeth. "You just moved here. Give it time."

"I don't see anyone else getting haunted," Hendricks said.

Eddie looked at her, a frown crossing his face. For the first time, she noticed the straight line of his jaw, the sharp cut of his cheekbone. When he stood up straight he was taller than her dad.

*He's sort of hot*, she realized. Anywhere else, he would've had his pick of moody chicks with dark eye makeup.

She stared at his mouth for a moment, distracted. He had a little scar just beside his lower lip. It curved toward his cheek like a backward J.

After a minute, Eddie cleared his throat and looked away. "Where's your brother now?"

"At the hospital with my parents." Hendricks felt a lump forming in her throat. "That thing, the ghost or whatever it was, threw him against the wall. The doctors think he's going to be okay, but it could have been so much worse."

"Jesus." Eddie dragged a hand over his mouth. "So where are you staying?"

"Park bench? Bus station? Anywhere but back there." Eddie frowned, and Hendricks added, "It's fine. I'll probably just go back to the hospital and curl up in the waiting room. I want to be there anyway, in case Brady wakes up."

"But you need clothes or whatever? Toothbrush?"

"I'm so not worried about that right now."

"You need a phone charger in case your phone dies and your parents need to get ahold of you. And books and stuff for school tomorrow. And a pillow, because those waiting rooms are uncomfortable as shit."

Hendricks chewed her lower lip. He had a point. "There's no way I'm going back there."

"I could go with you."

"Really?"

Eddie exhaled through his teeth, looking like he was trying to prepare himself for battle. "Yeah," he said after a beat. "I could do that."

There was a chill in the night air as they cut through Hendricks's yard, walking quickly past gnarly old trees, the empty pool, and the darkened windows of Steele House. Hendricks tried not to look up at those windows as she fumbled for her key. It was strange, but it sort of felt like the house was watching her.

"Let's do this quickly," she muttered, throwing the door wide.

"No shit," Eddie said.

They headed straight for Hendricks's bedroom. She took her book bag from her desk without bothering to turn on her bedroom light, hoping all the school stuff she needed was still inside. She grabbed a change of underwear and a fresh sweater out of her dresser, then pulled her phone charger out of the wall.

"I think that's everything," she said, looping her backpack over one shoulder. "Let's get the hell out of here."

Eddie had been waiting in the hall while Hendricks gathered her things, but now he crossed her room and plucked a pillow from her bed. "For the waiting room," he explained.

"Thank you," Hendricks said, touching his arm. Eddie glanced down at her hand, his posture stiffening.

"Careful," he said, suddenly sarcastic. "Haven't you heard that leprosy is contagious?"

"Ha, ha," Hendricks said. But she was pretty sure there was something beneath his sarcasm, something sincere.

*God, he must hate living here*, she thought and, without really thinking about it, she linked her arm through his, just to show him she wasn't listening to the gossip.

Eddie didn't say anything, but she felt a faint pressure on the top of her head and she knew without looking up that he was staring down at her. She kept her eyes trained straight ahead. For some reason, her cheeks felt hot.

They were halfway to the stairs. Hendricks was already anticipating the cool night air on her cheeks, the smell of chimney smoke in the air. And then—

*Stop.*

She froze, her skin crawling. "Did you hear that?"

"Hear what?"

Hendricks couldn't bring herself to answer. Her blood was thumping loud and fast in her ears, blocking out all other thought. The voice had seemed to whisper directly into her head, almost like it'd been her own thought.

Some impulse made her turn toward Brady's nursery. The door was open a sliver, the barest hint of moonlight spilling into the hallway.

*Look.*

There was something in there.

Hendricks moved slowly toward the door, her breath a dry rasp in her throat. Each step she took increased her dread, but she couldn't bring herself to stop. There was something *in* there, waiting for her. She needed to know what it was.

"*Hendricks,*" Eddie hissed. "What are you doing?"

*Just a quick look*, she told herself. And then they could leave.

The door hinges creaked slightly as she let herself in.

When she saw what was inside of Brady's room, Hendricks's legs quaked with fear and, for a moment, she thought she might collapse. She groped clumsily for the doorframe. It felt like her breath was knocked out of her. She couldn't speak, couldn't do more than release a weak whimper.

Scrawled onto the wall above Brady's crib was a message, written in big, dripping letters that looked black in the dim light but were actually, Hendricks knew, a deep, blood red.

ONE MORE

# CHAPTER 18

HENDRICKS WASN'T ENTIRELY SURE HOW SHE GOT BACK outside, but the next thing she knew she was kneeling in her backyard, staring into the empty swimming pool. She brought a hand to her chest and tried to steady her breathing.

"What the hell was that?"

Eddie was shaking his head. His eyes were wide and frightened, his skin near white. "*One more. One more what?*"

"Victim?" Hendricks had to suppress a shudder at the thought. "One more sacrifice?"

"That's not going to happen," Eddie said, and she looked up at him quickly. There was so much confidence in his voice, like he was going to make absolutely certain that nothing bad happened to her or her family. It was reassuring, and Hendricks couldn't help feeling a tiny bit better. It was nice to feel like there was someone looking out for her.

And just like that, the tears welled up behind her eyes as she replayed what had happened—the sound of her brother's body slamming into the wall. His broken, tearful voice.

*Ha-ha! Ha-ha!*

For a second Hendricks considered what it would be like to completely break down, to collapse against Eddie's chest and cry until there was nothing left inside of her. She hadn't cried since it happened.

She held it together for another fraction of a second before doubling over, hands braced against her knees, tears falling down her cheeks. She felt Eddie hesitate beside her, and then his hand was on her back. It was tentative, almost imperceptible.

"We're going to figure this out," he said. "I swear—"

"It's like they're . . . they're targeting my family. Like we did something to them."

Eddie shifted, seeming to make a sudden decision. He wiped a tear from her face with his thumb. He looked embarrassed about it a second later, as he mumbled, "I know. It felt like that, but—"

Hendricks looked up at him through bleary eyes. *Your sister died*, she wanted to scream. *Your brother committed suicide. I don't want that to happen to my family.* It was too cruel to say it out loud.

She straightened, wiping more tears from her cheeks. "I just don't know what they want from us," she said, her voice still thick.

"Maybe just this." He gestured between them. "Maybe they just want to scare you."

Hendricks pressed her lips together. She couldn't explain it, but she knew that wasn't quite right. The ghosts *wanted* something. She just needed to figure out what it was.

*One more.*

She shivered, hard.

Eddie's hand was still on her shoulder. He seemed to realize this at the same moment that she did and dropped it, awkwardly.

They stood there in silence for a few minutes, neither knowing what to say.

Finally, Eddie cleared his throat. "I think we're overthinking this.

We probably don't need to figure out what the ghost wants. We just need to find out how to get rid of him, right?"

"How do we do that?"

Eddie chewed at his lower lip. It looked like he was about to say something, but then he shrugged. "I don't know."

"Are you really going to hold back on me now?"

Eddie sighed. "We're not exactly friends—"

Hendricks felt a sudden surge of anger. "You're the only one I trust with this. I ran to your house in the middle of the night, begging for help," she pointed out. Then, because she'd already had one of the worst nights of her life, she added, "Maybe I shouldn't have bothered."

Eddie studied her for a moment. Hendricks wondered if he was thinking about what happened at Tony's earlier that day. Guilt squirmed through her again. No wonder he didn't trust her.

His thick eyebrows climbed his forehead and, in a rush, he blurted, "Okay, so I read about this ritual online. It's like a . . . a deghosting. I was thinking about doing it before your family moved in, actually. You light a few candles, wave around some burning sage, and leave crystals lying around." He shrugged with one shoulder. "Supposedly that'll convince the ghost to move on."

Hendricks frowned. "What do you mean, you read about it online?"

A pause, and then, "Reddit. There's a whole ghost forum. I've been reading it a lot since Kyle . . ." He exhaled, heavily. "Anyway, it's just an idea."

Hendricks swallowed. Her mouth and throat were both dry, so it hurt more than it should have. She brought her fingers to her neck, wincing.

She thought of the horrible sound her brother's body had made when it slammed into the wall. She could still remember how strained Brady's voice had been when he called out to her.

Eddie's idea sounded a bit crazy to her. Would it really work? But she had to do something.

"Yeah, okay," she relented. "Let's try it."

"Tomorrow night? I'd say we do it now, but we need supplies." Eddie looked sheepish as he added, "You know, crystals and candles and stuff."

Hendricks nodded, turning this over in her head. Her parents had said Brady needed to stay at the hospital for a few days while everything set and healed. And there was no way they'd leave him there by himself. So the house would be empty tomorrow night. The timing worked out.

"Okay." She sucked in a deep breath, filling her lungs, and then exhaled slowly. "Tomorrow night. Let's do it."

# CHAPTER 19

SCHOOL THE NEXT DAY WAS UNBEARABLE. HENDRICKS FOUND it impossible to follow any conversation for longer than a few seconds. She kept spacing out in class and—*twice*—she didn't hear the bell, and only realized that she had to stand up and start moving when a teacher came over to her desk to ask whether she was okay.

"Fine, just tired," she'd mumbled, cheeks flaring as she quickly gathered her things and hurried out of the classroom, trying to remember where she was supposed to go to next.

She *was* tired. She'd snuck back into the hospital waiting room after saying good night to Eddie, and curled up on one of the hard plastic seats to steal a few hours of sleep before leaving for school the next day. She'd cleaned up in the bathroom and changed her clothes before school so at least she didn't look like a total spaz.

Despite this, her skin still had a grayish cast that she was convinced came from the hospital's horrible overhead lights, and there were deep, purple circles around her eyes. Her clothes and her hair were mussed and creased in weird places.

And did she really just tell that teacher she was *fine?* Because that was a lie. She wasn't fine at all. Far from it.

Portia tried to ask her about her "hobo-chic" look at lunch, but Hendricks barely registered that she'd spoken.

"Sorry, didn't sleep well," she said when Portia poked her in the side. She knew she could tell Portia about what happened to Brady, but she didn't want to get into it just now. Not if it meant thinking about the ghosts.

Portia shook her head dramatically and looked like she was about to say something else, but the bell rang, cutting her off.

As everyone pushed back their chairs and headed for the hall, Connor knelt beside Hendricks and put a hand on her forearm. In a low voice, he said, "I wanted to say that you look nice today, but now I want to upgrade that to amazing since you didn't sleep well."

He flashed her a shy smile, leaving before she could say anything in return.

Hendricks felt warmth flare up in her chest. At least that part of her life was still working, even if everything else was falling apart.

Hendricks headed for the parking lot as soon as the last bell sounded, her eyes peeled. She and Eddie had agreed to meet there after school, but so far, she couldn't find him.

Then, at the corner of the lot, a beat-up old Buick flashed its lights.

Hendricks squinted and shaded her eyes with one hand. The Buick was a slate-gray color that was hard to make out against the flat, gray sky and asphalt. Now, though, she saw a shadowy figure hunched in the front seat.

She hurried across the lot and pulled the passenger door open. A burst of radiator heat rolled out of the car.

"Nice wheels," she said, sliding inside.

Eddie jerked his chin instead of saying hello. His dark hair was disheveled, and she was pretty sure he was wearing the same T-shirt as yesterday. Not that she had much room to talk, seeing as she'd bathed herself in a public bathroom this morning.

"Thanks," Eddie said. "It used to be Kyle's."

The Buick was ancient. It looked like it was at least fifteen years old, with holes in the interior and stains on the floor. Despite all that, Hendricks could tell that it had been impeccably maintained. There might be food stains on the floor, but there wasn't a crumb anywhere. The dashboard and cup holders looked like they'd just been wiped down.

Hendricks felt a little pang in her chest. She hadn't seen Eddie in any of their afternoon classes. That wasn't unusual, but . . . was it possible that he'd skipped school to clean his car, because he knew she'd be sitting in it?

Eddie put the car into drive and steered out of the parking lot. "We're not far from Devon," he said, turning onto Main Street. "It's this bullshit little tourist town about twenty minutes away. They have an occult shop."

Hendricks lifted her eyebrows. "Really?"

"Don't look so surprised. The whole New Age thing is *in* right now, apparently." He rolled his eyes. "Anyway, I think it's mostly greeting cards and dream catchers, but I called this afternoon and they have what we need."

"What *do* we need?"

"Sage. Crystals." Eddie ticked the items off on his fingers, even as he kept his hands balanced against the steering wheel. "A bunch of candles, some blessed salt, and the ritual itself, but I already got that printed that out."

Hendricks shifted in her seat, not entirely sure where she should put her hands, or where to look. She couldn't place her finger on why, exactly, but it felt weird being in such a small space with Eddie.

She'd never actually thought about it before, but cars sort of forced you to sit right next to someone. Hendricks didn't know Eddie that well, and she was suddenly intensely aware of that fact.

She could smell whatever he wore in his hair. It was a mix of baby shampoo and campfire.

She shifted her arm onto the armrest at the exact moment that Eddie reached for the gearshift. His arm brushed hers, and a heat like static prickled through her skin. She jerked back so quickly she nearly dislocated her shoulder.

"Sorry," she muttered when Eddie gave her a look.

God, she was such a freak.


The shop wasn't on Devon's Main Street but down a narrow residential road lined with run-down houses and scraggly yards. Hendricks studied the houses as Eddie brought his car to a crawl. It didn't look like people lived here. Windows were dark and boarded up, and the yards were unkempt.

Devon's Main Street had been cute, but the town seemed to fall to ruins as soon as you stepped outside of the area meant for tourists. Hendricks wondered if Eddie had gotten the address wrong.

They drove down the road twice before Hendricks noticed a small black sign near the curb: Magik & Tarot.

"Hold up. Is that it?" she asked.

Eddie pulled over and leaned across Hendricks's lap to squint at the sign. It was propped in the yard outside of a Victorian-style house that looked just as abandoned as the rest of the houses on the street. He frowned. "Is the shop supposed to be inside there?"

"You're the one who found it. You tell me."

Eddie scratched his chin. "There weren't any pictures online."

They got out of the car and cut across the yard. Now that they were closer, Hendricks noticed that there was a staircase to the side of the porch, and another sign indicated that the store was located in the basement. Hendricks chewed her lip as they made their way down the concrete steps. She felt a little nervous.

"Just be cool," Eddie said, shoving the door open with his shoulder.

The shop was darker inside than Hendricks had been expecting. Someone had slopped black paint over the windows, so the only outside light that drifted into the room was streaky and faint. Cluttered shelves lined the walls. Hendricks stopped at the nearest shelf and examined its contents.

Crystals. Tiny vials filled with murky liquid. Dried rose petals. Statuettes of naked women with snakes for hair. Hendricks saw a realistic-looking cow skull covered in sketchy symbols and resisted the urge to shudder.

"Whoa," she breathed.

"Yeah, not quite dream catchers and greeting cards," Eddie said. "But at least they have what we need."

Hendricks nodded, noticing one other person in the store, a woman sitting behind a cobwebby glass case that held a taxidermy fawn. The woman had dark skin and blunt bangs and wore a lot of black eyeliner.

Hendricks lifted her hand to wave, but the woman just stared at her, saying nothing. Her eyes were flat and black. She was so still that, for a strange, tilting moment, Hendricks thought she was taxidermy, too. A stuffed woman with marble eyes. The thought was unsettling.

Hendricks looked away, but she could still feel the woman's eyes trained on her.

She stopped in front of a table laden with all sorts of rocks and crystals and picked up a bundle of something that looked a lot like weed. She cautiously took a sniff and found it astringent but kind of earthy. "You said you had a list?" she asked Eddie. The sooner they got out of this place, the better.

Eddie dug a crumpled piece of paper out of his pocket. "That's the sage," he said, nodding at the bundle of green in Hendricks's hand. "And we also need clear quartz and black tourmaline."

Hendricks picked up a black, chunky stone. The sticker on the side said $27.50.

"Wow," she said. "Spiritual healing doesn't come cheap—"

Eddie cut in. "I've got some cash saved."

"Don't worry about it, I've got a credit card for emergencies," Hendricks said automatically. She looked up and saw that his face had gone stony.

"What?" she said.

"Nothing," he muttered.

"You're judging me because I have a credit card?"

"I *said* it was nothing."

But he didn't say another word to her as they gathered the rest of their supplies and piled them onto the glass case. Glancing down, Hendricks saw that the stuffed fawn inside the case had two heads growing side by side out of its fragile neck. Its eyes seemed to follow her. Both of its mouths were open, revealing sharp, brown teeth. Her nerves crept.

*One more.* The thought came unbidden.

She jerked backward, heart hammering.

"What?" Eddie asked, frowning, but Hendricks just shook her head.

"It's nothing," she reassured him.

The woman rose from her seat behind the fawn. She smiled faintly as she began checking them out.

"You have a ghost problem," she said. Her voice was softer than Hendricks had been expecting. It made her want to lean closer, worried she wasn't hearing every word.

"How'd you know?" Eddie asked.

The woman nodded at the materials spread out on the counter. "Sage, blessed salt, tourmaline." She picked up the quartz. "But, if I might make a suggestion, you should use amethyst instead. Quartz clears your own negative energy, amethyst clears the negative energy of others."

"Thanks," Hendricks said, as Eddie switched out the crystals. "You know a lot about this stuff."

"A bit." The woman handed over their bag, smiling slightly. "That'll be $122.50."

Hendricks reached for her credit card, but Eddie was faster. He tossed a wad of bills onto the counter. "That should cover it."

Hendricks dropped her hand, leaving her wallet where it was. If Eddie wanted to be petty, she was happy to let him. She didn't want to explain to her parents why she was spending a hundred bucks at a place called Magik & Tarot, anyway.

Hendricks couldn't be sure, but she thought she heard the woman call "Good luck" as they let themselves out.

# CHAPTER 20

IT WAS DARK BY THE TIME THEY REACHED STEELE HOUSE. Eddie pulled the Buick up to the curb and cut the engine. They sat there for a moment without speaking, the car growing cold around them.

Hendricks found her eyes drawn to the windows of the house. It occurred to her that they looked sort of like eyes, and the front porch was like a thin smile, almost as if the house was *watching* her.

The thought made her shudder.

Eddie's shoulder briefly nudged hers. "You cool?"

*No,* Hendricks thought, *I am not cool.*

But she glanced up at him, offering a weak smile. "I'm fine. So where are we doing this thing?"

"The ritual's supposed to be most effective when it's performed in a place of great supernatural energy." Eddie sounded like he was reciting something from a textbook. He cleared his throat and added, in a small voice, "I was thinking we could do it in the cellar."

Hendricks had been thinking they should do it in Brady's room, but at the mention of the cellar she blushed. Of course. That's where Eddie's little sister had died. It made sense to do it there.

"Yeah," she said, nodding. "That sounds right."

They got out of the car and walked around to the side of the house. Hendricks tugged the cellar door open with a grunt and held it while Eddie climbed down the stairs with their supplies.

Hendricks flipped the light switch, and the single raw bulb flickered to life, illuminating the cramped space and packed-dirt floor. Even though she and her father had cleaned up, wine still stained the walls a dark, crusty brown in spatters. It made the cellar look like a slaughterhouse. Hendricks glanced uneasily at Eddie.

Eddie started unloading the supplies. "Why don't you light the candles, and I'll draw the pentagram."

"Yeah," Hendricks said, taking the bundle of candles that Eddie held out for her.

He pulled a container of blessed salt from the bag and poured it in a star in the middle of a large circle. Hendricks placed the candles at the five points of the star. She went to light the match and noticed that her fingers were trembling. It took her three tries to coax a tiny red-orange flame to life.

When they were done, the cellar certainly looked spooky. The candles illuminated the white-salt pentagram and flickered in the dark glass of the few wine bottles sitting on the shelves. Her dad had been slowly trying to replace his collection.

Hendricks scanned the wine until she found a bottle with a twist top. She pulled it down and opened it, hoping it was cheap.

"Sacrifice," she said, pouring a little wine into the middle of the circle. Eddie grinned. He lit the sage with one of the candles, and thick, fragrant smoke quickly filled the air.

It smelled better than Hendricks expected. Not like weed at all, but sweeter, like cedar and grass. She took a small sip of wine, and felt her nerves fade, just a little.

Eddie's eyes darted to her face. "I'm going to start the ritual now."

Hendricks took another drink of wine, gathering her nerves. "Go on," she said, swallowing.

He pulled a crumpled paper out of his back pocket and unfolded it. Then, hesitantly, he began to read.

"Air, fire . . . um, water, and earth." He looked up. "Make this place clean again."

A cool breeze seemed to sweep through the room, raising the hair on the back of Hendricks's neck. The candles flickered—

Then, one by one, their flames died.

The wine suddenly felt stale on Hendricks's tongue. "Was that part of it?"

Before Eddie could answer, the light bulb above them popped and fizzled, plunging them into total darkness.

*Don't freak out*, Hendricks told herself. But her body didn't seem to want to listen. Sweat broke out on her palms. Her spine went stiff.

"Eddie," she whispered.

"I'm right here." His hand was suddenly on her back, his touch light. "This is supposed to happen. The ghosts will put up a fight, but that . . . that just means we're winning."

Hendricks cast her eyes to the side, searching for him in the darkness. "Did you get that off Reddit, too?"

Eddie didn't say anything. Hendricks hugged the wine bottle close to her chest, her skin creeping. The air was still thick with the smell of sage—

And something else. It was a sweet, dank smell. Dead leaves. Meat left to spoil.

Hendricks wrinkled her nose. "I don't think this is working," she murmured. "We should go."

"Quiet." Eddie's voice was barely more than a breath. "*Listen.*"

Hendricks listened.

At first she didn't hear anything at all.

And then—

Laughter.

It was soft, and it seemed to fade the second Hendricks started listening for it, like a radio going in and out of tune. Fingers shaking, she pulled her phone out of her pocket and turned on the flashlight app, casting a solid white beam at the wall across from her. She turned in place, and the soft pad of her shoes in the dirt sounded loud and close.

She sent the light from her phone bouncing over the brick walls and the wine stains. She had a hard time holding her hand steady, and the beam shook and bounced as she moved, making her feel slightly motion sick. There was nothing there. But she had the feeling of something stirring in the shadows where the phone's light didn't reach, taking shape the moment she moved the beam away.

She jerked the light around her more quickly now, wishing she could see the whole cellar at once, but she was going too fast, and it wasn't until she moved it away from the far corner of the cellar that she processed what it had just illuminated:

A boy standing in the corner with his head bowed, his hands clasped.

Hendricks's chest clenched. She spun back to the corner, one hand curled around the other to hold her phone steady. But the corner was empty again.

"Shit," she said. Her breath was a dry rasp in her throat. Her eyes darted from one side of the cellar to the other, but she didn't see the boy again. She turned in place, saying, again, "*Shit.*"

"Hey," Eddie muttered from beside her. She looked up and saw that his skin had gone completely white. "Do you feel that?"

Hendricks swallowed. She felt it. The temperature in the room had dropped. It felt like a cloud passing over the sun, and she shivered violently. "What are we supposed to do now?"

"We hold our ground. Show the ghost that this is our house." But Eddie didn't sound as confident as he had a few minutes ago.

Hendricks's heart pounded in her chest, and her ears felt like they were filled with static. She held her phone before her like a weapon.

*Stand your ground*, she told herself. *My house.*

The smell of dead leaves filled her nostrils. But now the scent seemed sweeter, muskier . . .

*Cologne*, she realized, and the smell set off an old terror in her, worse than anything else she could've found in the cellar. In an instant it grew so strong that it clogged her throat, stopping her breath. It didn't even seem right to call it a smell. It was a stench, a *reek*. It reminded her so strongly of Grayson that, for a moment, she expected to find him down here with her. The thought froze the blood in her veins, and she didn't realize that she'd let her fingers go slack until the cell phone slipped from her hand and hit the ground with a soft thump, the dim glow illuminating nothing but dirt.

*No.* Hendricks dropped to her knees, hands trembling as she groped for her phone—

155

Cold fingers closed tightly around her wrist. Hendricks felt a single moment of pure terror, and then her arm was being yanked behind her back, and she was lifted from the ground, shoved up against the wall. She felt the press of dirty bricks against her cheeks, tasted blood in her mouth.

"Hendricks? Holy shit! Hendricks! Get *off* her—"

Eddie's voice sounded far away, like he was speaking on the other side of thick glass. The fingers around her wrist were crushing now, and a solid weight leaned into her back, pinning her body against the wall. Hendricks was so completely stunned that she made no effort to move, to scream out. One thought circled her mind.

*This can't be happening to me, not again.*

Another cold hand snaked up the back of her neck and cupped the crown of her head. Hendricks barely had a moment to register what was about to happen before the fingers grasped a thick knot of her hair and *pulled*. She felt her head jerk back, and pain jolted up her neck like electric shocks.

"Did you think we really liked you?" hissed a deep, cruel voice, directly into her ear. "Poor Saggy Maggie."

Hendricks blinked into the darkness, unable to speak. She knew it was the ghost. But another part of her felt like it was Grayson's breath misting her face, Grayson pinning her arms to her side.

"You could be pretty if you tried," the voice continued. "We can help."

Something cold and sharp touched the side of her face.

A knife.

Hendricks's breath stopped and pure panic took over. She

flattened her hands against the wall and, with the last of her strength, she *pushed*, launching herself back against the force that had been holding her in place.

From far away, as though it was echoing down a long corridor, Hendricks thought she heard Eddie's voice,

*"Cleanse, dismiss, dispel."*

She expected to feel resistance, but the pressure behind her gave at once. She lost her balance and stumbled backward, her tailbone slamming into the packed-dirt floor. A fresh wave of agony rocketed up her spine.

Hendricks drew a long, sobbing breath as, all at once, the cellar grew warmer. The change was sudden, and so surprising that she felt the skin on her back grow damp. The smell quickly faded, the cologne replaced by the earthier scent of the floor.

The candles flickered back to life as one.

"Are you okay?" Eddie asked, crouching beside her.

Hendricks couldn't speak, she was breathing so hard. Little by little, she managed to get control of herself. "What just happened?"

"I don't know." Eddie met her eyes and then cut his away, a frown creasing the skin between his brows. "It said the ghosts would fight back, but I didn't think it would be like that."

"They tortured a girl down here," Hendricks said, her voice still weak with fear. She couldn't say exactly how she knew this, but as soon as the words were out of her mouth, she was sure it was true. *Saggy Maggie.* "I thought it was just one boy, but now I think there were a couple of them. He kept saying *we*, like he was talking about his friends, too." She brought a hand to the back of her neck, cringing when she touched the spot where she'd felt the cool blade of a knife. "They were going to hurt her."

"Who was talking about his friends?" Eddie frowned, studying her.

She blinked. "Didn't you hear him?"

"Hear who?"

Hendricks felt suddenly cold. The ghost boy's voice had been so clear, like there'd been another person standing in the cellar with them. "That *guy*," she said, insistently. "It sounded like he was talking to someone. He said something about how they never really liked her, and he called her *Saggy Maggie*."

"I didn't hear any of that, I swear."

Hendricks's skin was buzzing. She began backing toward the staircase. "Let's get out of here."

Eddie frowned, slightly. "We have to do the ritual three times for it to work."

Hendricks made a sound between a huff and a snort and groped for the staircase bannister behind her. "I don't want to be down here if he comes back."

"Then I'll stay." Eddie said this so quickly, so easily that, for a second, Hendricks didn't think she'd heard him correctly.

"You'll stay?" she repeated.

"I'm not leaving this house until I know for sure that you're—that *it's* safe." Eddie shrugged off his jacket, and settled on the ground. "You don't have to stay if you don't want to, but I'm not going anywhere."

Silence stretched between them.

Hendricks bit her lip. Was she really going to make him stay down here alone all night? His little sister died in this room. His brother had committed suicide in the room directly above it.

Eddie cleared his throat, drawing his knees toward his chest. Judging by the tense expression on his face, Hendricks knew he was thinking the same thing. Leaving now would be cruel.

She settled herself on the ground beside him, hugging her own knees to her chest in an unconscious imitation of his posture. She found her eyes drawn to the far corner of the cellar, where she'd been so sure she'd seen the ghost boy standing in the dark. There was no one there. For now, at least.

"All right," she said, finally. "Let's go through the ritual again."

# CHAPTER 21

THEY PERFORMED THE RITUAL TWO MORE TIMES ALL THE way through, but the ghosts didn't show up again. Hendricks still wasn't convinced they were gone, so they settled on the floor, the cell phone light shining up at the ceiling between them. Waiting.

After a few moments of silence, Hendricks grabbed what was left of the bottle of wine and took a swig. She cringed a little—she'd never liked the taste of wine, which was why she usually cut it with sparkling water—and then handed the bottle to Eddie.

"Thanks," he murmured, drinking.

"I don't get what this town has against you," she said, after a moment. "I mean, I know that your brother . . . that he's supposedly a . . ."

She let her words trail off so that she didn't have to say that word. *Murderer.*

"I don't think it's about Kyle," Eddie said. "I mean, that's a good excuse, but it's not the reason people around here hate my family."

Hendricks dropped her head back against the wall. "Then why?"

"They just always have." He shrugged. "My mom was bullied like crazy in high school, and my dad used to get in tons of fights." Eddie hesitated, mouth working like he was going to say something else, then decided against it. "Kyle and me mostly just hung out with each other," he finished.

"Kyle and Eddie," Hendricks mused.

"Short for Eduardo," Eddie explained.

"That's kind of odd, isn't it?"

"How do you mean?"

"Just that people usually name their kids things that go together. Like me and my little brother, we're Hendricks and Brady. They sound right together."

"*Hendricks and Brady* sounds like the name of an Etsy store that sells macramé plant holders and cross-stitched pillowcases."

Hendricks smacked him on the arm, and he released a soft snicker.

"You know what I mean," she continued. "Kyle and Eduardo don't go together."

Eddie was quiet for a beat. Hendricks noticed that he did that before saying anything real about himself, like he was weighing whether it was worth the potential backlash. After a minute he released a heavy breath.

"We're named for our grandfathers," he admitted. "My mom's dad was Kyle Becker, from Connecticut. My dad's dad was Eduardo Ruiz, from Argentina. My folks were really into the whole family name thing."

"What about your little sister?"

"Maribeth, after my mom's mom. You know, they used to talk about having another kid so they could round things out. Valentina, after my dad's mom. It was this ongoing joke when we were little. My mom would always say things like 'When Valentina gets here, you boys will have to share a room,' or if Maribeth grew out of a dress or something, she'd set it aside 'for Valentina.' She stopped mentioning Valentina after what happened, though."

Hendricks wasn't sure whether she was supposed to ask about this stuff. She'd never known someone who'd experienced such a loss before. But Eddie seemed okay to talk about it, so in a quiet voice, she asked, "Do you miss her?"

He nodded. "You want to know what's weird? I miss *both* of them. Maribeth and Valentina, even though Valentina was never real. It was like, for a while we had this big family, and then Maribeth died and Kyle committed suicide, and everyone stopped talking about Valentina. Now it's just me and my parents."

"What was she like? Maribeth, I mean."

Even in the darkness, Hendricks saw Eddie's face change. It was as if all the tension fell out of it, making him look younger. "Maribeth was different from the rest of us. She used to charm all the little old ladies at church group. She used to pronounce words wrong. Like, she'd say *smagetti* instead of spaghetti? And *wadder* instead of water. I swear she did it on purpose, because it made her seem younger, and then people would give her whatever she wanted." He smiled, the corners of his eyes crinkling. "Little con artist."

The smile faded so quickly, Hendricks almost thought she'd imagined it. "I'm sorry," she rushed to say. "I probably shouldn't have brought any of that stuff up."

"Don't be sorry," Eddie said. "I've never actually talked to anyone about it before. It's kind of nice to say it out loud."

His dark eyes met hers as he added, "I don't know. That might sound messed up to you."

He swallowed, hard, and she had the sudden impulse to touch his shoulder or squeeze his hand. And she might've tried it, too, if she hadn't thought of her school counselor back in Philly, how she'd tilted her head and pursed her lips after Hendricks told her what was happening, like she thought that might make her look sympathetic. Honestly, it always made Hendricks feel a little sick. She hated fake sympathy.

She was still thinking of that therapist when she said, "It doesn't sound messed up to me. I sort of know how that feels."

Eddie cocked an eyebrow.

"Not what happened with your brother and sister, of course," Hendricks said, her cheeks coloring. "But the other stuff. I know what it feels like to deal with something that you don't feel like you can talk to anyone about."

"So you really are hiding some dark and tragic secret?"

He sounded so much like Portia just then that Hendricks actually laughed out loud. "Where did you hear that?"

"You came here in the middle of the school year, and you aren't on social media, and you never talk about your old school, or your old friends . . ." Eddie shrugged. "People around here talk."

She fidgeted. Talking about Grayson felt dangerous for reasons that were tricky to explain. It reminded her of being a little kid and playing Bloody Mary at sleepovers. They'd all take turns going into a dark bathroom and saying the name "Bloody Mary" into the mirror. Rumor had it that saying the name three times caused Bloody Mary herself to appear.

It was silly, childish, but Hendricks felt like that now. Say Grayson's name out loud too many times, and it might call him here.

She glanced over at Eddie and saw that he was watching her, waiting for her to fill the silence with a story of her own. It was only fair, after all. He'd already told her his sad story.

"Okay," she said after a beat. "I was dating this guy back in Philadelphia. Grayson Meyers."

The name seemed to echo through the cellar. Hendricks hugged her arms close to her chest.

"Let me guess," Eddie said. "Quarterback? Homecoming king?"

"Close. He was actually the captain of our school soccer team.

163

He was good, too. Scouts used to come and watch him play. We were pretty sure he was going to get a scholarship.

"We started dating freshman year," she continued, "and we just . . . clicked. We liked all the same shows on Netflix, and we were both obsessed with Halloween. We were going to try every burger place in Philly and, like, rate them so we knew where to get the best burgers no matter which neighborhood we were in. People would talk about us like we were one person. *HendricksandGrayson*. I used to think we'd go to the same college, maybe even get an apartment together after school."

"So what changed?" Eddie asked.

Hendricks hesitated. She'd never tried to explain this part before, and now she realized she didn't know how to start. It felt like there was something lodged in her throat. "It was little stuff at first. *Tiny* stuff. Like, he hated it that I sometimes forgot to text him before I went to bed. We used to fight about it all the time. And then he'd start showing up places I was supposed to be, without telling me. Like, I'd see him at volleyball practice, or he'd stop by this diner where I used to work. It was like he was checking up on me. Like he didn't believe me when I said I was going to be somewhere."

There were other things, too. He'd get jealous when he saw her talking to another guy, even if it was just the checkout guy at the grocery store or someone she had to do a project with for class. He didn't like it when she wore revealing clothes, but he didn't like it when she looked "frumpy," either. He hated it when she drew too much attention to herself or contradicted him in public.

"Jesus," Eddie murmured. "So he was controlling?"

Hendricks pressed her lips together. *Controlling, yes*, she thought. But there was more to it than that. He had a way of making it seem like it was all her fault. If she forgot to text him, she was hateful and thoughtless. If she hung out with a guy friend without him, she was being too forward. Such a tease. When she told him it made her uncomfortable that he sometimes showed up places unannounced, he acted all suspicious. Like he thought she was hiding things from him.

She felt a rush of shame now, remembering.

"I was starting to think about breaking up with him," she went on. "But prom was coming up, so I figured I could wait until after. We used to have this joke about how all the cool kids lose their virginity on prom night, so we should just save ourselves for the after-party. It was so dumb, and I swear it didn't even mean anything, but I could tell Grayson sort of expected it to happen like that. It was like he thought that because we'd been joking about it for so long that I . . . *owed* it to him." Hendricks felt her cheeks grow warm. She'd never said that out loud before, not even to her parents, and it felt weird to be talking about it with Eddie. But the rest of the story wouldn't make sense unless she explained this part, and so she swallowed and forced herself to keep going. "So junior prom night came, and we went to the after-party and he . . . tried to make something happen, but I told him I didn't want to."

"I'm guessing he didn't take it well?"

Hendricks pressed her lips together, remembering Grayson's hand crushing her wrist, the way he'd blocked the door so she couldn't leave.

*Don't you dare embarrass me here.*

"He grabbed me," she told Eddie, speaking slowly, carefully. "He grabbed me really hard. He'd never done anything like that before, and it really freaked me out, so I—I screamed.

"I swear, every single person at that party came running. The next thing I knew there were all these guys pulling Grayson away from me, and my friends were forming this protective circle around me, like a barrier to keep him away." A puff of breath escaped her lips, not quite a laugh. "Someone even threatened to call the cops."

Eddie looked grudgingly impressed. "But that's a good thing, right? They stopped him. They stood up for you."

"Yeah, well, Grayson can get sort of obsessive about what other people think about him. He got a little scary after that."

Scary was an understatement. Hendricks had twenty-three text messages from Grayson by the time she got home after the party, each of them increasingly nasty.

*You totally overreacted. You know that, right?*

*Now everyone at school thinks I'm some sort of fucking rapist.*

And the worst of them all, the one that still sent shivers down Hendricks's spine:

*You'll pay for what you did.*

She'd written back only once: *We're over. Don't text me again.* And then she'd blocked his number.

So he'd started following her. He'd wait for her in the parking lot outside of school, or around the corner from her house, so he could catch her on the way to the bus. It got to the point where she didn't want to go anywhere without a friend, just in case he suddenly appeared. After he figured out she'd blocked his number, he'd text and call from other people's phones. It got so bad that she stopped answering calls or reading texts. Eventually, she'd had to change her number. But then he got the new number from a friend. She couldn't escape.

Hendricks didn't even think he wanted to get back together. He just hated that *she'd* been the one to break it off. That she'd done something without his permission.

And then, once, she'd gotten home from school and found Grayson in her bedroom. Waiting for her. To this day, she had never figured out how he'd gotten inside.

She'd called 911. It felt like a monumental decision at the time, but Hendricks couldn't think of anything else to do. She'd never been so afraid of anything in her life.

That's when her parents decided it was time for a change. Clean slate.

Hendricks breathed in deep, willing the memories away. "The most messed-up part is that I still miss him. Not *him*, I guess, but the way he was before all this happened. I'll drive past a burger place and think *Grayson and I haven't tried that one yet*. And then I remember and it's like it's happening all over again." She shook her head, her cheeks burning, and added, in a low voice, "I still have one of his old soccer jerseys in my closet. I can't bring myself to throw it out."

Eddie was quiet for so long that Hendricks almost thought he'd fallen asleep.

"After Maribeth died, I asked my dad if he believed in ghosts. He said he didn't know, but he figured the ghosts we made up ourselves were more dangerous than any real ones, anyway."

Hendricks's eyebrows drew together. "What does that mean?"

He shrugged. "I always figured it meant that we let the bad things that've happened to us have too much power. If we could just figure out how to move on, we wouldn't be haunted anymore."

"So all I have to do is forget about Grayson, and the Steele House ghosts will leave me and my family alone?" Hendricks meant for this to sound like a joke, but there was an edge to her voice. "That makes it sound easy."

Eddie raised an eyebrow without looking at her. "You really think *that* would be easy?"

She started to reply, and then merely pressed her lips together. She remembered the stench of Grayson's cologne. His grip crushing her wrist.

Eddie was right. Moving on was never easy.

Hendricks wasn't entirely sure when she drifted off. It happened gradually. At some point her head seemed heavier, and then her thoughts slowed down, growing soupy. She imagined that Eddie put his arm around her shoulder, letting her rest her head against his chest.

But no, it wasn't Eddie. It was Grayson. They were curled up in his basement, watching old horror movies like they used to. Grayson loved horror movies, but Hendricks hated them, so Grayson would put his arms around her and let her hide her face in his shoulder.

"Shhh . . . ," he whispered in her ear. "You'll pay for what you did."

Hendricks opened her eyes, her heart hammering. She blinked for a few moments, her mind still groggy from her dream. She lifted a hand to her face and found that her cheeks were damp, and her eyes were sticky with tears. She wiped them away, angrily. When did she become such a crybaby? She never used to cry.

She started to take stock of where she was, and that's when she realized that her head really was resting on Eddie's shoulder, and Eddie actually did have his arm wrapped tightly around her. When did that happen?

She sat up, and Eddie jerked awake.

"What time is it?" he moaned, rubbing his eyes with his free hand. He didn't seem to have any intention of moving his arm off Hendricks's shoulder. The warmth was pleasant. Comforting, even.

"Early," Hendricks murmured. She shifted to the side and Eddie stretched both arms over his head, yawning. She missed the weight of his arm now that it was gone.

"I didn't mean to fall asleep," he said, pushing himself to his feet. "Any more ghostly visitors?"

Hendricks shook her head. "Nope. None."

Eddie grabbed his jacket from the ground and threw it over one shoulder. "Seems like the ghosts have been busted."

"Are you leaving?" Hendricks didn't know why she was surprised. Eddie didn't live here.

She thought, again, of how nice it had felt to have his arm wrapped around her shoulder. How safe. Heat spread through her cheeks.

"Yeah." Eddie was looking at her, frowning slightly. "Well, we've got school, you know?"

*School*, Hendricks thought. Right.

"You sure you don't want breakfast or something?" she blurted. "Coffee, maybe?"

Eddie hesitated. "I better not."

"Why not?" Hendricks asked.

At the exact same time he explained, "You don't want anyone to see me coming out of your house this early in the morning. People would talk." He smiled, but this time it was tinged with something. Sadness, maybe. "It's a small town."

"Right," Hendricks said. "Well. I guess I'll see you at school, then."

Eddie just laughed, darkly. "Sure."

He said it like it was a joke. Hendricks wanted to argue, but the words died on her tongue.

What was she going to say? That she'd be cool blowing off her new friends and being his cafeteria buddy during lunch? That she'd give up popularity and acceptance because he'd told her about his little sister?

She slumped slightly, shifting her eyes down to her knees.

Eddie made a sound at the back of his throat. A laugh, or a cough. "That's what I thought," he said, pushing himself to his feet.

Hendricks couldn't bring herself to look at him. "Thank you," she said, hoping he knew she was sincere. "I mean it."

She finally looked up and saw Eddie hesitating near the stairs. For a moment, Hendricks thought he might say something else. But then she heard his boots on the stairs, and the cellar door creaked open and closed. And he was gone.

# CHAPTER 22

PORTIA WAS WAITING AT HENDRICKS'S LOCKER WHEN SHE got to school.

"Are you stalking me now?" Hendricks asked, fumbling with her combination.

Portia didn't seem amused. "Where the hell *were* you last night? Connor was seriously pissed."

"Last night?" Hendricks pulled her French book out of her locker and shoved it into her book bag. "What are you talking about?"

"What am I talking about? Have you been spacing out all week? Yesterday was Connor's *birthday*. We were all coming to my place for his party, remember? Jesus, we've only been talking about it every single day at lunch."

A sinking feeling opened up in Hendricks's gut. She vaguely remembered joking around about something that might have been a birthday party. And hadn't she heard something about a clown?

"Portia, I'm so sorry," she sputtered, cheeks burning. "I had a family thing, an emergency, and—"

"Really?" Portia snapped, cutting her off. "Because Raven saw you get into Eddie Ruiz's car after school."

Hendricks looked at Portia and then back at her locker. *Shit.*

She could still feel Portia's eyes boring into her, waiting for an explanation.

"That wasn't, like, a social thing," she said. "It was for school or whatever. We had a project."

Portia gave her head a little shake. "Whatever," she said. "I'm not the one you owe an apology to, anyway."

Hendricks and her friends back in Philly used to have a system. And that system was cupcakes. Sometime around ninth grade, they'd all agreed that instead of doing the whole silent treatment or passive-aggressive thing that everyone else did when they were pissed off, they'd start a new tradition. Fights meant cupcakes. If you did something shitty to the other person, all you had to do was show up at their door with a dozen cupcakes and all would be forgiven.

Hendricks believed in the cupcake system. So she did a Google search for bakeries in Drearford, and was psyched to find that there was a cute little shop called Mae's Treats & Things within walking distance from school.

She set out after last period and picked out a dozen cupcakes in all different flavors since she didn't know what Connor liked. While she was waiting for Mae to wrap the cupcakes up, she texted Raven to get Connor's address.

*He's at 2496 Elm*, Raven wrote back. *Good luck!*

Hendricks rolled her lip between her teeth. She didn't know whether to be heartened or depressed that apparently everyone in her new social circle already knew that she was on the outs with Connor—but she decided to go with heartened. She wanted to feel good today.

*You already got rid of the ghosts*, she told herself as she pulled her hood over her topknot and started toward Elm. *Salvaging your social life will be a piece of cake.*

She glanced down at the box of cakes in her hands and smiled at her pun.

*Literally.*

Connor lived in a ramshackle, two-story house that looked both well-loved and well overdue for a facelift. There was a tire swing hanging from the tree out front, and a bunch of cars parked in the driveway. Sporting equipment littered the porch, and the grass had clearly been flattened by many people running and tumbling through it over the years.

And maybe even parking on it, Hendricks thought, noticing two deep ruts in the lawn that looked suspiciously like tire tracks.

She grinned to herself as she rang the buzzer. Even if Connor hadn't already told her about his brothers, it would have been obvious that a bunch of boys lived here. Although she might've guessed he had a dozen brothers instead of just three.

A little girl in a soccer uniform opened the door.

"Who're you?" she asked, frowning.

"Um, my name is Hendricks," she said, kneeling so that she was eye-to-eye with Connor's sister. "You must be Amy?"

Amy tugged on one of her blond pigtails and said nothing.

"Um, Connor told me all about you," Hendricks said. Would it be weird of her to offer this little girl a cupcake? She glanced over Amy's shoulder, suddenly anxious. "Is he here?"

"Connor!" Amy screamed. "There's a girl here!"

And then, without saying another word, she turned and fled down the hallway.

Hendricks didn't quite know what to do. She hadn't been invited inside, exactly, so she stayed on the porch, but it felt weird to be standing directly in front of an open door without even bothering to close it.

Luckily, she heard the thud of footsteps on the staircase about a second later, and then Connor appeared, smiling shyly at the sight of her.

"Hey, you," he said. He motioned toward the hall. "Come on in."

Hendricks followed him into the hallway as he casually swung the door shut.

She sheepishly held out the cupcakes. "Peace offering?"

Connor frowned and peeked into the box. "They look like a cupcake offering. Why peace?"

"Portia told me you totally hated me for missing your party last night, and I just wanted you to know that I didn't mean to at all." Hendricks chewed her bottom lip. "I really wanted to be there. I'm so sorry."

Connor hesitated for a moment, then gave her a small smile. "Hey, if you feeling sorry means I get to eat cupcakes, then I'm all for it." He nodded toward the kitchen. "Come on, let's get some milk."

Hendricks followed Connor down the hallway to a small kitchen with a beaten wood table and seven mismatched chairs. She sat down and began carefully taking the prettiest cupcakes out of the box while Connor went to get the glasses.

"You drink dairy, right?" he asked, putting a plastic jug of whole milk on the table. "I know a lot of you city girls only drink milk that comes from almonds and oats and grass and stuff."

"I'm pretty into the stuff that comes out of cows," Hendricks said, "but don't knock oat milk until you've tried it."

Connor laughed. "Noted." He grabbed a chocolate-on-chocolate cupcake. "So."

"So," Hendricks repeated. She took a vanilla-lavender cupcake and began picking at the wrapper. Connor cleared his throat.

"So, what happened?" he asked after a beat.

Hendricks knew she should have come armed with a reasonable explanation, but she suddenly didn't know what to say. Connor had been nothing but caring and respectful. She just didn't know how to start to explain the horror of the past few days at home.

"What's the deal?" he prompted again. "Because I kind of thought you liked me."

Connor shifted a little, so that his knuckles brushed against the back of her hand.

Hendricks glanced down at their hands, her breath catching in her throat. She realized she genuinely *did* like him.

But Grayson had seemed nice, too. At first. It was hard for her to trust her intuition when she'd been so wrong before.

Heat rose in her cheeks. "I did," she blurted, pulling her hand away. Then, feeling awkward, "I mean, I *do*."

Connor asked, "But, what?

"I don't remember saying *but*."

"Strange, because I definitely heard it."

Hendricks took a deep breath. "*But* things with my last boyfriend got really intense, really fast," she admitted. "I guess I'd always wished we'd taken more time to get to know each other as friends before we got involved. I don't want to make that mistake again."

That was all true. It just wasn't the whole truth. She thought of Eddie and their night in the cellar. Her cheeks grew hot.

"Friends first, huh?" Connor scratched the back of his neck. "I guess there's some logic to that."

"You'd be cool with that?"

"Of course I would. If it's what you want."

"It is," Hendricks said on an exhale.

She took a bite of cupcake, waiting for Connor to ask her about Eddie. But he didn't.

"Is this why you didn't you come to the party last night?" he asked instead.

"Actually, my little brother's in the hospital," she said. "He hurt his leg pretty bad. My parents have been staying with him at the hospital. We're all pretty upset and, anyway, that's why I didn't come last night. It's not that I didn't want to go, obviously, it's just . . ."

Hendricks ended her sentence with a sigh, once again not sure how to explain the strange mix of guilt and terror and everything else she'd been feeling since Brady got hurt.

Sensing her unease, Connor thankfully saved her from having to continue. "If one of my siblings was in the hospital, I'd be a total mess," he said, taking a drink of milk. "There's no way I'd be going to parties. In fact, I'm impressed that you're here right now."

"Yeah." Hendricks's voice cracked, betraying her. "I just feel so bad for him."

"I really hope he gets better."

Hendricks lifted her eyes to his. He sounded sincere. Which was funny considering that he had a milk mustache.

"Thanks," she said. "You got a little . . ." She touched the top of her lip, and Connor's ears turned pink. She dug a crumpled napkin out of the cupcake box and handed it to him.

"Thanks," he said, wiping the mustache away.

"So tell me about the party!" Hendricks said brightly, wanting to change the subject. "Were there really clowns?"

"No, thank God. But Portia and Raven passed out bright red clown noses to all the guests, so it sort of felt like we all got to be clowns for the night."

Connor told her about how they'd set up all the old-school kids' games—pin the tail on the donkey, musical chairs, and a cakewalk. Portia and Raven had filled Portia's basement with streamers and balloons and rented a snow-cone machine—which they'd spiked with vodka, of course.

"There was even a piñata," Connor said. "Although my brothers got ahold of the stick thing you're supposed to use to break it open, and then they spent more time chasing each other around with it than trying to get the candy."

Hendricks laughed and, for a moment, she felt like she had right after she'd leapt off the cliff into the quarry: wholly and perfectly herself.

Her smile flickered as she realized this wasn't as comforting as she'd hoped it would be. There was a shadow looming over her that she couldn't quite shake. Even when she knew she was perfectly safe, there would always be a part of her that was a little bit afraid.

# CHAPTER 23

STEELE HOUSE WAS EMPTY WHEN HENDRICKS GOT HOME. She eased the front door open. It swung smoothly, without a creak. It was late, but there were no lights on in the house. Hendricks's mom had called while she was walking back from Connor's, to tell her they wouldn't be home tonight.

"We had that meeting in Boston today, remember?" she'd said. "Train ride back will take forever, so we're staying at a hotel and heading back sometime tomorrow."

Hendricks had heard the sound of cars zooming past, and the distant murmur of voices, and pictured her mother on some busy street corner in Boston, hailing a cab.

Her chest twisted. "You actually went to that?"

"Yeah, well, rescheduling was going to be a pain, so we just brought Brady with us. You'll have the place to yourself tonight."

"Goodie," Hendricks murmured, but if her mother noticed the sarcasm in her voice, she hadn't mentioned it. They said goodbye soon after, with her mother first assuring her, again, that they didn't blame her for what happened to Brady. And Hendricks had reluctantly walked home.

Now, a thrill of fear went through her as she stood in the doorway, listening to the groan of the old house settling around her. The air felt stale, and the room was dusty and tinged with cold. She couldn't help shivering.

She dropped her book bag by the door and began making her way through the rooms. Her mother had left a note on the counter in the kitchen.

*Be home around ten tomorrow morning!*
*Love you!*
*xo Mom*

There were twenty dollars for pizza tucked beneath the note. Hendricks touched the bill, and then moved her hand away. Thinking about pizza made her think about Eddie picking up a pizza from Tony's, and that made her feel strange and jumpy. Her eyes reflexively moved to the windows that looked out onto her unfinished backyard.

Eddie was on the other side of those trees. If she wanted to see him again, she didn't have to go get pizza. She could just walk outside, cross her backyard, knock on his door.

Instead, she rummaged around in the freezer and pulled out a pint of Peanut Butter Marshmallow Crunch. She grabbed a spoon but didn't bother with a bowl, opting to eat straight from the carton as she walked from room to room of the empty house, turning on lights, studying the shadows, listening for noises. It was hard to believe that the danger could've passed so easily, but the house felt different than it had even the night before. She spooned ice cream into her mouth, exhaling as it melted on her tongue.

It felt . . . quieter.

Satisfied, she headed back into the living room and curled into the corner of the couch with her ice cream, digging between the cushions for the remote. From this angle, she could see through the kitchen, to where the plastic sheet covered the stairs to the second floor. She glanced at the plastic sheet, and then away, her skin prickling.

She wasn't ready to go upstairs yet.

Hendricks settled in with an episode of *Vampire Diaries* that she'd seen before, automatically spooning ice cream into her mouth as her eyes glazed and her body sank deep into the couch cushions. She hadn't realized how tired she was. It'd been a few days since she'd gotten a good night's sleep.

She was drifting, and so it could have been one of those surreal, half-dream moments, but she could've sworn she heard the front door open. There was the sound of hinges creaking, and then the sudden, cool sweep of wind over her cheeks.

She jerked upright, heart hammering, her eyes still blurry with sleep.

The front door was still closed.

But the television had been switched off.

Hendricks felt a sick twist of fear. Had she switched the television off? She didn't remember doing that.

Sitting up, she noticed she'd dropped her pint of ice cream when she'd fallen asleep, and now it was on its side on the floor, spilling a goopy layer of Peanut Butter Marshmallow Crunch onto her mother's vintage rug.

"Shit," Hendricks muttered, leaning over the side of the couch to pick up the sticky pint. Her mother loved that rug. She dabbed a finger at the ice cream, wondering if it would come out if she scrubbed it.

All at once, every light in the house flicked off. Hendricks lifted her head just in time to watch the living room lamp blink out, leaving her in perfect darkness.

Fear prickled through her. She sat, frozen, for a long moment, staring intently into the darkness. Listening for the sound of movement. But there was nothing.

Outside, a cloud passed over the moon, allowing a faint stream of light through the living room windows. Hendricks's eyes adjusted enough that she could see the edge of the television set, the outline of the front door. The muscles in her shoulders tightened. She imagined racing to the door, throwing it open, running outside. Her leg twitched.

But she couldn't do it. She was too scared. She had the unsettling feeling of being watched. It was as though the house itself had eyes, as though it were waiting for her to move and then it would . . .

*What?* she thought, desperately. What did she think the *house* was going to do to her?

*One more.*

The thought came to her so clearly that it was as if someone had spoken it out loud. Her heart plummeted into her stomach. She was too frightened to breathe. Too frightened to blink.

A tear traced, slowly, down her cheek.

Time passed. Hendricks listened to the sound of the wind moving through the trees outside, the sharp tap of rain on the windows. Her hands unclenched. Slowly, she began to realize that it was storming, that the wind must've knocked out the electricity. She lowered one foot to the floor, and then the other. The melted ice cream was warm and sticky beneath her toes. Very slowly, she stood.

Hendricks used to play a game with herself, when she was little and scared of monsters hiding under her bed. Whenever she needed to get up in the middle of the night to use the bathroom, she'd clench her eyes shut and walk to the door.

*If I can make it out of this room without anything touching me, then there's nothing there,* she'd tell herself.

It was a childish game, like trying to make it across a room without touching the floor, but it always used to make her feel a little bit better.

She played the game now, walking slowly across the living room, toward the front door. Her skin crept, and her breath felt lodged in her throat.

*If I can just make it out the front door,* she told herself, *if I can make it outside . . .*

The rug beneath her feet gave way to the cold tile that surrounded the entry. She reached forward, groping in the darkness for the door. Relief welled up inside her as her fingers brushed against the cool, brass knob.

The sound of metal scraping metal broke through the silence. The dead bolt had clicked shut.

All around her, the air filled with the scent of cologne.

Hendricks screamed, the sound seeming to reverberate through the air for a long time after she closed her mouth. She gripped the doorknob firmly and turned, but the door wouldn't open. She hammered on the door with one hand, still twisting the knob with the other, and then fumbling for the dead bolt, trying to force it open again. She wrenched it to one side and then the other, cold metal digging into her fingers. It would not open and would not and would not—

She opened and closed her mouth, unable to emit a sound. Tears fell hard and fast down her cheeks.

"Please," she said finally, her voice very quiet. She didn't know who she was talking to, but she said the word again. "Please, *please.*"

The house answered.

*Come with me.*

Hendricks went still. Just like before, the voice seemed to come from both the inside of her mind and from the house itself, as though the house had spoken directly into her brain. Largely against her will, Hendricks turned around.

The ugly cat sat in the middle of the entryway floor, his tail twitching, his eyes glassy in the darkness. As Hendricks watched, the cat turned and bolted across the kitchen, slipping past the plastic curtain and upstairs.

Hendricks knew that she was meant to follow him.

She walked across the kitchen, her body feeling slow and heavy. From the corner of her eye, she saw curtains jerk in place, closet doors swing silently on their hinges, kitchen drawers roll open. But when she turned to look at them directly, the drawers and doors were all closed, the curtains still.

Hendricks's hand twitched, horror growing inside of her. She took a ragged breath in, pushed the plastic curtain back, and started upstairs. She noticed she was trailing blood onto the stairs, the color garish and red against the raw wood. But when she stopped walking and examined the prints a little closer, she saw that it was only peanut butter ice cream.

A voice echoed from just above her: "You crazy . . . you, you *assholes*. You think you're so cool, that the world revolves around you, but you're *nothing*. I'll show you."

It was a high rasp of a voice that seemed to grow higher and thinner as Hendricks listened. She stood, frozen, on the staircase. That voice didn't sound human at all. It didn't sound like anything she'd ever heard before.

Sweat broke out on her palms. She was crying again, her breath hitching in her throat, her eyes clouded with tears. She didn't want to go up there, didn't want to see what was waiting for her in Brady's room, but her legs seemed to move on their own, carrying her up to the second floor and around the corner. The voice had stopped talking, but that didn't ease her fear.

Hendricks reached for the doorknob of her little brother's room. Holding her breath, she pushed the door open . . .

Brady's baby doll sat on the windowsill, its glass eyes seeming to glow in the dark, jabbering away.

"A . . . B . . . C . . . D . . . come sing with me!"

Hendricks peered around the room, her heartbeat hammering. There was nothing there, nothing but that damn doll. She wiped a hand across her mouth, trying to catch her breath. Her skin felt cold and clammy to the touch, still damp with tears. She closed her eyes, and then opened them again, expecting the room to change. But it didn't.

"Sing with me!" the baby doll sang.

Hendricks hurried across the room, grasping the toy with shaking hands. She turned it over, intending to switch it off, but her hands were thick and clumsy and it smashed to the floor instead.

She blinked down at the ruined toy and felt her heartbeat slow as its low, gravelly voice petered out. Then she turned around and saw the boy lying in the doorway.

Hendricks's hands flew to her mouth. The boy was on his side, his arms and legs tied. His lips had been stapled shut, and blood ran down his chin in thick rivulets, pooling on the ground below his cheek. He writhed around on the ground, struggling to get free.

Hendricks stared in horror, too shocked to scream. She took a quick step backward—

And her foot banged into something.

Something that *wriggled.*

She felt her whole body constrict. *No*, she thought, but she was already turning, a hand balled at her mouth.

A second boy was lying on the floor behind her, his arms and legs tied just like the first boy's had been. His mouth had been duct taped shut, instead of stapled. Someone had carved the word loser into his chest, the lines thick and deep. Thin strips of skin peeled away from the wound, and the blood had crusted up around it, brown and scabbed. Fresh droplets still oozed out from where it had dried, tracing thick, red lines down the boy's front.

Hendricks felt her stomach lurch and pressed her hand tighter over her mouth. She felt like she was going to be sick. She turned and—

*Oh God.*

There, just a few feet away from where she was standing, was a third boy. This boy had been tied, too, and his mouth duct taped, but no one had mutilated him. His eyes were bugged and red. He moaned against the duct tape covering his mouth and, though Hendricks couldn't hear what he was saying, his meaning was clear.

*Don't hurt me.*

Hendricks took a step toward the bound and frightened boy, and said, "I didn't do this to you, I swear!" She dropped to her knees and began fumbling with the bindings around the boy's wrists.

When she raised her hand, she saw that she was holding a stapler.

# CHAPTER
## 24

HENDRICKS'S HANDS SPRANG OPEN, BUT THE STAPLER vanished before it hit the floor.

She spun in place, eyes moving anxiously over Brady's stuffed animals, and the baby-animal pictures hanging on his wall. The boys had vanished. Brady's room looked just like it always did, except that his crib was still overturned from his accident the other night. Hendricks stared at the blankets spilling onto the floor for a long moment, waiting for her heartbeat to steady.

It was good that the crib was messed up. It made it easier to believe that everything she'd seen had really been there.

She turned back to the door, her eyes drawn to the place on the floor where Brady's nursery met the hall. While the hall floors had been replaced, Brady's were still the original wood, and it always looked a little funny where the old, creaky floorboards met the fresh, raw wood of the hall. But now, looking closer, Hendricks noticed that there was a spot that looked a little darker than the rest. Stained.

It was *blood*, she realized. That's where the ghost boy with his lips stapled shut had been lying. Hendricks pictured how the blood had dripped from his mouth, pooling between his cheek and the floor.

What she'd seen had really happened.

She pressed her trembling fingers to her lips and took a few horrified steps away from the door. There was a part of her that expected

**186**

the ghost boys to blip back into existence again. But the door stayed empty. Sucking down a deep, uneven breath, she bolted. She didn't slow until she was down the stairs and out the front door, cutting around the side of her house and through the yard.

She nearly collided with Eddie's back door. "Help!" she screamed, fists pounding on the wood. "He's back, they're back!"

Eddie yanked the door open and pulled her inside. He locked the door behind her, checking the window like he thought the ghosts had chased her across the yard.

"You okay?" he asked.

Hendricks started to nod, struggling to catch her breath. She could still feel the strange weight of the stapler between her fingers. There, and then gone.

She stopped mid-nod and started shaking her head instead.

She was *not* okay. She didn't see how she could ever be okay again.

"Oh my God," she spluttered, raking her hands through her hair. "I feel like I'm going crazy."

Eddie took her by the arm. For a second, it looked like he might hug her, and then he froze, shifting his eyes away. He was still holding on to her arm, but now he repositioned his hand, like he was trying to lead her out of the room. "Come on, let's go upstairs," he said.

Hendricks's skin was warm where he was touching her. Her voice felt lodged in her throat, so she just nodded.

It was too dark for her to see much of the room around her, but she could tell that the layout was different from her house. Eddie's back door seemed to open into a sort of basement bedroom. She saw a mattress on the floor, piled with sheets and clothes, and then Eddie was leading her up a narrow staircase with tacky, wood-paneled walls and orange carpet. The staircase opened up into the kitchen.

Hendricks had been preparing herself. She didn't know what

Eddie's family situation was, but, between what had happened to his sister and what went on with his older brother, she couldn't imagine it was great. She didn't want to come across as a total snob if things were a bit hectic.

Still, when Eddie flicked on the kitchen light, she stood frozen in the doorway, shocked by what she saw.

The kitchen was clean. Not tidy, like her kitchen back home, but *clean*. Like someone had gotten down on their knees and scrubbed the floors by hand. The linoleum floor was old and peeling, but spotless. The stainless steel sink gleamed.

And that smell . . . Hendricks's nose wrinkled. Bleach, she realized after a moment, mixed with some sort of lemon-scented cleaner. The entire room reeked of it.

Eddie motioned for her to sit. There was only one chair at the card table set up in the middle of the room. Hendricks had the feeling that this wasn't the sort of home where the family ate together.

"Tell me what happened," Eddie said, getting a glass from a cupboard above the sink. Hendricks noticed that the array of cheap-looking coffee mugs had been arranged according to color, but Eddie closed the door quickly, before she could see anything else.

He filled a chipped blue mug with water from the faucet, and handed it to her.

"Thanks," Hendricks murmured. And then, haltingly, she told him everything she could remember about what had just happened. "It—it felt like they were re-creating something. And then, the ghosts just . . . vanished."

Eddie leaned back against the sink. "That's messed up."

Hendricks took a sip of water. "The night Brady got hurt was the same. It felt like something that had happened before." She shuddered, remembering.

Eddie stared off into space. After a long moment, he said, "Okay, so I read somewhere that this can happen. A ghost will re-create the events leading up to its death. Can you put all the . . . scenes, or whatever they are, together?"

Hendricks closed her eyes and pressed a finger to the skin between her eyebrows. The things she'd seen seemed to morph together until all she could remember was that awful laughter. That voice whispering to her: *You'll pay for what you did!*

And then a pair of yellow eyes popped into her head.

"Okay, this might be something," she said, sitting up straighter. "There was this cat in the basement, right? And then the night Brady got hurt, the first ghost boy was holding him, but not like you'd hold a baby. He was holding him like this."

Hendricks curled her arms in front of her chest, showing Eddie.

Eddie's brow furrowed. "So he was holding Brady like *he* was a cat."

"Yeah, and kind of stroking his head, like this," Hendricks said, demonstrating.

"And then what?" Eddie motioned for her to continue.

"And then he—" Hendricks's voice got caught in her throat. She swallowed and tried again. "He threw Brady against the wall. That's how he got hurt."

Eddie was staring at her, a look of sympathy in his eyes. "Hendricks, I'm so sorry."

But Hendricks just shook her head. She couldn't think about that right now. "And then, tonight, the cat led me upstairs." She frowned. "I didn't see him after that, though. He wasn't in the same room as the boys."

Eddie ran a hand through his hair, ruffling it. "Look, I'm really hungry. Are you hungry?"

Hendricks nodded. She was about to reach into her pocket for the money her parents left for pizza, but Eddie was already opening up his fridge and rummaging around inside. He pulled out a frozen pizza.

"Pepperoni?" he asked, holding it up.

Hendricks was relieved that he hadn't said bacon mushroom. "Perfect."

Eddie popped the frozen pizza into the oven.

"Here's the thing. I've never been big on the supernatural." He fumbled with an egg timer that had been on the fridge. "Most of what I know comes from Reddit or old movies."

"Which clearly isn't enough." Hendricks sighed heavily. "I really thought that ritual was going to work."

"So maybe that's what we need." Eddie paused. "An expert."

"You know a lot of ghost experts?"

"Just one," Eddie said. Hendricks cocked an eyebrow and he continued, "Remember when we were at the occult shop? That woman at the counter knew about our ritual just from the stuff we bought." A shrug. "So let's go talk to her."

"I'm not telling some random weird chick about my ghosts."

"Why not? What have we got to lose?" He placed the egg timer on the table between them, and for a moment, the only sound in the kitchen was its steady ticking. Hendricks stared at it for a long moment, trying not to think of it as a metaphor. They were running out of time.

"Fine," she said, her eyes flicking back up to Eddie's. "I guess I'm desperate enough to give it a shot."

"Tomorrow, then?"

Hendricks nodded. "Tomorrow."

As they were eating, the kitchen door swung open with a creak, and a small, rail-thin woman poked her head into the room. She was wearing yellow cleaning gloves that gaped around her skinny wrists, a red bandana holding her thick, dark hair away. She smelled strongly of lemon-scented floor cleaner.

For a moment, she stared at Hendricks without seeming to see her.

"Uh, Mom, this is Hendricks, she's a"—Eddie glanced at her—"uh."

"I'm a friend of Eddie's from school," Hendricks finished. She shot him a look, daring him to contradict her.

He shifted his eyes to the table and added, "Her family just moved into Steele House."

Eddie's mom's eyes flickered to the kitchen window, as though trying to catch sight of the house through the trees that separated the two yards. Some emotion that Hendricks couldn't place passed over her face, but then she shook her head, and the look was gone.

"Margaret," she said, by way of introduction. She adjusted her gloves. "Nice to meet you, Hendricks."

And then she ducked back into the living room. A moment later, Hendricks heard a sound like a vacuum cleaner turning on.

Eddie cleared his throat. "Look, you can stay here tonight, if you want."

"Thank you," Hendricks said, and Eddie stood, clearing their plates and loading their things in the dishwasher before heading back to the basement door.

Hendricks pushed her chair back and followed him. But she paused at the living room and peered in.

Margaret Ruiz was running the vacuum cleaner over a spot on

the carpet, back and forth, again and again. She didn't seem to notice Hendricks standing there, watching.

Eddie offered his bed, but Hendricks insisted on taking the floor.

"I'm not kicking you out of your bed," she said. "It's enough that you're letting me stay here at all."

Eddie rubbed his neck, mussing the back of his hair. "My dad would kick my ass if he knew I let a girl sleep on the floor."

"Well, tell your dad it's not the 1950s anymore."

Eddie raised an eyebrow. "What?"

"Girls are tough enough to spend a night on the floor." Hendricks thought of all the nights she'd spent in her closet back in Philadelphia, crouched behind coats and shoes, because she was too scared to sleep in her actual bed. "Besides, I've had worse."

Eddie frowned at her, and then shrugged. "Suit yourself," he said, then grabbed some pillows and blankets from his closet.

"Thanks," Hendricks said, and she settled herself on the floor as Eddie flicked off the lights and crawled into bed. She pulled the blanket up to her chin and, even though the room was dark and Eddie had his back to her, she wiggled out of her jeans below the blanket and placed them on the floor beside her.

"Good night," she murmured.

"Good night," Eddie said. His voice sounded very close.

Hendricks peered into the darkness, listening to his ragged breathing. The taste of peanut butter ice cream was still on her mind. Every time she swallowed, she remembered the footprints she'd trailed upstairs, how they'd looked so much like blood . . .

She shivered, hard, and pulled the blanket tighter around her shoulders. Goose bumps popped up along her legs. For a moment, she considered pulling her jeans back on, but then decided against it.

She just needed to close her eyes and go to sleep. Everything would be easier in the morning.

She squeezed her eyes shut and tried to steady her breathing.

A minute passed. And then another. This wasn't working.

She opened her eyes again and stared up at the ceiling. A crack ran through the plaster, and if Hendricks looked at it for long enough, it began to take shape. Two ears, and two eyes, and a long, twitching tail . . .

*Meow.*

She sat bolt upright, breathing hard.

It wasn't real.

A sob hitched in her throat and she pressed her lips together, desperate not to cry.

There was a creak of mattress springs, and then Eddie's voice, closer than before: "Hey."

Hendricks swallowed, not quite trusting herself to speak. "Hey," she croaked.

"You all right?"

"Yeah?"

"You don't sound too sure about that."

"I—I'm not, really," Hendricks admitted. She pressed the heels of her hands to her eyes. *Don't cry, don't cry.* "This is just a lot. I feel like I'm going crazy."

There was a beat of silence, and then Eddie said, "This is a queen-sized bed, you know."

Hendricks thought she knew what he was trying to say, but she didn't want to assume, in case she was wrong. She lowered her hands, sniffing. "So?"

"So, it's plenty big enough for both of us."

Hendricks didn't say another word. She scrambled into bed

193

beside him, huddling down in the blankets. The bed was big enough that she wouldn't have known Eddie was in it with her, except that the mattress shifted when he rolled over.

She lay very still for a long moment, imagining his body in the darkness. Was he facing her? Looking at her? She wanted to reach out to him, touch his arm or his shoulder, just so she knew how he was positioned beside her.

*This was the second time they'd slept together*, she realized, and, without meaning to, she remembered how it'd felt to curl up against his side, his arm wrapped around her shoulder, his chest rising and falling beneath her cheek.

Her skin flushed with heat. She was suddenly glad for the darkness, glad that Eddie wouldn't be able to see how badly she was blushing. She shouldn't be thinking like this, anyway. *She had a boyfriend.*

Or, she sort of had a boyfriend. She had a Connor. And she'd *just* seen him that afternoon, just told him that she liked him.

So why couldn't she stop imagining how it would feel to roll a little closer to Eddie, to feel the warmth of his chest against hers. To—

"You're not sleeping," Eddie said out of nowhere.

Hendricks stiffened, feeling caught. "You can see me?"

"The moonlight is reflecting off your eyes."

"Oh." Hendricks tried to make out the shape of Eddie's face in the darkness, but it was no use. The window was behind him, so all she could see was an outline of blankets. "That's not fair, I can't see you at all."

There were several beats of silence. Hendricks blushed again, worse this time, as she realized how she must've sounded.

And then she felt the mattress move, felt the heat coming off Eddie's body as he shifted closer to her. His face separated from the dark, and now she could see the line of his jaw and nose, the shape of his eyes. They were open, watching her.

"Better?" he asked, his voice thick.

"Yeah," Hendricks said. She wanted to reach for him. She dug her fingernails into her palms. "You're not sleeping, either."

He swallowed, his Adam's apple bobbing up and down in his throat. "No," he said. "I'm not."

Neither of them said anything for a long moment. Hendricks could feel him watching her and wondered what he was thinking, wondered if he was imagining the same things she was imagining. Her breath had gone shallow . . .

She rolled closer to him, pressing her chest to his chest, burrowing her head under his chin, her arms pinned between them.

For a moment he just lay there, stiff, and she knew she'd made a huge mistake, that she'd misjudged the moment. Shame washed over her . . .

And then Eddie wrapped his arms around her, pulling her closer. Hendricks relaxed into him as he lowered his face to the top of her head, his exhale tickling her ears.

"You're not crazy," he whispered.

She closed her eyes, his words releasing something inside of her. "Thank you," she said. She felt safe for the first time in weeks.

And then, finally, she was able to drift to sleep.

# CHAPTER 25

THE NEXT MORNING, HENDRICKS WAS FACED WITH A seemingly impossible decision: throw on yesterday's clothes? Or brave Steele House for something clean?

Wrinkling her nose, she grabbed her rumpled jeans from the floor and pulled them back on.

"Wakey-wakey," she said, nudging Eddie with her elbow.

He groaned and covered his head with the pillow. "Five more minutes."

Hendricks sat up, scraping her hair back into its usual messy knot. "Come on, wake up," she said, standing. "I want to get a move on."

Eddie didn't say anything for a moment. Then, moaning, he tossed his pillow aside, mumbling something that sounded like "okay."

Twenty minutes later, they were loaded up in his car. Magik & Tarot didn't open until ten a.m., so Hendricks insisted that she treat Eddie to coffee, as a thank-you for letting her crash the night before.

Eddie reluctantly agreed, though Hendricks could tell that he didn't like the idea of letting her pay. But when they drove past Dead Guy Joe, the coffee shop on Main, Hendricks saw Portia, Raven, Connor, Blake, and Vi crowded around a table just inside.

Eddie kept driving.

"What about coffee?" Hendricks said, twisting around in her seat. "I don't think you understand how badly I need caffeine."

Eddie shot her a look. "There's a shop in Devon."

Hendricks hesitated, trying to ignore the tiny ball of relief growing inside of her. She knew it was shitty to hang out with Eddie in private but not in front of her friends. But when she tried to imagine walking into Dead Guy together and explaining how they came to be hanging so early in the morning, she just couldn't do it. Better to avoid that problem, for now.

They picked up coffee at a shop called The Sparrow in Devon, and then walked the block and a half to Magik & Tarot, arriving at ten a.m. on the dot.

There was a sign taped to the door:

*Closed for Imbolc*

"Imbolc?" Hendricks said as Eddie leaned past her to try the door. "What's *Imbolc?*"

Eddie found the door locked and leaned back on his heels, shoving his hands into his jacket pockets. "I dunno. Maybe it's like Groundhog Day?"

Hendricks raised her eyebrows. She couldn't picture the occult woman from the other day closing her shop in honor of something like Groundhog Day. "We could check the store's website for a contact number. Or maybe this place has a Twitter—"

"Check it out." Eddie jerked his chin, and Hendricks looked up at a curl of black smoke hanging in the air just above the old house, looking a little like an upside-down question mark against the gray sky. It seemed to be coming from directly behind the shop.

"Come on," Hendricks said.

They followed the smoke down a short cobblestone alley that led to a small overgrown yard. The remains of a wooden fence separated the yard from the rest of the alley. Or, at least, it tried to. The fence had long ago been overtaken by moss and weeds and rot. Grass wove through the slats, and gnarled trees grew up alongside the fence itself, their ancient roots bursting from the ground below and splintering the wood and pushing up the cobblestones.

Hendricks looked around for a gate, and that's when she noticed the dolls. They were small, no larger than her hand, and crudely fashioned out of straw and twine. Now that she knew to look for them, Hendricks saw that the dolls were everywhere: hidden behind leaves and twitching from tree branches and wedged between the slats of the fence. There were dozens of them—maybe *hundreds*—all faceless and strange. Watching her. When the wind blew, the dolls spun, like they were dancing.

"Shit," Hendricks muttered, taking a quick step backward. Nerves crawled, very slowly, up her spine.

Eddie nudged her in the side with his elbow, murmuring, "Look."

Hendricks followed his gaze past the trees and the fence, and saw a woman standing in the middle of the yard. For a moment, Hendricks didn't think it was the same woman they'd met in the shop but someone much older, with long, white hair and deep wrinkles. And then a cloud moved past the sun and Hendricks's eyes adjusted to the dim, gold-tinged light. She'd been mistaken; it was the same woman after all. She wasn't that old, maybe only a few years older than Hendricks herself. She wore ripped jeans and combat boots, and a sleeveless black T-shirt supporting a band called Dead Man's Bones. There was a flower crown perched in her dark hair, somewhat inexplicably.

Hendricks watched as the woman lifted a clay pitcher from the ground and began pouring something that looked like milk into the grass. A small bonfire crackled beside her.

Hendricks glanced at Eddie. This didn't seem like something they should interrupt.

Before either of them could decide what to do next, the woman looked up. "Can I help you?"

"We didn't mean to bother you," Hendricks said quickly. "We can come back later, if you're busy."

But the woman was already walking toward them, still clutching the clay pitcher. She had lovely hands, Hendricks noticed. Long, thin fingers with rounded nails. A snake tattoo wrapped around her thumb.

She stopped just inside the wooden fence. "You came into the shop the other day."

"Yeah," Hendricks said, holding out her hand, "I'm—"

"You're Hendricks." The woman didn't shake her hand, but only frowned, slightly, like she didn't know what it was for. "I'd recognize the girl who moved into Steele House anywhere." She said this in a strangely flat voice. "My name is Ileana. And you're Eduardo Ruiz, of course. I was very sorry to hear about your brother."

"Y-yeah," Eddie sputtered, clearly surprised.

"He never should've been convicted." Ileana didn't blink as often as she should, and her gaze had begun to wander over the line between intense and creepy. "But I suppose 'ghosts killed my little sister' wasn't exactly a good defense?"

"You already know about the ghosts?" Hendricks asked.

Ileana only shifted that intense gaze to her, eyes dark and massive. "A nine-year-old died in your cellar," she pointed out. "It's unnatural for a child to die so young. Her death would have left marks on the place."

A shiver crept up Hendricks's arms. She kept her eyes trained on Ileana so she wouldn't have to look at Eddie. "Maribeth isn't the one haunting my house."

Ileana still hadn't looked away. "No, I don't suppose she would be. We think the haunting at Steele House started long before that."

"I'm sorry, *we?*" Eddie asked, at the same time Hendricks said, "What do you mean, *started?*"

Ileana finally dropped her eyes. She touched a weed growing up through her fence. "Other supernatural enthusiasts," she said. "Steele House might not have the national reputation of a place like Amityville, but regional enthusiasts have always been drawn to it as a place of deep spiritual energy. We think it started out as a baby haunting at first. Flickering lights, cold drafts, that sort of thing. It would've only progressed as the house took more victims."

"You talk about the house like it's alive," Hendricks said, and Ileana lifted her eyebrows without looking up. Hendricks exhaled through her teeth. "What I've seen is definitely not a *baby* haunting."

Ileana pursed her lips. "I'd have to see what's going on there myself to know for sure. But that's why you came to find me, right? So I would look at your ghosts?"

Hendricks blinked. She wasn't sure she wanted this incredibly strange woman inside her house. "Well—"

"Yes," Eddie cut in. "We want you to take a look."

Ileana pulled the weed out of her fence and began twisting it around her finger. Distantly, Hendricks heard a phone ringing. It seemed to be coming from inside of Ileana's house, but Ileana made no move to go inside to answer it.

"I'll need to get a few supplies first," Ileana said once the ringing had stopped. "Wait here."

# CHAPTER 26

ILEANA ENTERED STEELE HOUSE LIKE SHE WAS ENTERING a church. She walked slowly through the living room and into the kitchen, seeming to see beyond Hendricks's parents' furniture and paint colors and the family photographs hanging on the walls.

"There's definitely something here," she said, dropping her duffel to the floor with a thud that made Hendricks jump. "I can feel its energy in the air."

"So, uh, what do we do first?" Hendricks asked, her eyes on the duffel. It contained the supplies Ileana had brought. And it smelled strange. Like incense and sour milk.

Ileana said nothing but reached into her pocket and pulled out a stack of dog-eared cards, like playing cards but larger. The tops were pure black. As Hendricks watched, she began to shuffle, moving the cards easily between her long, thin fingers.

Ileana flipped a card over, frowning down at a smudgy image of a skeletal figure holding a scythe. *Death*, the card read.

"There are lots of different types of ghosts," Ileana murmured, studying the card.

She shook her head, and slid the *Death* card back into the deck, beginning to shuffle again. "Residual hauntings are like echoes, or reflections. They can't hurt you or interact with you in any way. But you're dealing with some real rage here, which usually means murder."

She paused and, this time, she slid three cards out from the middle of the deck.

More smudgy images. *The Tower*, one of the cards read, and Hendricks thought the picture looked like a woman hanging from a noose. *Queen of Swords*, read the next card. And the third, *Judgment*.

"Something happened here that no one ever found out about," Ileana said quietly, frowning at the cards. "A terrible crime. That's why the energy in this place is so tainted."

"Some boys were hurt here," Hendricks said, pulling her eyes away from the image of the woman hanging from the noose. "Three, I think."

"Interesting." Ileana tapped her fingers against the deck of cards. She took a deep breath in and slowly exhaled while surveying the room. Hendricks got the sense that she wasn't looking for something but feeling for it with her breath. Hendricks shivered. After a moment, Ileana said, "If those boys were murdered here, they might be angry that no one ever punished the person who did it. Which means they'll want vengeance." Her eyes flicked up to Hendricks. "Anything else?"

"There was a message on the wall," Eddie cut in. "It looked like it'd been written in blood."

"It said *one more*," Hendricks said. "We thought it meant that the ghosts wanted one more victim. Like, as a sacrifice."

"Mmm." Ileana nodded, shuffling the tarot cards again. "An eye for an eye. The ghosts want one sacrifice for each of their deaths. Maribeth and Kyle were sacrifices one and two. Which means they'll need one more before they can rest."

Hendricks felt a chill work its way down her spine. "So one of us has to die before they'll leave us alone?"

"A sacrifice doesn't necessarily mean a death," Ileana said calmly. "For a sacrifice to work, you need to give up the thing you hold most dear. That doesn't always have to be your own life."

Eddie was frowning. "But Maribeth and Kyle—"

"Maribeth sacrificed her future when she died," Ileana explained. "And Kyle gave up ever being able to prove his innocence. Those are two very powerful sacrifices. The ghosts would have liked that."

Ileana held the deck of tarot cards out to Hendricks. Her eyes seemed a much deeper brown than they had a moment ago. Almost like they'd darkened the second she'd stepped inside this house.

"Cut the deck," she said.

Hendricks hesitated, her fingers twitching. She didn't want to touch those black cards. "Why?"

"People who've been murdered are looking for vengeance," Ileana said. "Most of the time their ghosts want to punish the person who murdered them. But if that's not possible, they're going to find a proxy. I believe they've decided that you will be their proxy, Hendricks."

Hendricks's throat felt dry. "Proxy?"

"A stand-in. Someone who reminds them of their murderer." Ileana nodded at the tarot deck. "These will help me read your energy. I want to know why the ghosts have chosen you."

Steeling herself, Hendricks took the deck from Ileana's hands and quickly split it in half. She flipped a card over.

The card showed a woman bound and blindfolded, a man

pressing a sword to her back. Her mouth was warped in a silent scream.

Staring down at it, Hendricks felt her eyes sting. She remembered cold fingers crushing her wrist. Grayson's voice in her ear.

*Don't you dare embarrass me here.*

She suddenly felt like there was something lodged in her throat.

"Interesting," Ileana said, taking the card from Hendricks's hand. "Eight of swords."

"What does it mean?" Hendricks asked.

"It's the card of jilted and abused lovers. It seems to indicate that you're a person who's been . . ." Ileana hesitated before saying, "Broken. Trapped. They want to make you pay because they can't make *her* pay."

"So it's my fault this is happening?" Hendricks asked. The injustice of it made her want to scream. When would she ever be done paying for what Grayson did to her? "What am I supposed to do? Sacrifice myself?"

Ileana tilted her head. "Think about the thing you're most reluctant to give up, and cut again." She held out the deck. Hendricks thought for a moment, and then flipped over another card.

This one showed two people, side by side in matching coffins.

"*Two of cups.* Interesting," Ileana said. "This card could indicate that the thing you value most is either love itself, or a particular person you're in love with. Now that would make for an interesting sacrifice."

With effort, Hendricks tore her eyes away from the card. *Love itself?* How was she supposed to sacrifice that?

She nodded, trying to look like she was unbothered by this sudden revelation. She'd already given up her freedom, her sense of safety, even her home—all because of Grayson. And now she'd have to give up more? It wasn't fair. Her eyes began to sting.

Ileana knelt beside her bag. "We can start with a smudging while you think about your sacrifice."

Hendricks nodded again, but now her eyes were on Ileana's long fingers, which were slowly pulling the silver zipper on her duffel. It seemed to take forever for the bag to fall open.

Ileana removed several thick bundles of fragrant, white herbs, a vicious-looking silver dagger with a jewel-encrusted hilt, and a reddish-brown fur crusted with blood.

And now the sour-milk smell was so bad that Hendricks had to take a step backward, her nose wrinkling. She pressed a hand over her mouth and nostrils. "What is that?"

"Fox pelt," Ileana explained, spreading it out across the floor. For a moment, she was perfectly motionless.

Then, in one swift move, Ileana took the dagger and jabbed it into the flesh of her right ring finger.

Hendricks released a small yelp, and Eddie flinched. "Jesus," he murmured.

Blood rose to the surface of Ileana's skin, forming a perfect red bubble before tipping over the side of her finger and winding down around her wrist.

"The ritual you performed was probably fine, but I'm guessing it didn't have any direction." Ileana crouched over the fox pelt and, wielding her bleeding finger like a pen, began drawing on the hide. "This will tell the spirits what we want from them. The smudging ritual will show them the path to follow out of your house, and your sacrifice will release their anger, compelling them to move on."

Hendricks watched with gruesome fascination as strange drawings and symbols began to appear. She wondered where Ileana had learned all of this.

Ileana sketched one last symbol onto the fox pelt, and then sat back on her heels, wiping her bloody finger on her jeans. She gathered the bundles of herbs from the floor and stood, passing one each to Eddie and Hendricks.

"Either of you got a light?" she asked.

Eddie tugged his lighter out of his pocket, and Ileana motioned for him to light the bundles.

Once they were all smoking, she said, "Smudging only works if you get the smoke into every corner of the house. You'll have to open every door, every closet, even the kitchen cupboards. The ghosts will hide if you give them the chance. You want the smoke to permeate the house, so they have no choice but to follow it."

Hendricks felt cold somewhere deep inside of her. She nodded.

Ileana turned and began walking carefully through Steele House, the softly smoking sage held out in front of her like a beacon. Hendricks couldn't have said exactly what the smoke smelled like, but it reminded her of being in the cemetery for her grandmother's funeral. A strange mixture of packed earth and flowers.

First, they headed outside, and around the side of the house, to the cellar.

"This is where you did your original ritual, right?" Ileana asked, as Hendricks and Eddie spread their smoke to the far corners of the room. "Was there any particular reason you chose this place?"

"Maribeth died down here," Eddie said.

Hendricks dropped to her knees so she could spread the smoke into the darkness beneath the staircase. She almost expected the shadows to move, like they had the night the wine exploded, but they stayed still. "And I saw a cat," she added. "A ghost cat, not a real one."

She felt a little stupid admitting that, but Ileana stopped moving, and looked over at her. "You *saw* the cat?"

Hendricks nodded at the wall. "It ran through those shelves."

"Hmm," Ileana murmured.

They headed to the first floor next, spreading out so that they could smudge every room and closet and bathroom. The smoke was thick and white. It gathered in the corners near the ceiling. If Hendricks breathed too deeply, she knew she'd start to cough.

Finally, they took the stairs to the second floor.

"I'll take the bathroom," Hendricks said, starting down the hallway. Ileana nodded and gently pushed the door to Brady's bedroom open, while Eddie stayed in the hall, waving his smudging stick behind the half-finished, plastic-covered walls.

The door creaked slightly as Hendricks let herself into the bathroom, and then there was cold tile beneath her bare feet, and cold air creeping in from around the window frame. Shivering, she stopped in front of the sink and set the smoking sage down on the counter.

*Love itself*, she thought.

She tried to breathe, but she could only manage short, shallow inhales that left her head swimming. Every muscle in her body felt pulled tight, like rubber bands about to snap, and her pulse was fast and fluttery. She kept expecting something to jump out of the shadows at her, hands reaching for her neck, teeth bared.

It didn't help that nothing had, so far. It only made the anticipation worse.

With a slow exhale, she switched the faucet on, letting the water grow warm and fill the basin.

Her reflection stared back at her, her hair swept into a messy bun, her face clear of makeup so that she could easily see the dark shadows beneath her eyes and the gray cast to her skin. She looked terrible. Tired. She leaned closer to the mirror, squinting at her pores, running her fingers along her hairline. Steam rose up from the sink, fogging the mirror.

Shaking her head, she leaned over the sink and gathered water in her hands, splashing her face a few times.

Something rustled behind her.

She jerked her head up, water still dripping from her cheeks. She'd moved too quickly, and accidentally bit down on her tongue. The taste of blood filled her mouth.

Cringing, she brought a hand to her lips, scanning the room reflected in the foggy mirror.

There were the freshly painted, lilac-colored walls, bare because they hadn't yet gotten around to hanging pictures. The toilet was to her left, and above it was a small window with the blinds drawn. The bathtub was behind her, the wall hidden by the shower curtain she'd brought from their old house. It was white and covered in a repeating pattern of jungle cats in profile, all mid run. Everything looked exactly like it was supposed to.

So why was her heart beating just a little bit faster?

*Look closer.*

She fumbled along the sink without moving her eyes from the rest of the room, jerkily switching off the faucet, and then leaning forward to wipe the fog from the mirror with her palm. The silence seemed to gather more thickly around her. She frowned, her eyes meeting the eyes of her reflection. What was it she'd thought she heard, exactly? It had only been a sort of quiet swish, like fabric moving. She'd probably kicked the bathmat across the floor, or bumped into the shower curtain.

*One more.*

The voice was back. It spoke directly in her head. Her breath stopped in her throat.

Her eyes drifted back toward the shower curtain, narrowing.

The curtain didn't move, but Hendricks thought she saw shadows shifting behind it. The shape of someone who'd been crouched inside the tub slowly standing up.

"No," she whimpered. She whipped around, breathing hard. Her hands groped for the edge of the sink, and she held tight, the sharp corner digging into her palms. Her back was to the mirror now, and she was facing the shower curtain directly.

There was no shadow. There was no one there.

Hendricks stood frozen, terror building in her chest. She was shuddering all over now. She inched away from the sink, one hand reaching for the door. She needed to get out of here, get back to Ileana. She lowered her hand to the doorknob and, when it wouldn't turn, she glanced down at it, turning her back on the tub.

There was a sound behind her, metal scraping metal.

Hendricks jerked her head around. The sound she'd heard had been the sound of the metal rings scraping across the bar as someone yanked the shower curtain back.

Sure enough, the curtain was open now. But the tub was still empty.

Hendricks's heartbeat was cannon fire. She groped for the doorknob behind her back, but she couldn't get it to turn. Her nostrils twitched as the air around her slowly filled with the scent of cologne.

She looked away from the tub for a fraction of a second, and when she looked back, there was a boy standing in the tub, watching her with wide black eyes, her razor clutched in one hand. He tilted his head, his upper lip twitching.

Hendricks could feel the scream building in her chest. Her mouth opened, and she managed to release a choked whimper before an invisible force wrapped around her throat, squeezing.

The boy spoke, his voice a deep rasp that sent fear shooting down Hendricks's spine. "Do you want to play a game?"

The bathroom lights flickered.

And now he was climbing out of the bathtub, his fingers tightening around the razor, his lips pulled back from his teeth so that he almost looked like he was grinning. He placed one foot and then the other onto the floor. Hendricks saw that his feet were bare, something oozing from beneath his toes. His toenails had grown long and yellow, and they clicked against the bathroom tile.

She grasped for the doorknob, wrenching it from side to side, but it only jangled in the door, refusing to budge. The invisible force wrapped around her throat seemed to be pinning her in place.

The lights flickered again, and now the ghost boy was closer, just a few inches away.

"The game is called make-over," the ghost said in that same deep, shivery voice. "Doesn't that sound fun?"

His face looked wrong, his eyes too far apart and pure black, his lips pulled too tightly over his teeth.

*Those teeth.* Now that the boy was so close, Hendricks could see that they were sharp, as though someone had filed them to points.

Hendricks's hands curled into balls. Her shoulders hunched in fear. She was going to die, just like Maribeth had died. She began to cry, weakly, as she clawed at the invisible hand that held her pinned to the door, choking her.

The scent of rotting flesh and cologne was overwhelming now, clogging her nostrils, crawling down her throat and into her eyes.

She couldn't breathe, couldn't move, couldn't scream . . .

And then the lights went out.

# CHAPTER
## 27

**"HERE, KITTY, KITTY . . . HERE, KITTY . . ."**

The voice rose from the darkness, cold and flat and close. Hendricks pressed herself against the bathroom door, the invisible force around her throat squeezing still tighter. She felt light-headed, like she might pass out. She curled her hands into the door, her fingernails pressing into the wood.

"Here, kitty . . ." the boy said again, and now Hendricks heard the sound of toenails clicking, followed by the dry scrape of the boy's dead skin dragging over the tile.

Her breath stopped in a gasp. The boy was coming toward her. Tears leaked down her cheeks. She knew that he was close, but it was too dark for her to see just where he was. At any moment she would feel him reach for her, his cold hands wrapping around her arm—

"Help," Hendricks choked out, barely able to force her voice out of her throat. Her hands twitched against the door. "P-please help . . ."

Cold metal touched her face, and she froze. It was her razor, the razor the ghost had been holding. Hendricks felt it drag over her skin, almost lovingly, the edge of the blade not yet cutting her.

"You're such an ugly bitch," said the boy, his breath tickling

Hendricks's ear. It smelled of rot and damp and things that were long dead. "But you could be pretty if you tried."

Hendricks thrashed, and the blade nicked her ear, drawing blood. The ghost hissed, and there was a slashing sound in the air, followed by bright pain as he brought the razor down hard across her shoulder. She felt her skin split open, felt the sharp edge of metal dig into her. She gasped and arched her back, soundless. Her skin smarted as blood rushed from the gash.

Frantic now, she struck out with every part of her body she still had control of. She felt the blade cut into her again, and then again, but the ghost seemed to have a harder time when she was moving. She kicked into the darkness, and her foot connected with something. She heard the soft *thwump* of a body hitting the floor.

The lights blinked on, again, and Hendricks saw the boy lying in a heap on the tile.

The lights flickered.

The boy lifted his head. Moving jerkily, like a spider, he crossed the room on all fours and was in front of Hendricks again. His appearance shifted again, giving way for something dead and wrong. Mold grew up along the side of his face, and his teeth and lips were black. There was only a gaping, bleeding hole where his nose should be.

Hendricks gathered her strength and kicked with both feet this time, sending the ghost skittering backward again.

A low growl seemed to bubble up from beneath her.

*Hold still.*

Hendricks froze. The voice didn't come from the boy but seemed to speak directly into her head. It was as though the *house itself* was talking to her.

It wanted to hold her here, she realized. It wanted to keep her forever.

Hendricks grasped at the force around her neck with both hands and pulled, her muscles straining. The lights above her flickered more quickly now, turning on and off like a strobe light. The grumbling sound grew louder.

And then Hendricks was on the ground, sobbing, the taste of blood thick in her mouth. She was alone in the bathroom now, the ghost boy gone. Her razor lay in the middle of the tile, still dripping blood.

Hendricks lifted a hand to her throat, but whatever had been gripping her was gone, too. She could breath. She could *speak*.

She thought she heard footsteps on the other side of the door, or maybe it was just the sound of her own blood pounding in her ears. She couldn't tell. Scrambling to her feet, she threw the door open, and tore down the hallway, immediately colliding with Eddie and Ileana.

Eddie said, "What is it? What happened?"

"Did you see something?" Ileana asked, at the same moment.

Hendricks's mouth flapped open and closed, like a fish. She couldn't speak. "Ghost," she managed, after a moment.

"In the bathroom?" Ileana asked. Hendricks nodded and Ileana raced past her.

"Come here." Eddie wrapped his arms around her shoulders. Hendricks closed her eyes, breathing steadily. She realized, in a detached sort of way, that he was patting the back of her head, murmuring into her ear, "It's okay, you're safe now . . ."

She felt her heartbeat begin to slow. *Whatever that was, it's gone now*, she told herself, burrowing into Eddie's chest. His hands moved down her back, rubbing in small, comforting circles, and she felt her head fit easily under his chin. His T-shirt was soft beneath her cheek, smelling of fabric softener and something else, something sweet.

Hendricks's nose twitched. That smell . . .

Eddie kissed the top of her head. She could feel how cold his lips were, even through her hair. "It's okay," he said, "it's okay, kitty."

Hendricks stiffened.

*Cologne*, she realized.

Her skin crawled. Acid climbed her throat.

Hendricks jerked away from him, her blood running cold. "What did you call me?"

Eddie began to laugh. "What's the matter?" His voice was different now. It was the ghost's dry rasp, like the rustle of dead leaves.

Hendricks felt her terror deepen. She was frozen to the spot, her arms and legs numb with fear.

"Why are you doing this?" she asked. "What do you want?"

The false Eddie was grinning. Dark blood oozed between his teeth and dripped over his chin. As Hendricks watched, horrified, his face began to change. His eyes moved farther apart and darkened, his hair grew long and thick.

It wasn't the same ghost she'd seen in the bathroom. This ghost had longer, darker hair and a wicked grin. The word loser had been carved just below his neck, and blood dripped over his chest, gathering in the folds of his tattered clothes.

"We already told you," he said. "We want one more."

Hendricks felt the blood rush back into her veins. She screamed and jerked backward so violently that she lost her balance, collapsing onto the floor just at the top of the staircase. She struggled to regain her balance, to get back to her feet, but this new ghost was faster. He leaned over her and curled his fingers through her hair, fingernails scraping her scalp. Hendricks screamed as the ghost hauled her off the floor—and threw her.

Hendricks didn't have time to catch her breath before she slammed into the top of the staircase. And then she was falling, rolling, tumbling down the stairs. She couldn't see, couldn't grasp hold of anything to stop herself. She felt something hard and sharp hit the back of her head, just above her spine—

—and then everything went black.

Eddie's screams cut through Hendricks's thoughts, waking her. She lifted her head, and forced her eyes open. The room swam in and out of focus, and it took her a long moment to figure out that she was lying in a heap at the foot of the stairs. Everything hurt.

Grimacing, she tried to push herself to sit, but sharp pain cut through her ribs, stopping her. Tears sprang to her eyes. She must've broken something.

Eddie's voice cut through her thoughts. "Get off me, you psycho!"

"Eddie?" Hendricks said. She tried to sit and, again, pain shot through her body, nearly sending her tumbling back to the ground. She whimpered, gasping. She couldn't do it, she couldn't stand. It hurt too much.

But she couldn't leave Eddie to face the ghosts alone, either.

Breathing hard, she lifted her hand to the bannister above her head, wrapped her fingers around the raw, splintery wood, and *pulled*. Everything inside of her screamed, but then she was standing, her other arm wrapped around her side, and it wasn't so bad.

"It's okay," she said to herself. "You can do this."

Taking shallow, sharp breaths, she forced herself back up the stairs, following the sound of Eddie's screams.

Eddie was lying on the nursery floor, his shirt torn open, his arms pinned to either side of him. The boy she had seen in the hall was sitting on his chest, Hendricks's razor gripped in one hand. Seeing him caused her to freeze, breathing hard. She could still remember the feel of that ghost's cold lips on her head. Her knees knocked together.

She caught the edge of Brady's dresser, her other hand still clutching the doorframe. Eddie's eyes swiveled over to her, widening.

"Hendricks," he yelled, bucking beneath the ghost. "What the fuck is happening?"

"Can't you see him?" Hendricks hissed. The ghost brought the razor to Eddie's chest, and Eddie screamed as a bright line of blood appeared on his skin.

*One more*, she thought desperately.

The ghosts needed a sacrifice, and they were going to take Eddie if she didn't do something *now*. But Ileana said that a sacrifice didn't have to mean a death. *Love itself*, she'd said. That's what Hendricks had to sacrifice.

With a groan, she pushed herself off the dresser and hobbled down the hall, to her bedroom.

She'd sacrificed a lot over the last year, but there was one thing she hadn't been able to get herself to get rid of, even though she'd known it was messed up to keep it.

She threw her closet door open, her eyes skating over the clothes still piled on the floor until—

*There.* She felt a rush of triumph as her eyes snagged on the familiar orange fabric of Grayson's old soccer jersey.

She'd tried to explain to Eddie why she'd kept it, but she didn't think she'd done a very good job. It wasn't because she'd wanted Grayson back. She was far past ever wanting him back. But that didn't mean she wanted to forget how things had been in those early days, when they'd been in love. It had been those same strange, complicated feelings that'd kept her with Grayson even after things started to go so wrong. Those same feelings had driven her to Connor, even though she wasn't sure she was ready to be with someone new.

Hendricks didn't miss Grayson. She missed love.

Her heart ached. If she sacrificed the jersey, it was like she was sacrificing what Grayson had once meant to her. She was giving up the dream that she'd ever feel like that again.

She only hoped it would be enough.

The pain in her ribs stabbed at her, but Hendricks clenched her jaw, ignoring it as she made her way back to Brady's nursery, jersey in hand.

The ghost looked up as she stepped into the room, his black eyes zeroing in on her. He growled and snapped his teeth.

"Eddie, give me your lighter," Hendricks said.

Gasping in pain, he pulled his lighter out of his pocket and tossed it to the middle of the room. Hendricks knelt to pick it up.

The ghost stood up. "Don't do that."

Hendricks flipped the lighter open. A flame leapt between her fingers.

The ghost moved too quickly, standing over Eddie one moment, and then hovering beside Hendricks the next. His lips were pulled tightly over his teeth, making his smile wide and garish. His eyes had disappeared, so that there were only two deep, rotted holes in the middle of his face. A maggot squirmed out of his skin and dropped to the floor, wriggling beside Hendricks's feet.

The ghost grabbed her shoulders, his fingernails digging deep into her flesh. "Don't!"

Hendricks touched the flame to Grayson's jersey.

*I sacrifice love*, she thought.

The slick fabric was slow to catch the flame, but once it took hold, the stink of melting and burning overwhelmed the room, in a blinding flash of red and orange.

The boy let out a thundering roar.

*I sacrifice love*, she thought again and again, tears streaming down her face. Hendricks wasn't sure if she was speaking the words out loud or in her head, but she knew the boy could hear her.

He vanished in a cloud of smoke.

Hendricks dropped what remained of the jersey to the floor and stomped out the smolders. Then she collapsed against the wall, gasping.

The light in the hall was on, and it threw a long, yellow rectangle into the dark nursery. Hendricks could see that there was blood splashed across the floor and matted into the fibers of Brady's rug.

Across the room, Eddie was pushing himself to his knees, one hand pressed to the gash on his chest. Hendricks's heart ached. She wanted to go to him, to comfort him, but she didn't think she could move. Her ribs throbbed.

"Eddie," she croaked, trying to sit up straighter.

"Don't move." He stumbled, fell, and then picked himself up again. His hair was plastered to his forehead with sweat. "You could break—"

There was movement in the hallway, and they both froze instantly, like prey animals in the wilderness. Hendricks's heart was beating fast and hard.

They waited.

Nothing.

And then . . .

A sound, just outside of the door to the nursery. Like footsteps but slower, dragging. Hendricks met Eddie's eyes and saw her own fear reflected back at her.

*Not another one, please no, please God.*

Ileana appeared in the doorway, gasping. "There were two of them in the bathroom, but they just disappeared. What did you do?"

# CHAPTER 28

EDDIE COLLAPSED AGAINST THE WALL, EXHALING IN RELIEF. Hendricks slid to the floor beside him. Her legs felt weak and shaky. She wasn't sure she'd ever stand again.

"I made a sacrifice," Hendricks explained. "That's how I got rid of them."

She expected Ileana to ask her what the sacrifice was, but the woman only blinked at her. "You see them, don't you?" she asked after a moment. "The ghosts."

Frowning, Hendricks looked at Eddie. "We *all* saw them."

But Eddie was staring at her, mouth agape. Hendricks's heart stuttered. "Didn't you?"

Eddie frowned. Ileana shook her head.

Hendricks turned to Ileana. "You're, like, some mystical ghost hunter," she sputtered. "You honestly expect me to believe you've never seen a ghost?"

Ileana made a sound between a huff and a snort. "Sometimes, in a really intense haunting, the temperature in a room will drop, or maybe I'll see a strange shadow or a spot of light or feel a presence. But I don't see actual figures. No one does. Except you did, didn't you? You said you saw a boy in the bathroom."

Hendricks swallowed, her throat feeling suddenly dry. "I've seen three, so far," she said. In her head, she thought, *Four if you count the cat.*

Ileana pressed her lips together. "Your sacrifice must have been pretty powerful," she said very solemnly. "My fox pelt is still downstairs. I'll need to douse it in rosewater to complete the ritual." Her eyes moved from Hendricks to Eddie, and one eyebrow went jagged. "Will you two be okay?"

Hendricks nodded, and Ileana walked out the door. A second later, Hendricks heard her boots thudding against the stairs.

Eddie pressed a hand to the wound on his chest, blood dripping between his fingers.

"God, you're hurt." Hendricks crouched beside him. "Can I see?"

He nodded, and she carefully moved his hand away from his chest. The cut was long but shallow, and the bleeding had mostly stopped. "You need a bandage. I think we have some in the bathroom, but—" She glanced at the door to the hallway, hesitating. She didn't want to go to the bathroom alone.

Eddie seemed to read her mind. "We'll go together."

Clumsily, he pushed himself to his feet, his free hand moving back to the cut on his chest. Despite her aching ribs, Hendricks pulled his other arm over her shoulder, and the two of them stumbled down the hallway to the bathroom.

Hendricks flipped the light switch near the door, her eyes immediately moving to the shower curtain. Everything looked normal, but she still felt something in her chest tighten.

She wondered if she would ever feel truly safe here.

"Sit," she said, pulling her eyes away from the curtain. Eddie lowered himself to the toilet seat as she shuffled through the medicine cabinet, pulling out gauze and antiseptic and cotton balls.

"Can you, um, move your hand?" she asked, motioning with a cotton ball.

Eddie's eyes flicked up to hers. For a moment it looked like he might say something, but he just nodded and dropped his hand. Hendricks crouched between his legs.

"This might sting a little," she said, dabbing his skin with the antiseptic.

Eddie cringed, then blushed.

"I know . . . I hate this stuff, too," she told him. Hendricks's voice felt strangely tight. She cleared her throat. "When I was little, like nine or ten, I took a bad fall on my bike and completely shredded the skin on my knees. My dad made me put this stuff on every night until the cuts all closed up, so I wouldn't get an infection. I swear it hurt worse than messing my knees up in the first place."

Neither of them spoke for a beat. Hendricks kept dabbing until her cotton ball turned pink. Eddie's chest was warm beneath her fingers. Distractingly so.

"So you're saying I'm about as manly as a nine-year-old girl?" he murmured.

She grinned. "To be fair, I was a pretty badass nine-year-old."

"I believe it." After a moment, Eddie lowered his hand to hers, his fingers lightly brushing the tops of her knuckles. She paused.

Hendricks's fingers had been touched a million times before. They were probably the most frequently touched part of her body.

But this was different. She felt the heat of Eddie's hand burn through her, spreading up her arm and into her shoulders, down her back, until it was as though he were touching all of her, all at once. Her skin hummed.

She stopped dabbing, her eyes lifting. Eddie was already watching her, and she felt her cheeks flush as she held his gaze.

"Hendricks." He said her name slowly, like he was savoring the taste. "You saved my life tonight."

"I—I didn't," she breathed. She grabbed a bandage, unwrapped it, and awkwardly pressed it to his wound, letting her hand hover over his chest for a moment longer than necessary, holding it into his skin.

"Yeah, you did," he said.

Hendricks stared at his mouth for a moment, distracted. She could feel his heart beating beneath her palm. She looked at him, and he looked at her, and when she couldn't stand the silence any longer, she said, "Eddie."

The name worked like a spell. He slid to the ground in front of her, his knees gently easing hers apart. He took her face in his hands and pressed his mouth to hers. Their chests touched.

Hendricks was still for a moment. And then she kissed him back.

She couldn't seem to get close enough to Eddie, couldn't seem to touch enough of him. His fingers traced down the line of her back and then hooked into the waistband of her jeans, thumbs brushing, tantalizingly, against her bare skin. Electricity shot through her. She snaked her fingers up his neck, through his hair—

She remembered holding Grayson's jersey above the flame, watching the orange fabric go up in smoke, and the words that had seemed so clear inside her own head.

*I sacrifice love.*

She pictured herself teetering on the edge of a great cavern, pebbles crumbling beneath her feet. One misstep and she'd plummet down and down and down.

She jerked away from Eddie, blushing. "I'm sorry. I—I shouldn't have done that."

Eddie blinked at her. "What?"

"I can't." The words tumbled out of her mouth, and she regretted them immediately. But she didn't know how to explain what she'd just sacrificed. She wasn't sure she understood it herself.

Would the ghosts come back if she fell in love again?

The weight of all that she'd just given up pressed down on her shoulders, and for a moment, Hendricks wasn't sure she'd be able to hold herself upright. She thought of all the years still left ahead of her, years she now knew she'd be spending alone, thinking about this exact moment.

What had she done?

Eddie stared at the tile floor, as though he couldn't bear to look at her. He cleared his throat, fingering the edge of the bandage she'd just pressed to his chest.

"I should probably go," he said, his voice low.

Hendricks felt something lodge itself in her throat. "Yeah."

He stared at the floor for several more seconds. When his gaze returned upward, she could see some sort of struggle going on behind his eyes. "See you around, Hendricks."

Without another word, he stood and brushed past her, hurrying into the hallway.

Hendricks let her eyes close, adrenaline churning inside of her. She was dimly aware of the hair rising on her arms, the steady thrum of her heart. Every part of her body felt alive and raw.

She'd sacrificed love so that the ghosts wouldn't take Eddie, or her little brother, or *her*.

Kissing Eddie was dangerous now.

But that didn't mean she didn't want to do it again.

# CHAPTER 29

"WE'LL BE BACK FIRST THING IN THE MORNING,"
Hendricks's mother was saying. "There's money for food on the table,
and a list of phone numbers for emergencies. Although, why would
you need a list? You have all our numbers in your phone already."

She seemed to say this last part to herself, so Hendricks didn't
bother answering, or even looking up from her phone. "Uh-huh," she
murmured.

"It's just a checkup," her dad added. "The doctor just wants to
touch base with the specialist in New York. Nothing's seriously wrong."

*This* was directed at Hendricks's mother, who had been anxious
for the last few days. The only thing wrong with Brady was that he
hated his tiny baby cast and desperately wanted it off.

Hendricks glanced up and saw her dad massaging her mom's
shoulders, encouragingly, while her mom buried her face in her hands.

She put her phone down and flashed what she hoped was a
bright, confident smile.

"Brady is fine," her mother stated, sounding like she was trying to convince herself. She slid her hands down, so that they
were only covering her mouth instead of her whole face. The skin
between her brows had creased. "You really don't mind staying
here alone?"

Her fingers muffled her words, so that it sounded like *reallydonminstayinherlone?*

Still, Hendricks caught her meaning. "Nope," she said. "I'm perfectly okay."

And that was the whole truth. She *was* perfectly okay.

It'd been two weeks since she, Eddie, and Ileana had gotten rid of the ghosts. Fourteen days where the only noises in the hall came from her parents trying to sneak past her bedroom without waking her up. While she didn't sleep for the first two nights, she was slowly beginning to trust the new quiet that surrounded her. She even picked up the phone the last time Grayson called and told him that if he didn't delete her number she was going to call the cops on him again. After that, she stopped seeing his name on her screen. She thought about him less than she had before, and when she did, she didn't feel nearly as guilty.

*Progress*, she thought. Maybe sacrificing love wasn't all bad.

"Portia said she might come over to study later, but that's all," Hendricks said. Her phone *pinged* and she slid a hand over it, not bothering to pick it up. No sense clueing her parents into the real plan now. For the first time since moving to Drearford, she was starting to feel normal.

And normal girls threw parties when their parents went out of town.

She inched her smile wider. "I'll be totally fine. Now *go*."

Raven showed up an hour after Hendricks's parents left for the city, carrying two shopping bags filled with Jell-O shots. Portia was only a few seconds behind her, tapping at the screen of her phone.

"I put in an order for a bunch of pizzas from Tony's," she

said, breezing past Hendricks as if she owned the place. "They'll be ready in about an hour, but we can send one of the boys to pick them up." She looked up from her phone and flicked a finger. Blake and Finn trailed in after her, carrying a keg. "Where do you want this?"

"A keg?" Hendricks asked, stunned. "Since when do we have a keg? I thought we were keeping this thing pretty small. You guys, me, Connor, Vi, and that drama club guy Raven's into."

"Quentin," Raven said dreamily. Portia rolled her eyes and Raven smirked. "You have to tell her."

"Tell me what?" said Hendricks.

"Portia invited a few more people," Raven said. Portia shot her a look.

Hendricks could feel dread creeping over her. "How many is a few?"

"This wouldn't have happened if you were on Facebook," Portia muttered.

"Portia!" Hendricks snapped.

Raven grimaced. "She put out an open invite for the whole school. Everyone's coming."

"*Everyone?*" Hendricks's stomach dropped. Their class at Drearford had at least two hundred people in it. There was no way everyone was going to fit inside her house.

"You were the one who said you want to cleanse the juju in this place," Portia pointed out.

Hendricks swallowed. She *did* say that, but all she'd meant was that she wanted to have some friends over to talk and hang out and help her forget that just two weeks ago she'd been terrorized in her own home. "This wasn't what I'd had in mind."

Portia threw her hands up in the air, exasperated. "Well, I can't be expected to read your mind. I just figured, you know, nothing cleanses juju better than a good old-fashioned house party."

"What do you know about juju?" Raven asked.

"My grandma back in Nebraska has a psychic phone line."

"And she told you a house party cleanses juju? Really?"

The doorbell rang. Hendricks dug her fingernails into her palm. *Here we go.*

Over the next few hours, people filtered into the house regularly. Hendricks played hostess, telling them they could throw their jackets into the spare room and making sure to direct them to the keg sitting on the kitchen counter. Portia and Raven, meanwhile, set up the Bluetooth speaker by the still-empty pool and started the dance party.

Hendricks was about to join them. She was hurrying down the front hall, to the kitchen, when a voice stopped her in her tracks.

"Hey."

She stiffened. That voice was achingly familiar. She turned and found Eddie standing behind her, leather jacket slung over his shoulders.

He looked so good. She'd forgotten how his T-shirts were so worn-in and soft looking, begging you to run your hands over the fabric. When he stood this close, she could just make out the smattering of freckles on his nose and the campfire smell of his skin.

He stared at her with those dreamy dark-fringed eyes, but otherwise, his face was impassive. Guarded.

Hendricks straightened. "Hi," she said, and her voice sounded so breathy that she grimaced, hating herself a little. She cleared her throat and tried again.

Eddie kept his eyes fixed on her, but they were no longer guarded. He looked . . . hopeful.

Something inside of her thrummed. "What are you doing here?"

*That* came out sounding accusatory. But at least it was better than seeming like some lovestruck schoolgirl.

"Sorry." He shook his head, the hopeful look instantly gone. "I didn't mean to crash your party."

"That's okay," Hendricks said quickly.

"I'm looking for my lighter," he explained, cupping a hand around the back of his neck. "You know that silver one? It used to be Kyle's, and I haven't seen it since I was here, so I figured it might be up in Brady's room. Is it cool if I go look for it?"

"Of course," Hendricks said. And then, before she could lose her nerve, she rushed to add, "You're welcome to stay, you know. If you want to."

"I don't—" Eddie started, and then stopped. Something in his face changed, though Hendricks couldn't say what it was. He took a breath and said, carefully, "I think I'll just find my lighter and go."

He gave her a tight smile, and then he turned and hurried up the stairs to the second floor without another word.

Wanting to avoid another awkward interaction, Hendricks made her way out to the yard, where her friends were hanging out around the empty pool. She'd barely seen Eddie at all over the past two weeks. They passed in the hall at school sometimes, and they'd smile or nod at each other, but they didn't talk or hang out anymore. Every time Hendricks saw him she felt strangely empty. Like she'd lost something she hadn't realized she'd wanted.

"Portia and Vi look like they're having fun," she said, doing her best to push Eddie from her mind as she dropped into a lawn chair next to Connor and Raven.

Raven had been staring up at the night sky, but now her gaze swung around to the side of the pool, where Portia and Vi were dancing. Her eyebrows knit together.

"Just pray that Vi calls her after this," she said. "I don't think I can take another two hours on the phone with Portia dissecting her every facial expression."

Connor leaned back in his chair, blinking up at the stars. "Hey, I think I can see the bigger dipper," he murmured.

"You mean the *Big* Dipper," Hendricks said.

"No, like that one but bigger." Connor squinted, and pointed up at the sky. "See? It's right there."

Hendricks leaned over to see what he was pointing at. "There's no such thing as the bigger . . ." She trailed off, her eyes landing on a slim red book that was leaning against Portia's chair. She cocked her head. "What's that?"

Connor blinked, blearily. "The yearbook? Portia brought it to show Raven earlier."

"It was her mom's," Raven explained. "Remember how I didn't believe that story about those guys who disappeared when her parents were in high school? Well, Miss 'I can't stand to be wrong about *anything*' just had to bring the yearbook to your party so she could prove to me that it'd really happened."

Hendricks felt her breath go still.

*Guys who disappeared?*

All at once, she remembered the story Portia had mentioned during her first days at Drearford High. *My mom told me that her freshman year, three of the coolest boys in school just vanished, and no one ever heard from them again. They were gone, just like that.*

Her heart thumping, Hendricks grabbed the yearbook and began flipping through the pages. Raven said something, but Hendricks didn't hear what it was. A strange, buzzing sound had filled her ears.

*Where is it . . .*

It was on the very last page. At first glance, it just looked like a collage of photographs. But when Hendricks looked closer, she saw snippets from poems about loss, well wishes, and sad messages from parents.

It was a memorial page.

The inscription at the top read:

*For Jason Hart, Eric Hughes, and Chris Adams. We hope you found peace, wherever you are. Lots of love, Drearford High Class of '99.*

Hendricks lifted a hand to her mouth, her eyes scanning the three faces shown in the photo collage below. Cold sweat gathered on the back of her neck. She recognized those faces.

"Oh my God," she said out loud. "I—I know what happened to these guys."

Raven snorted. "Um, how would you know anything about three teenage boys who disappeared, like, twenty years ago?"

But Hendricks wasn't listening. If the boys who were haunting her house were in this yearbook, then it probably meant the girl who'd killed them would be in here, too.

Her stomach warped as she flipped through the book again, more slowly this time, carefully scanning the lists of names next to the blocks of photographs.

*Kevin Brooks, Kelly Bishop, Amanda Bell . . .*
*Margaret Bailey.*

Hendricks felt her body temperature drop. Maggie was short for Margaret. She followed the name to the corresponding photograph, and a new horror settled over her as she realized that she recognized Margaret Bailey's bugged eyes and lanky brown hair. She lifted a trembling hand to her mouth.

She'd *met* Saggy Maggie.

Only now, her name was Margaret Ruiz.

Hendricks jerked her hand backward, her chest hitching. She looked up, staring into the darkened windows of Steele House. If she concentrated, she could feel something pulsing. An angry, insistent energy. Like swarming bees.

All this time, she'd thought the ghosts were after her. She'd been so sure that they'd sensed something in her, something that Grayson had broken.

But she'd been wrong. They'd wanted *Eddie*. They'd already punished Maggie by murdering two of her children, and now they needed the third.

Three sacrifices, for their three lives, just like Ileana had said.

Hendricks pushed herself to her feet, her legs trembling beneath her. She saw movement behind the window of Brady's nursery and remembered, suddenly horrified, that Eddie had gone upstairs to look for his lighter. She was pretty sure the rest of the party was outside by now, which meant he was alone in Steele House. Alone with the ghosts of the boys his mother had murdered.

*No,* she thought, digging her fingernails into her palms. *No . . .*

There was a sudden crash of thunder and, a second later, lightning lit up the sky. A breeze tore through the trees with a sound like rattling bones, and Hendricks flinched, feeling rain prick the top of her head, her shoulders, her cheeks.

The rain came faster now, creating rivers in Hendricks's backyard. The party devolved into chaos. People were leaping to their feet, laughing and shouting as they rushed for the house One kid finally reached the back door and frantically tried to pull it open, but it was locked.

Connor and Raven and Portia had been dragged along with the crowd, but Connor stopped when he saw that Hendricks wasn't following them.

"Hendricks!" he shouted, squinting to find her in the confusion. "Come on!"

She shook herself from her stupor, stumbled after him, and almost fell. There was a crunch beneath her sneakers. She looked down to see that the earth beneath her feet had begun to *shift*.

Like something was trying to crawl up from the ground beneath her.

She hurried faster, but it was too late. The ground writhed and moved. And then something poked up through the earth, wriggling like white worms. Hendricks stared for a long moment before she realized, with horror, what she was seeing.

*Fingers.* Not the fingers of a living hand but the bony, decayed fingers of a long-buried skeleton. They were reaching up from the ground below her feet, *grasping*.

And then they were whole hands, *six* of them, opening and closing like claws. One of the hands curled around Portia's ankle, dragging her, screaming, to the ground. Tears streamed down her face as she tried in vain to kick the hand away.

Arms appeared next, and the tops of skulls. Then full skeletons were dragging themselves up from the mud. Their bones were glowing an eerie white in the erratic flashes of lightning. Bits of old clothes and half-rotted skin still clung to their skeletons. Maggots wriggled through their empty eye sockets. Their smiles were wide and gruesome.

There were three of them.

Hendricks's heart dropped as a voice filled the night, seeming to leak out of the wind and creep up from the ground below her.

*ONE MORE.*

# CHAPTER 30

HENDRICKS STOOD WITHOUT MOVING AS THE DECAYING bodies crawled out of the ground around her.

*Eddie's mother tortured and killed these boys*, she realized with growing horror. All this time they'd been right *here*. Buried in her backyard.

How many times had she walked over their bones without ever knowing they were there?

Her mouth filled with the taste of something sour. Goose bumps climbed her arms.

The three skeletons circled Hendricks, Portia, Connor, and Raven, forcing them into a tight huddle at the center of the yard. Portia was crying. Raven's face was pale and pinched.

"Holy shit," Connor kept saying. "Holy *shit*."

The skeletons didn't speak. But their yellow jaws snapped open and closed, gnashing broken teeth. They raised their bony arms in front of them, fingers twitching.

One of the skeletons leapt for them. Raven screamed and stumbled back as Connor threw himself into the skeleton's path. Hendricks felt a lift of hope as Connor began to wrestle the skeleton away from them. But it only bared a gruesome smile. It caught Connor by the shoulder and wrist, and then Hendricks heard a sickening *snap* as it wrenched his arm out of its socket.

Connor dropped to his knees, the color draining from his skin. The skeleton didn't let go of his arm—

Another skeleton had grabbed Portia from behind, pinning her arms to her sides. She tried to scream, but it covered her mouth with its dead, decaying fingers. The sound came out muffled and hoarse. As Hendricks watched, frozen with fear, the skeleton sunk its broken teeth into Portia's shoulder—

And the third was dragging Raven to the ground, its fingers curled in her hair—

Hendricks shrank back, her breath coming in harsh little gasps. Her instincts told her to run. But if she didn't do something, and soon, all of her friends would die.

The lights inside Steele House began to flicker. On and off. On and off.

Through the windows, Hendricks could see the shapes of three ghosts moving through her living room. Her kitchen. Up the stairs to the second floor of her house. The smell of cologne was suddenly so strong that it burned the insides of her nostrils.

Something came to her with a sudden, dawning clarity:

All of this would be over once Steele House had its final sacrifice.

*Eddie*, she thought. She couldn't let Eddie die.

She needed to give the house something else.

Feeling like she was in a dream, Hendricks tore past the skeletons, her legs trembling beneath her. She crossed the yard and pulled the back door open with a screech of hinges that sent a shiver straight down her spine.

*You can't save him.*

The buzzing she'd heard earlier was louder now. It rattled her bones and made her skin creep.

Hendricks stepped inside, and the door moved on its own, whizzing out of her hand and slamming shut behind her. The walls trembled.

She felt a scream rise in her throat. She swallowed it down, worried that the house would hear her, and hurriedly tried to open the door again. She couldn't. It was locked.

The kitchen flickered in and out of focus. It reminded Hendricks of a faulty light bulb, except the house itself changed. The familiar walls and furniture of her family home blinked out and, underneath, Hendricks saw a different house. An older house.

It was empty, and rotten, with moldy floorboards. Words had been scrawled across the walls in something that looked an awful lot like blood. SLUT. LOSER. WHORE. Hendricks shivered, reading them.

Somewhere in the dark, someone began to laugh, the sound causing fear to drop through her like a stone. She felt a tickle at her ankles and screamed, jerking backward.

A cat wove between her legs, mewing.

*"Poor Saggy Maggie . . . What are you going to do about it . . . ? You going to cry?"*

The voice was like a radio signal fading in and out. Hendricks felt weak with terror.

The lights flickered back on, and the kitchen looked normal again. Gone were the moldy floorboards, the mewing cat, the words painted across the walls in blood. In its place was the house Hendricks knew. Boxes stacked in the corner and freshly painted drywall and the gently rustling plastic curtain. The buzzing sound had stopped, too, and in the sudden quiet Hendricks could make out the sound of Eddie's strained, strangled voice echoing down the stairs.

"Please, no, please don't! Oh God!"

Hendricks drew a long, sobbing breath. She raced for the stairs.

But each step she took forward made her more aware of the friends she was leaving behind.

*I'm doing this for them,* she told herself. Once she gave the house its sacrifice, the ghosts would leave for good.

She pushed the curtain back—

*YOU CAN'T SAVE HIM.*

With a sudden *bang!* every single window in Steele House shattered. Glass filled the air, twinkling like diamonds.

And then it began to fall, cutting into Hendricks's face, slicing her arms. With a shriek, she threw her hands over her head, trying to protect herself.

Rain rushed into the house in a torrential flood. It poured in from the second-story windows and cascaded down the stairs, sweeping Hendricks's feet out from beneath her. She fell to her knees, one hand grasping for the bannister. She knew that if she let go, the rain would sweep her away.

The house didn't want her to reach Eddie. It would do everything it could to keep her from getting to him.

As soon as the thought entered her head, the walls around her burst into flame. The paint bubbled and caught, and fire raced up the stairs and leapt to the second floor, where it quickly consumed the plastic curtains, the drywall, the bare wooden beams of the walls. The hall and staircase filled with smoke.

Coughing, Hendricks dragged herself back to her feet. The flames were still low enough that the heat wasn't burning her, but she knew how fast fire spread. She needed to get Eddie out of there now, before the whole house came down.

Ash and blood rained down around her in equal measure, making it impossible to see more than a few feet in front of her. The blood was past her knees now and growing higher with every second. Glass floated on the surface, reflecting the firelight dancing over the stair-well's walls.

Hendricks kept moving. It took all of her energy to force her feet up the stairs, to keep moving.

The smoke made her dizzy and left her eyes clouded and itchy. She grew light-headed and fuzzy. Her knees knocked together, and then gave out entirely. As Hendricks's breath stopped, pure panic took over.

*This is it*, she thought, the last of the energy leaving her body. *This is how I die.*

The flames around her danced higher, but Hendricks's eyesight grew darker, darker, darker.

And then everything went black.

When Hendricks awoke she was lying on her stomach in Brady's nurs-ery. The floor was warm beneath her cheek and her head pounded, like someone had struck her with something heavy. The fire hadn't reached this floor yet, but the air was thick with smoke.

She choked, and tried to roll over, but there was a pressure on her back, like knees driving into her spine. Her arms had been wrenched behind her, and she felt fingers moving, twisting thick, coarse rope around her wrists.

"Don't move," said a deep voice. Hendricks lifted her head, and whoever—or *whatever*—was on her back gave her wrists a violent jerk, sending pain flaring up her arms and through her shoulders. "I *said* don't move."

Hendricks tried to say *okay*, but there was something covering her mouth. She worked her lips up and down, recognizing the sticki-ness and the strange, almost vinyl texture. *Duct tape.*

The pressure released from her back. She tried to inhale, but the smoke was too thick. It coated her nostrils, making her feel sick. She turned her head.

Through the smoke, she could just make out Eddie lying a few feet away, curled on his side. His eyes were wide and horrified over the duct tape covering his mouth.

Two of the boys stood over him. They were so good-looking, Hendricks realized. Just like their photographs in the yearbook. Their skin was clear and unblemished. Their hair was tangled, but still thick and shiny, one of them a brunette, the other blond. Hendricks could easily picture them being friends with Grayson and the other soccer guys back at her old school. Except for the fact that they were dead.

She couldn't say for certain how she knew they were dead. They *looked* alive, at least at first glance. But if she studied them a little closer she thought she could see something pulsing in their eyes, something writhing and wriggling beneath their skin. Something that hinted at decay.

In fact, the longer she stared, the more clearly she could picture maggots pushing through their cheeks, mold growing up over their hair, teeth and nails yellowing, curling, rotting away . . .

As Hendricks watched, the third boy crossed the room, joining them. He didn't look as alive as the other two. His face was hollow-eyed, his black teeth bared in a gruesome smile, his lips thin and bleeding. There was a pair of scissors in his hands.

"You can't save him," he said, his voice a deep rasp.

And then he knelt beside Eddie, yanking his head off the ground. Hendricks struggled to scream, but the duct tape kept her from uttering a sound.

"Don't be afraid," said the ghost. "We're just teasing, remember? Like how Maggie teased us?"

Eddie stared at the scissors above him, the rise and fall of his chest growing frantic.

The ghost flicked the scissors open, moving toward Eddie's chest. The top few buttons on his shirt ripped off, pinging across the room, and then the ghost lowered the blade to the skin just below Eddie's collarbone, digging a long thin line.

L...O...

Hendricks felt something sour rising in her throat. She shifted on the floor, surprised to find that the ropes tied around her wrists weren't quite as tight as she'd expected them to be. She worked her thumb into a knot, trying to pull them loose.

The boy had finished carving up Eddie's chest. *loser*, it read, dripping blood. Eddie's eyes lolled. He didn't seem to be able to lift his head.

There was a clatter of metal as the scissors fell to the floor.

Now, the ghost held a stapler. Leaning forward, he ripped the duct tape from Eddie's lips.

"Stop. *Please*." Eddie's voice was weak. "Please, you have to let me go. *Please*."

"I thought this was just a game? Remember? That's what your mother told us when she killed us."

Eddie's face creased with confusion. "What are you talking about?"

The stapler lowered to Eddie's face and snapped shut an inch from his nose. He flinched and drew in a long, shuddering breath.

"What does this have to do with my mother?" Eddie asked, unable to move his eyes away from the stapler. "What—"

The stapler closed over his mouth and—

*Snap!*

A metal staple shot straight through his skin.

# CHAPTER 31

EDDIE'S SCREAM WAS A STRANGLED, GRUESOME THING.
He couldn't open his mouth past the staple or the metal would rip
straight though his skin, tearing his lips in two. Thick streams of blood
trickled down his lips and over his chin.

*Snap!*

*Snap!*

*Snap!*

Hendricks flinched each time the stapler snapped closed. She
clenched her eyes shut, unable to watch anymore. Tears streamed
down her face. Behind her back, she kept working on her ropes, pulling and tugging, her arms trembling with nerves. The smoke in the
air was growing thicker. The skin around her fingers felt rubbed raw.

*Come on . . .*

Hendricks yanked one last time, and the ropes binding her hands
unraveled. She felt them drop from her wrists, landing on the ground
behind her. For a moment she just lay there, shocked.

Then she leapt to her feet, her heart racing. Her brain felt foggy
and slow.

Clumsily, she grasped Eddie by the arm, half-pulling and half-
dragging him.

The ghosts stood between them and the door to the hallway. Their
eyes were deep, solid pits of black, and their mouths weren't moving,

but Hendricks could still hear them speak. Their voices were whispers and shouts and hissing, all layering one over another. Sometimes they spoke backward, and sometimes their voices seemed to seep out of the walls and drift up from the floor.

*You'll pay for what she did to us*

*You'll pay for what she did*

*You'll pay*

*You will you will*

Hendricks threw her hands over her ears, but the voices kept speaking into her head. She couldn't catch her breath. It wasn't just the stench of the ghosts, it was the air itself; the smoke had left it feeling thin and hot. There wasn't enough of it.

The boys' eyes were growing larger, the black taking over their faces so that their noses and eyes and lips seemed to cave inward, sucked into the darkness. They reached out for Hendricks and Eddie, their long, bony fingers grazing her face. She backed away from them, felt the closet behind her.

There was nowhere else to go.

Desperate, Hendricks threw the closet door open and shoved Eddie inside, jumping in behind him and slamming the door.

For a few moments she just stood there, her heart hammering, waiting for her eyes to adjust to the darkness. The smoke was thinner in here, and Hendricks could finally draw a full breath. A sliver of light came in through the crack at the bottom of the door, and it illuminated the outline of Eddie's face, his mangled lips, and the blood dripping down his chin.

He was bent over in pain, his expression pinched and pale, his arms still bound at the wrists.

Hendricks's heart lurched. "Let me get those." She began to fumble with his ropes. After a moment of struggle she managed to dig her thumb into the knot and yank the bindings loose. Eddie pulled his hands away and went to work on his lips.

"*Ah*," he moaned, grimacing as he dug the staples out of his skin. Hendricks heard the soft click of staples hitting the floor.

"Are you okay?" she asked.

"I'm bleeding pretty badly." Eddie's voice still sounded strangled. His eyes moved to the closet door. "Do you think they're gone?"

Hendricks held her breath and cocked her head, listening.

Wood creaked in the nursery. And then there was a shuffle, like dry leaves sweeping across the floor. Hendricks's skin crept.

"Eddie," she murmured, the word coated in terror. Flames appeared, lighting the dim closet. They crackled along the corner where the wall met the floor, and then slowly crawled up the walls.

The house was coming alive.

"Listen to me," she continued. "You have to find a way out of here."

"I'm not going anywhere without you."

"The ghosts didn't accept my sacrifice. They want . . ." Hendricks paused. She couldn't bring herself to tell Eddie that the ghosts wanted *him*, and so she murmured, "Something else."

"What did you sacrifice?" Eddie asked.

Hendricks shook her head, tears pooling in her eyes. She remembered how powerful she'd felt as she held Grayson's jersey over the flame. It had seemed monumental at the time, but now she could see that it hadn't been a sacrifice at all. It'd been a release.

"Love itself," she said, her cheeks flaring. "Like Ileana told me to. Didn't work, though. I think maybe I never really loved Grayson, so it wasn't really a sacrifice."

She didn't know how to say the rest of it. She knew she couldn't have been in love with Grayson, because what she felt for Eddie was so different. It wasn't passion and fear and anger and want, the familiar roller coaster of emotions she'd mistaken for love before. What she felt now was so much simpler than that. Trust and acceptance and warmth. A desire to do better, to be better.

It embarrassed her that she'd ever settled for such a pale imitation of the real thing.

There was a crushing sadness in Eddie's face as he looked at her, but all he said was "Oh."

The flames had reached the ceiling and were stretching over their heads, hot and crackling. Hendricks's lips trembled. She thought of her friends outside, wrestling with the skeletons in her backyard. Was it possible that they were still alive?

Or was she already too late?

Horror rose up inside of her. "If we don't sacrifice something soon, we're all going to die."

"The ghosts . . . they kept talking about my mother," Eddie said. "They said, *you'll pay for what she did.*"

Hendricks sensed movement from the corner of her eye and whipped her head around, pulse thudding. But there was nothing there.

The sound of laughter drifted down from the ceiling.

"She used to talk about these boys who bullied her in school." Eddie sucked in a deep, uneven breath. He was shaking a little. "They killed her cat. And then they just disappeared, and no one ever found out what happened to them. Except . . . she—she killed them, didn't she? They bullied her, and so she killed them in revenge?"

The closet door blew open with a crash. Three figures hovered just outside, fire dancing around their feet. Hendricks huddled closer to Eddie.

The lights in the nursery blinked off, on, off again.

*You can't save him.*

The ghosts floated, their toes black and dangling. The fire grew, spreading across the floor and chewing its way up through the drywall and insulation. A piece of plaster crumbled from the ceiling and crashed to the ground in an explosion of white dust, fire sparking and crackling around it. The room was suddenly stifling. Hendricks felt her skin start to burn.

The ghosts lifted their hands, pointing at Eddie.

"They need one more," Hendricks said, choking on the smoke.

He stared at her. Her heart crashed in her ears. He opened his mouth to speak.

"Eddie, no," she said, cutting him off before he could say a word. "They can't have you."

"They already took Kyle and Maribeth."

The smoke had made Hendricks dizzy. She blinked, hard, trying to refocus on Eddie's face. She could feel the ghosts coming closer. The fire was everywhere now, the air shivering in the heat. Hendricks realized she could no longer see the door to Brady's room through the smoke.

"Three lives for the three lives my mother took," Eddie said. His eyes had glazed over, and he didn't seem to notice the smoke or the ghosts any longer. "I'm the third."

Hendricks shook her head. "There has to be another way."

No.

Eddie turned to her, curling his hand around hers. "I love you, Hendricks," he said in a rush. "That's why your sacrifice didn't work. I was already in love with you, so you couldn't sacrifice it."

Hendricks's throat felt thick. "Eddie . . ."

Eddie took her face in his hands. "I love you," he said again. "I just need you to know that. Before."

He lunged past the ghosts, fumbling for the pair of bloody scissors lying on the nursery floor. And then he drove them into his chest.

Hendricks felt her heart stop.

*No.*

For a moment, Eddie stared back at her, dazed. And then he fell to his knees.

"No!" The word burst out of her like a command as Hendricks dropped onto the ground beside him. She grabbed his arm and pulled it around her shoulder. "Come on, we have to get out of here. Come on."

Eddie's eyes flickered. "I'm not leaving, Hendricks," he murmured. "It's over."

She drew a long, sobbing breath. She was dimly aware that the air in the room had grown considerably warmer.

Desperate, her eyes swiveled to Brady's window.

Her own words rose in her memory, bringing with them a sudden jolt of adrenaline: *I used to be fearless.*

*Not used to be,* she thought, hauling Eddie to his feet. *I am* fearless.

Eddie was fading, but she managed to drag him over to the window. She shoved the half-broken window open with her shoulder—

There was a low popping sound, and then a blast of stifling air swept through the hallway outside of Brady's room, blowing the nursery door open with a thud. A cloud of orange and red flame billowed into the room, slamming into Hendricks's back.

Holding tight to Eddie, she pushed herself out the window, flames licking at her feet. Gravity took hold and they rolled, one over another, onto the low-hanging roof and then over the edge, into nothing. For a moment, it felt like flying—

—and then the ground rose up to meet them and they slammed into the muddy yard below. In the pouring rain, the soft give of the mud broke her fall. She lay there, her body stinging, unsure if she could move. Eddie was no longer in her arms. Panic rose within her, and she rose to her hands and knees, wiping the mud from her mouth. She could see his unmoving figure lying a few feet away.

"Eddie," she choked out. The rain continued to pour relentlessly. She slipped as she clawed her way to him.

He was horribly pale. Blood coated his chest and neck. His eyes didn't focus.

Tears choked Hendricks's throat. She grabbed Eddie by the shoulders, shaking him.

"Don't leave me," she sobbed.

Eddie's lips parted, as though he were about to say something. His eyes went still. Something inside of Hendricks crumbled and broke. He was gone.

Behind her, there was a series of explosions. She glanced up just in time to see sparks light up the Steele House windows, and fire spew up through its chimney and belch out the back door, lighting the night. Black smoke filled the sky in a great, roaring cloud. Both stories of the house were flaming now, its freshly painted exterior cracking and peeling under the heat, its shutters hanging from blackened hinges. A deep, yawning darkness stared out from beyond the shutterless windows. It reminded Hendricks of lidless eyes.

For a moment, she thought she saw movement in that darkness. Three shapes standing at the windows, watching.

And then a breeze blew through the yard and into the house, drawing Hendricks's eyes as it upset the flickering embers and ash. By the time Hendricks looked back up at the windows the ghosts were gone. Steele House was empty.

# EPILOGUE

HENDRICKS STOOD ON THE SIDEWALK ACROSS THE STREET from Steele House, staring at the ruins. She couldn't see much from here—just blackened brick and splintered wood and broken glass—but she didn't dare move closer.

She knew it was childish, but she thought that if she got any closer, the house might see her.

It had been one month since Steele House had burned to the ground, although sometimes it felt to Hendricks that only minutes had passed. The last four weeks had the surreal quality of a dream she couldn't wake up from. It was hard to believe that anything was real.

Raven was still unconscious in the hospital. Connor had been released, but his arm would never be the same. Portia was hobbling around on crutches. She and Hendricks saw each other in the halls at school, sometimes, but neither of them spoke. Then again, Portia didn't really speak to anyone anymore. She stared into space with wide, unblinking eyes. Her lips always seemed to be trembling.

And Eddie was dead.

That was the part Hendricks was having a hard time believing. She kept expecting to wake up and find herself on the floor of Brady's old nursery back at Steele House, the ghosts surrounding them, Eddie by her side. But that wasn't going to happen.

Eddie had died to pay for his mother's crimes. He'd sacrificed himself to save Hendricks and everyone else in Drearford. He was really, truly gone.

Hendricks scuffed the toe of her sneaker into the sidewalk, releasing a deep sigh. So why did she keep coming here? If Eddie was really gone, why did she keep haunting the place where she'd lost him?

Her parents had moved across town, renting a small house while they tried to figure out whether to stay in Drearford or move on to someplace else. There was no reason for Hendricks to walk all this way so she could stand on the other side of the street from her old house. Except—

It pained her to admit, but there was a part of her that expected Eddie to come back. To try and see her one last time.

A soft breeze, thick with the smells of fresh dirt and smoke, swept across the street, making Hendricks shiver. It was getting darker. Time to head back home. She turned, felt something crunch beneath her shoe.

Glancing down, she saw a small silver lighter lying in the street.

She stared at it for a long moment. Eddie's lighter hadn't been there when she'd first come back here. She would've noticed it. He'd loved that lighter.

She looked around, eyes skating over the yard, half expecting to see Eddie himself materialize from the shadows, familiar beat-up leather jacket hanging from his shoulders. But there was no one. She was alone.

Heart hammering, she knelt and picked the lighter up.

It was still warm.

# ACKNOWLEDGMENTS

I'm so lucky to have a truly brilliant team behind me for all of my books, and this one was no different.

Thank you to my wonderful Alloy family—specifically Laura Barbiea and Josh Bank—for supporting me from the prologue to the final pages. I couldn't do this without you.

Thanks times about a million to my team at Razorbill. This book has benefitted immensely from Jessica Harriton's brilliant notes, and Casey McIntyre's endless support. Additional thanks go to Bri Lockhart, Felicity Vallence, Elyse Marshall, Kristin Boyle, and the rest of Razorbill's sales, marketing, and publicity team. I'm continually blown away by how hard you work to help people find my books.

In addition to the people named here, there are so many others working behind the scenes to make this book happen. I am grateful to all of you. I couldn't have done it without your support.

And finally, as always, thanks to my fabulous, supportive family and friends and, specifically, to Ron, who really believes in this one.